Honey Girl

Center Point
Large Print

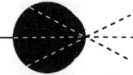

**This Large Print Book carries the
Seal of Approval of N.A.V.H.**

Honey Girl

MORGAN ROGERS

CENTER POINT LARGE PRINT
THORNDIKE, MAINE

This Center Point Large Print edition
is published in the year 2021 by arrangement with
Harlequin Books S.A.

The text of this Large Print edition is unabridged.
In other aspects, this book may vary
from the original edition.
Printed in the United States of America
on permanent paper.
Set in 16-point Times New Roman type.

ISBN: 978-1-64358-965-7

The Library of Congress has cataloged this record
under Library of Congress Control Number: 2021935058

Dedicated to the girls with claws.
Let them fear you.

Honey Girl

Prologue

In Las Vegas, they sell cheap replicas of the love locks from the Parisian bridge for twenty-five dollars. You can buy them on your way out of a chapel, drunk and giggly and filled with champagne bubbles. There is someone on your arm, a girl whose name you cannot remember, or perhaps never knew.

She says, "Let's get one of these," and points to the locks. Their shiny surfaces barely echo the originals, but a pretty girl asks, and you say yes.

It's the second time you've said *yes,* but you don't remember that yet. So, you say yes to this, to this replica lock in a replica city.

In your hazy, champagne-pink reality, you find somewhere for these locks. You won't remember where later, but now—

But now.

This place is sacred. This place has two people, bound together by ceremony and glittering bands around their left ring fingers. This place has roses that bloom purple and pink and red that can be seen even at night. This place has links in a fence, and the lock clicks into place with finality.

"Where should we put the keys?"

In your dream or your champagne-pink reality, you decide to make a swap. The girl's key hangs warm around your neck, and yours around hers.

In Paris, the love locks made the bridge bend and buckle.

In Las Vegas, they are light. Was it your whole heart that has been locked away, or just a piece?

It's a ceremony. Two locks hang from a fence neither of you will remember in the morning or the months that follow. All you have are keys, warm metal from where you gripped them in the meat of your palms.

There, a ceremony finished.

It's a good dream. Or, it's a hazy, champagne reality. Perhaps, it is a memory, made up of the two.

As an alarm buzzes, loud and bright, it is hard to tell the difference. Maybe there is none. Maybe there is no difference between the weighted, heavy locks in Paris and the knockoffs in Las Vegas tourist shops. Maybe there is no difference between dreams and the things you barely remember. They say the things that happen here, stay here, and perhaps that is the same for your midnight dreams and fizzy memories.

An alarm buzzes. You wake up. Or maybe you just remember.

One

Grace wakes up slow like molasses. The only difference is molasses is sweet, and this—the dry mouth and the pounding headache—is sour. She wakes up to the blinding desert sun, to heat that infiltrates the windows and warms her brown skin, even in late March.

Her alarm buzzes as the champagne-bubble dream pops.

Grace wakes in Las Vegas instead of her apartment in Portland, and she groans.

She's still in last night's clothes, ripped high-waisted jeans and a cropped, white BRIDE T-shirt she didn't pack. The bed is warm, which isn't surprising. But as Grace moves, shifts and tries to remember how to work her limbs, she notices it's a different kind of warm. The bed, the covers, the smooth cotton pillowcase beside her, is body-warm. Sleep-warm.

The hotel bed smells like sea salt and spell herbs. The kind people cut up and put in tea, in bottles, soaking into oil and sealed with a little chant. It smells like kitchen magic.

She finds the will to roll over into the warm patch. Her memories begin to trickle in from the night before like a movie in rewind. There were bright lights and too-sweet drinks and one club after another. There was a girl with rose pink cheeks and pitch-black hair and, yes, sea salt and sage behind her ears and over the soft, veiny parts of her wrists. Her name clings to the tip of Grace's tongue but does not pull free.

The movie in Grace's head fast-forwards. The girl's hand stayed clutched in hers for the rest of the night. Her mouth was pretty pink. She clung to Grace's elbow and whispered, *Stay with me,* when Agnes and Ximena decided to go back to the hotel.

Stay with me, she said, and Grace did. *Follow me,* she said, like Grace was used to doing. Follow your alarm. Follow your schedule. Follow your rubric. Follow your graduation plan. Follow a salt-and-sage girl through a city of lights and find yourself at the steps of a church.

Maybe it wasn't a church. It didn't seem like one. A place with fake flowers and red carpet and a man in a white suit. A dressed-up priest. Two girls giggled through champagne bubbles and said *yes.* Grace covers her eyes and sees it play out.

"Jesus," she mutters, sitting up suddenly and clutching the sheets to keep herself steady.

She gets up, knees wobbling. "Get it together, Grace Porter." Her throat is dry and her tongue sticks to the roof of her mouth. "You are hungover. Whatever you think happened, didn't happen." She looks down at her T-shirt

12

and lets out a shaky screech into her palms. "It couldn't have happened, because you are smart and organized and careful. None of those things would lead to a *wedding*. A wedding!

"Didn't happen," she murmurs, trying to make up the bed. It's a fruitless task, but making up the bed makes *sense,* and everything else doesn't. She pulls at the sheets, and three things float to the floor like feathers.

A piece of hotel-branded memo paper. A business card. A photograph.

Grace picks up the glossy photograph first. It is perfectly rectangular, like someone took the time to cut it carefully with scissors.

In it, the plastic church from her blurry memories. The church with its wine-colored carpet and fake flowers. There is no Elvis at this wedding, but there is a priest with slicked back hair and rhinestones around his eyes.

In it, Grace is tall and brown and narrow, and her gold, spiraling curls hang past her shoulders. She is smiling brightly. It makes her face hurt now, to know she can smile like that, can be that happy surrounded by things she cannot remember.

Across from her, their hands intertwined, is *the* girl. In the picture, her cheeks are just as rose pink. Her hair is just as pitch-black as an empty night sky. She is smiling, much like Grace is smiling. On her left hand, a black ring encircles her finger, the one meant for ceremonies like this.

Grace, hungover and wary of this new reality, lifts her own left hand. There, on the same finger, a gold ring. This part evaded her memories, forever lost in sticky-sweet alcohol. But there is it, a ring. A permanent and binding and claiming ring.

"What the hell did you do, Porter?" she says, tracing it around her finger.

She picks up the business card, smaller and somehow more intimate, next. It smells like the right side of the bed. Sea salt. Sage. Crushed herbs. Star anise. It is a good smell.

On the front, there is plain text.

ARE YOU THERE?
brooklyn's late-night show for lonely
creatures & the supernatural.
sometimes both. 99.7 FM

She picks up the hotel stationery. The cramped writing is barely legible, like it was written in a hurry.

I know who I am, but who are you? I woke up during the sunrise, and your hair and your skin and the freckles on your nose glowed like gold. Honey gold. I think you are my wife, and I will call you Honey Girl. Consider this a calling card, if you ever need a—I don't know how these things work. A friend? A—

Wife, it says, but crossed out.

A partner. Or. I don't know. I have to go. But I think I had fun, and I think I was happy. I don't think I would get married if I wasn't. I hope you were, too.

What is it they say? What happens in Vegas stays in Vegas? Well, I can't stay.

Maybe one day you'll come find me, Honey Girl. Until then, you can follow the sound of my voice. Are you listening?

It all barely fits, the stops and starts, but Grace finds herself holding the paper close and tight. A calling card with no number, a note with no clarity.

Someone knocks on the door, and all of Grace's adrenaline snaps like a stretched rubber band. She shrieks, heart thumping as she swings the door open.

"Stop screaming," Ximena says. She's already dressed, burgundy-red hair slicked into a bun and outfitted in what she calls her airport clothes. Grace wonders how Ximena can make edge control work in this heat. "If anybody should be screaming, I should be screaming. You know why I should be screaming?"

I got married last night, Grace thinks. *To a girl with rosebuds on her cheeks. To a girl whose name I don't even know. I should be screaming.*

"Why should you be screaming?" Grace asks instead. "Why are you already dressed?"

"I should be asking the questions," Ximena says, eyebrows raised.

"Oh my God." Agnes peeks her head from behind Ximena's shoulder. "We have to be at the airport in an hour. The fact that you're not dressed and ready means you're actually an evil doppelgänger. So that means I, in fact, should be screaming. Are you going to let us in? Rude."

She shoves past, and Grace sets the photograph and the business card and note on the little nightstand by the window and covers them up with a stray Bible.

Ximena follows more primly, perched carefully on the edge of the bed where Agnes has already sprawled on her back. They stare at her, and Grace stares back.

"Well?" Ximena asks. "Aren't you going to tell us where you were last night?"

Grace frowns. "I was here."

Ximena stares in disappointment at the blatant lie.

Agnes props herself up on an elbow. "Nice shirt," she drawls. "Now, what did you really get up to when we left?"

Grace plucks at the shirt. The gold ring on her

16

finger feels heavy and damning. *Someone has laid claim here,* it says. *This person is not yours now, but mine.* She hopes they don't notice. "Not much after you guys left," she says. "Hung out."

Ximena blinks. "Hung out," she repeats.

Grace blinks back. "Yes." She tries to remember when exactly Ximena and Agnes left. Was it before or after the girl smiled at her over shot glasses? The girl that tangled their fingers together as they walked through crowded streets, past theater lights and clubs with rhythmic music. Grace danced, she remembers now, right there in the street. She clung to the girl and *laughed,* like it was uncontrollable. "We just walked around, I guess."

Agnes sits up abruptly. Her mouth curls, a glinting, knife-sharp thing. "You're lying," she says. Agnes's hangover is apparent in her messy, bleached hair and the shadowed crescent moons under her eyes, but excitement brightens her up like a dog after a bone. "Grace Porter, you are *lying.* Oh my God, I'm putting this in my calendar." Her black, pointed nails click frantically against her phone screen.

"*Dr.* Porter," Grace says weakly, trying to run fingers through her own tangled hair. She should have tied it up last night. "If you're going to slander my good name, at least address me correctly."

"Sue me," Agnes says distractedly, still looking down at her phone. "Sue me in court, you liar."

17

Ximena narrows her eyes and examines Grace like she is one of the patients she must keep careful watch over. "You have flowers in your hair," she says. She watches as Grace reaches up and feels dried petals in her honey-dipped strands.

"We were outside," Grace says. *We were outside an illuminated, plastic church. We were behind roses and weeds and long lilac stems with just the smell of blooming desert flowers and sage and cheap metal.* She remembers the keys suddenly; it burns like a brand against her skin, hidden under her shirt. "I think I was so drunk I fell over."

"You fell over." Ximena looks unimpressed. "You came back with that girl? The one you met?"

"Yeah?"

"Was she here, too?" Agnes asks, looking around like someone will jump out of the closet. "It was loud when you came in for the night."

"After ignoring our texts," Ximena adds. She gears herself up for a rant. "What the hell would I look like on *Dateline* talking about how you disappeared in Las Vegas? Colonel would *kill* me for losing his kid. And when would I have time to film my segment? I work soul-crushing hours, Porter. No time to get my hair and nails done before I make my television debut as the distraught best friend."

"Why am *I* not the distraught best friend?"

18

Agnes asks. "I can cry on command. What can you do?"

"You need help," Ximena says seriously, but doesn't move when Agnes smiles and leans on her shoulder.

"My therapist would be thrilled to hear you say so," Agnes says. She looks at Grace, who straightens up under sharp eyes. She keeps her face blank. *You have a secret,* Agnes mouths, and Grace looks away.

"As you can see, I made it back just fine," Grace says dryly, "and alone. So, now that nobody will have to mourn me, tell me again when we have to be at the airport?"

"Again?" Ximena ask incredulously at the same time Agnes yells, "Doppelgänger!"

"An hour," Ximena repeats. She stands up, hand coming up over Grace's forehead. "Did that girl give you something? You made us memorize the travel schedules, Porter."

"We had to recite them before we could leave the apartment," Agnes adds. "What was her name anyway? You're fucking lovestruck."

Grace jerks back, away from Ximena's probing fingers and Agnes's eyes. "I don't have time to be lovestruck. It was only one night."

"One hell of a night," Agnes murmurs, hidden from view as Ximena plucks petals from Grace's hair and inspects her pupils. "Let it be known to the court that my question was not answered."

"They'd never let you be a lawyer," Ximena mutters, a smile just for Grace hidden between them. "You didn't answer, though," she says, face softening once she confirms Grace is Grace and is not drugged or cloned. "And you did look a little smitten. Mostly drunk, but kind of smitten."

Grace sighs. She hears the echoes of laughter from dancing in the middle of a sidewalk. Giggling like—like newlyweds, pressed close together as they left the church. "I was not smitten," she says, suddenly desperate to keep it—*this*—to herself. "And I don't think I even found out her name."

"Ugh," Ximena says. "For all you know she could have been The One, and you don't even know her name. How can I live vicariously through your relationship without a name?"

Grace rolls her eyes. "You don't," she says simply. "You can live vicariously in the lobby while I get dressed."

Everything rushes back to her, all the things that make up Grace Porter. Diligence. Efficiency. Details. "God, we have to be at the airport in an *hour*. Have you guys packed? Agnes, check under the bed, I don't feel like calling back here to have them ship one of your shoes or something. And, if you took anything from the minibar, you *are* paying for it. Ximena—"

"There you are, conejito," Ximena cuts in,

patting her cheek and smiling. "I'll get our brat together. You get dressed. I'll call for a cab in—"

"Fifteen minutes," Grace says. "That's all I need, swear."

"Fifteen minutes," Ximena repeats, back in their natural rhythm. Grace feels her chest loosen and her breath return, slow and steady, as Ximena kisses her nose quick and disappears out the door. "C'mon, little demon."

Agnes crosses her arms, reminding Grace of the three years between them. "Why do you get a cute nickname, and I get 'little demon'?"

Grace laughs. "The better question would be *why* are you a little demon?"

Agnes humphs. She takes her time as she leaves the room. Grace turns her back, trying to get everything in her bag, folded and tidy. "Hey, Porter," she says.

"Hmm?"

"You might wanna hide this from Ximena." She pauses. "Unless you're ready to explain why you have a ring on your finger."

Grace whirls around. Agnes is holding *the* photograph, one eyebrow raised.

"Don't—" Grace starts, her mind moving faster than her tongue. Don't what? Don't tell anybody about the accidental marriage? The nameless girl that carries a matching black ring on her left hand? *Don't,* she says, but there is no finish.

"Hey," Agnes says. She comes close, and

21

she's trembling and—*no, that's you trembling*—goes eye level with Grace. "The good thing about putting up with me for so long," she says carefully, "is that now you have my morally gray and questionable loyalty. You get me?"

"Please don't," Grace says again, and she trusts that Agnes hears all the things within it.

"I won't," Agnes promises. "But for Christ's sake, get a little better at lying. I know I've taught you better than that."

She leaves, and Grace buries the photograph and the business card and the note under her silk hair scarf for safekeeping. She buries her rosebud girl and her calling card.

She closes her suitcase.

Agnes sticks close in the cab. On the plane, she whines until Ximena agrees to switch seats, and she gives Grace the window seat. She pulls Grace's nails out of the tender skin on her palms. In the air, the clouds mold themselves into different shapes. A dog. A bunny. A human heart.

Grace thinks, *Can you see these, too? Wherever you are, can you look up and think of me, hidden behind a heart made out of clouds?*

Agnes grabs her hand. It pulls Grace from her daydreaming, the grounding squeeze of Agnes's fingers. She grabs back.

What happened in Vegas is tucked away in her suitcase. It is under her shirt in the shape of a key. It is hidden in her hair with the last little bits of dried petals. It hides in the gold ring wrapped around her finger like a brand.

It travels back home with Grace. It does not stay.

Two

How is the job search coming along? The text from Colonel burns hot in Grace's hand. She puts her phone away in her apron pocket.

After eleven years of chasing the brightest stars and relentlessly working toward her PhD, she was done.

She'd stood in front of her panel of professors. They did not know her as Grace Porter, tall and freckled and raised by a soldier to be the best. They knew her as Grace Porter, Doctor of Astronomy. Hardworking, detailed, Black.

Her deep brown skin dotted with sweat while Professor MacMillan and her peers, all white, studied her as she hid her trembling hands after defending her dissertation. With Colonel's voice in her ears, urging her forward, she'd grappled to the top of this mountain. Mom urged her to *follow her dreams,* so she chased the stars. She poured blood and sweat and tears into her work and here was the proof. Here was her vow of success to Colonel completed.

Professor MacMillan had asked her a final question with a wide, completely unprofessional smile, and Grace had answered, holding her bound defense against her chest. She waited with choked breath as they validated what she already concluded. There was more to be seen in the sky; there was more to be seen in her.

Congratulations, Dr. Porter, they'd said, and there she stood, feeling as expansive and terrifying as the universe itself.

And now she stood in this tea room, wiping sweaty palms on her stained apron and not responding to her father's messages.

"Are you okay?" Meera asks, and Grace blinks back to the White Pearl Tea Room. "Are you daydreaming about the end of your shift, too? If I make another masala chai for a white guy I'll scream."

"I'm fine," Grace says. "Daydreaming, like you said." She blows her curls out of her face, and Meera squints. "I'm going to do an inventory check. Be right back."

She escapes to the back room and stares at her metal reflection in the large fridge. "Get it together," she mutters, palms pressed to her eyes. "Stop thinking. Do your job. A Porter always does their job. A Porter does every task with precision."

"Grace!" Meera hisses from the door. "I have a code red customer. He might get his tea dumped on his head."

"That bad?" Grace asks, carefully pulling herself back together. She folds it all up into something small, something she can tuck between her ribs and feel its sharp edges poking her, but

25

no one else will be the wiser. "Taking down the patriarchy one third-degree burn at a time."

"Baba would love that," Meera says. She moves closer. "You sure you're okay, Space Girl?"

"Hmm?" Grace asks, not looking up. "Yes. What makes you ask?"

Meera scoffs. She opened this morning, and Grace can see exhaustion around her eyes. The bitter smell of loose tea leaves clings to her dark umber skin and hair. Up close, you can see she is young and tired and hardworking, and Grace sighs. She doesn't want to burden Meera with more worries.

"It's nothing," she tries. "Nothing I can't handle, at least."

"You've been so quiet," Meera points out. "You didn't gossip about customers at all today. Not even that woman that tried to smuggle her dog in with her coat."

"Really, that spoke for itself—"

"A goddamn bichon frise! Under her coat!"

"Emotional-support bichon frise?"

Meera groans, grabbing two of the tea containers. "You've been like this since you got back. Not even talking my ear off about your space stuff."

Grace raises an eyebrow. "I just got a PhD in my space stuff, you know."

"I know," Meera says meaningfully. "And then you left me here all alone while you celebrated in

Las Vegas. You haven't even mentioned it! You haven't given me any details! Did you get super wasted? Gamble away all your savings?" She moves even closer, voice low and eyes big. "Did you *score?*"

"Absolutely not, Meera."

"Meera!" Baba Vihaan calls from the front. "We have customers."

"God," Meera says. "Pray I make it through the day. Baba would hate it if I threw a fit."

"Which god am I praying to?"

"Pick one," Meera tells her, straightening her kurti as she steps out of the kitchen. "Choose wisely."

Grace stays in the back most days. She lets Meera be the face of the tea room. The white liberals of Portland flock to the White Pearl to aggressively compliment Meera on the tea selection and the jeweled bangles that wrap around her wrists like planetary rings. They love her thick, arched brows and her intricately decorated kurtis and the way she smiles as they leave.

They do not care about Grace in the back: not Indian, not draped in beautiful fabric. A Black father and a white mom. Old news for the diversity quota in Portland.

Today, it's good. It's quiet. No one is going to ask why Grace presses the key and gold ring at the end of her necklace tight in her palm. *Can*

27

you feel this? Did you keep yours, too? She sends her thoughts into the universe, and she hopes someone, *her* someone, is listening.

It remains calm and quiet until closing. Meera lets out mournful little sighs between the MONSTA X playlist she blasts out of the speakers.

"You sound like a broken record," Grace teases while they tag-team the last of the dirty dishes.

"I've given you, like, ten chances to open up to me today! I'm being emotionally available."

Grace snorts. "I don't think that's how it works, but thank you."

Meera crosses her arms in a childish pose. "Whatever it is, did you at least tell Ximena?"

Grace puts down the dishrag. "I'm not confirming there's anything wrong, but why would Ximena have to be involved?"

Meera gives another frustrated huff. "Because," she says, like it's the most obvious thing in the world, "Ximena is beautiful and smart and can fix anything."

"All true," Grace concedes, "but why do you think I need fixing?" Meera lifts herself up onto the counter and shrugs. It's another surface they'll have to wipe down, but for once, Grace doesn't complain. "I'm good," she says.

"If you say so." Meera frowns. "But something is going on. People are supposed to be relaxed after vacations, but you came back so on edge. I've known you too long. I can always tell."

Grace grits her teeth, then forces her jaw to relax. "I just have—*things* on my mind, okay?" Things like rose pink girls and blooming flowers and a man that held their hands together while Grace said *yes* and *I do*. Things like pieces of paper with *Dr. Grace Porter* on them with no directions on where to go next. She wonders how those things intersect, and if she can find herself in the point between. "I'm fine," she says, and the folded-up edges of her feelings poke at her ribs.

"Okay," Meera says quietly. She opens her arms. She smells like bitter tea and steam water and soap. Grace rests her head against Meera's chest and for a moment, the world stops spinning. She lets herself breathe as Meera starts to lament about yet another customer and "Did you see the shoes she was wearing? Suede pumps in the rain. Is this her first time in Portland?"

Eventually, Raj emerges from the back office where he and Baba Vihaan have been reconciling the till.

"Ready, Gracie?" he asks. He grins when Meera makes a face at him. She's always hated that nickname for Grace.

Grace extracts herself. Meera gently shoves her toward the door, even though the dishes aren't done, and they haven't swept the floors yet. "You can owe me one," she says. "Go tell Ximena I said hi."

Grace flicks the end of Meera's braid and kisses the side of her cheek as a goodbye. She follows Raj outside. "You know you don't have to walk me home. I'm a big girl."

It's raining, and he pulls an umbrella out of his front hoodie pocket. His wavy, black hair hangs in his eyes, and his nose ring shines in the dark. "Now that you're a doctor, you don't need any company walking home?" he asks.

Grace rolls her eyes and pushes closer so the two of them can fit underneath the umbrella. She's tall, but Raj is taller. "I don't need you to walk me home, because I learned self-defense when I was eight."

"Okay, Danger," he says, linking their arms together. "If someone runs up on us, I'm fully expecting you to protect me. I'll be your damsel in distress."

"That's not a new thing."

"Ouch." He clutches his chest. "Will you tell me what's up, or are you just going to roast me?"

The two of them have come a long way. He didn't always like Grace, but once he did, once he started calling her "little sister," they could talk about anything on their walks home. Even still, she hesitates.

Raj and Meera are so alike as brother and sister, and they both know her too well.

"I've been thinking too much," she says eventually. "It's just—" *Have you ever gone to bed thinking of someone you only knew for a night? Have you ever stared up at the sky and wondered where it was you saw yourself, all those years ago? Which star it was you followed here?* She doesn't say any of that.

She tries to find the words to encompass her tangled thoughts. The words for missing sheets that smell like sea salt and wondering if the girl that left it behind misses her, too. If she regrets leaving or is glad to have escaped when the sunrise and sobriety revealed what they'd done. The words for not wanting to talk to Colonel about jobs and the *future* when her pride is still stinging from the interview she has not gathered the nerve to tell anyone about yet. The words for wanting things to be as simple as they were on a desert night with just two girls and a locked promise.

"Sometimes I wish," she starts, staring blankly out at the road in front of them, "I didn't have to have everything figured out. I wish I could turn off the part of my brain that needs perfectly executed plans, you know?"

Raj laughs lightly, his mouth curling in his beard. "I thought the great Grace Porter loved her plans." He bumps her shoulder. "Colonel had one set out for you, and you were determined to follow it."

"It wasn't just that," Grace says, looking at him.

"You were gonna make sure your dad was proud of you," he says. "A Porter always does their best." His voice goes wry with Colonel's echoed words.

"Yes. A Porter always does their best," she repeats, staring down at her hands. "Maybe I don't know what my best is anymore. Maybe my best is doing something completely reckless Colonel wouldn't approve of." Her fingers tighten around the umbrella. "Something absurd and ridiculous and all mine. What if that's my best?"

They stop in front of her building, and Raj searches her face. "If it's *your* best, then it's *the* best," he says, voice sincere. "You need to talk more?"

"No." She shakes her head. "I can handle it. I always do, don't I?"

She looks up at the apartment. The lights are on. Everyone is home but her.

"Thank you," she says, getting her keys out. "For listening or whatever."

"Or whatever," he teases. "If you change your mind and do wanna talk, call Meera instead. I need my beauty rest."

"Will do." She salutes from the door. "Night, big brother."

"Night, little sister," he says, and he disappears

into the night, as Grace heads into her apartment.

The stars glimmer above her. They gleam under the gaze of people like Grace, searching for meaning in their formations. They are doing their best for all the people that stare up at the dark and do not know that they, too, shine brilliantly.

The door shuts behind her. The universe says, *Places, everyone,* and its inhabitants gather. They are doing their best.

Three

Grace didn't grow up in Portland.

She grew up in Southbury, Florida, on family land turned into orange groves. There were always people out in the early morning with sticky citrus fingers, dropping fruits into basket after basket until the picked oranges were trucked away.

Grace remembers playing hide-and-seek in the groves. Giggling behind big, wide trees as Mom called her name. She remembers the smell, *oh,* the smell of oranges in the evening. When the sky turned pink, then purple, then midnight blue.

Mom called out for her, and Grace hid for hours in those grove trees.

She was thirteen when she and Colonel jumped in the rumbling pickup truck and left. Mom stood on the veranda with a trembling smile on her face.

"You be good for your father," she said, as Grace held back angry tears. "Listen to what he says." She pulled lightly on one of Grace's curls, and it sprang back into place. "Call me as soon as you land."

Grace remembers worrying about the trees. Would they still grow big and strong without her there to watch them? Would they still grow plump fruit? Would it still taste as sweet?

She asked Colonel about that once, about the trees.

"Your mother will watch over the trees," he said carefully, as gentle as he knew how to be. "They'll be fine." He said, "They'll still grow as long as she's there."

Grace looked at him. "And who will watch over her?" she asked, and Colonel went silent.

Eventually, she stopped asking Colonel about the trees. She listened when Mom talked about the grove on the phone. She waited at the mailbox for letters with pictures of the harvest. Those didn't come as often. Mom was busy, after all, taking care of all the oranges and trees and the earth beneath her feet. Then, she was busy during the off-season, traveling around the world in search of meaning and spirituality and holistic retreats that made Colonel scoff when the postcards came.

Soon enough Grace was busy, too.

So, she didn't grow up in Portland. But Colonel's house, with its winding driveway and pebbled walk and Victorian porch, eventually made itself home.

Sharone answers the door with fresh box braids, her dark brown skin gleaming in the setting sun. She smells like shea butter and vanilla when she leans in for a hug.

"Porter," she says, smile in her voice, and Grace relaxes into her embrace. From her mouth, her name has a different harmony. *Porter* doesn't sound like a rebuke, a resignation, a demand, like it does from Colonel. From her stepmom, it just sounds like a name of a person you love. "We miss you. I wish you'd spend some time here now. You graduated in January, and we still barely see you. I know Colonel would enjoy it."

Grace rolls her eyes, following Sharone into the house. "Right," she says. "He enjoyed my graduation, too. Must have been ecstatic when they called me Dr. Porter, and he stormed out."

Sharone sighs. There's a process to dealing with Colonel: excuses, rationalization, defeat, attempting to change the behavior, sighing and finally acceptance. Grace is still trying to reach acceptance. She thinks she might always be trying to reach acceptance when it comes to her father.

"Is he home yet?" she asks. He was the one who invited her for dinner. A formal email, signed off with all his military honors and titles, as if Grace needed reminding.

In the kitchen, Sharone has her famous butter rum corn bread laid out on the counter. A pan of mac and cheese sits heavy on the stovetop.

"You know damn well he gets home at five thirty on the dot," Sharone says, pouring an

36

oversize glass of sangria. "He's in his study, but he can wait. I need wine first."

"Cheers," Grace says, cutting into the corn bread. "You know, you could always come live with me. I am *Dr.* Porter now. I'm a catch." Sharone rolls her eyes. "Is that a no?"

"It's also a hell no," she says, humor twisting her lips, "unless you start making the same money he makes."

Grace shrieks, the laugh carrying through the echoes of the big home. She and Sharone fall into each other, laughs eking out into little cackles. "After almost ten years," Grace says, "you've finally outed yourself as a gold digger."

"Oh, honey." She lifts her glass. "That was never a secret."

A cleared throat announces the arrival of another person, and instinctively Grace straightens up, brushes the crumbs from her mouth and her lap. Colonel stands tall in the doorway, leaning against the frame as he rubs at the titanium that makes up most of his right leg.

"I heard laughter," he says. It still takes Grace aback after all these years, the deep bass of his voice. He can still command her attention. "Thought we agreed that wasn't allowed in this house."

"That's just you," Sharone says, but she moves gracefully toward him, reaching up on her toes to give him a quick, chaste kiss. She offers her arm, but Colonel brushes it off, limping stiffly inside. "Porter and I know it's laughter keeping us young."

"Is that right?" he asks. "What do you think? Is it laughter keeping you young, Dr. Porter?"

"Don't start," Sharone says, hovering as Colonel lugs himself onto a stool at the kitchen island. "Ain't nobody tell you to come out of your study to nag."

Grace picks at the remains of her corn bread.

"All right, sweetheart," he says. He's like a pod person sometimes, with how normal he is with Sharone. "No nagging. We'll have a nice dinner." He winks at Grace, and she squints back. "What are we talking about, then?" he asks while Sharone starts bringing over pans of food.

She's been gearing up to tell Colonel about her big interview. Professor MacMillan set it up with a private company in Seattle. They'd discussed for weeks ahead of time. Grace wore her best suit. She slicked her hair back and practiced answering questions in the mirror. She showed up twenty minutes early.

She doesn't quite know the Porter way to say, *I put on my best voice. I sat up with my back straight. I made eye contact, but not enough to seem threatening. I said 'yes, sir,' and 'yes, ma'am,' and I hated every second of it.* She doesn't know the Porter way to say, *They picked*

*me apart, questioned me until my eyes stung and
I stormed out. I saw one person of color on the
way to the door.*

Maybe instead she could say she got drunk-
married in Vegas. How she drank away the
memory of her interview. And at the bottom of
a cocktail she discovered the world did not end,
it just felt like it did. There was so much more
work, more climbing to be done. And then the
rose-petal girl took her alcohol away, and they
danced, and they got married.

Colonel breaks the silence. "Okay," he says,
looking at her over the rim of his glass. "I've
been wanting to talk about what's next for you."

"Well, we're watching *Waiting to Exhale* when
I get home," she says. "It's movie night."

Sharone lays a hand over Colonel's, straightening out his clenched fingers. "What he
means, baby, is what's next for *Dr.* Porter? You
worked so many summers doing research for
Dr. MacMillan's lab. Are you going to stay with
her for a while? What were you working on last
year?"

Colonel would have her head if she slumped at
the table, but she wants to. "Using Gaia's data for
high-speed observation of white dwarf binaries,"
she mumbles.

Sharone squints. "Will you keep doing—that?"

Grace exhales deeply. In her head, she thinks
of the most efficient way to get through this.

Colonel taught her how to turn a stressful situation to her advantage. Sometimes you do that with deflection, with questions, with subtle manipulation. Sometimes you just lie.

"I had an interview before I left for Vegas," she admits. "With a company in Washington. Kunakin."

Colonel narrows his eyes. "How did it go?"

Grace almost shrugs before she catches herself. "They said I wasn't the right fit for the company culture." She looks down at her plate. They didn't say that, but they thought it. They probably said it aloud when they checked back in with Professor MacMillan. "But, it's fine," she says quickly. "They were good, but not the best. A Porter always goes for the best."

"We do," Colonel agrees. "Perhaps you and I should sit down with your mentor. She advised me—"

"You talked to Professor MacMillan? Why would you do that?"

Colonel blinks. "Admittedly, I know less about the trajectory of employment in—" he pauses here, mouth twisting "—astronomy than in medicine. I wanted to know your degree isn't being wasted. It's not as stable a field as medicine would have been."

"No," Grace says, voice rising, "but it's mine." She hides her clenched fists. The way she pinches the thin skin on her wrists. Sharone watches the two of them carefully. "It's mine, Dad." *Dad,* not Colonel. Not some distant military figure that sends her a formal email for dinner at the house she grew up in. No, it's Dad, who taught her how to ride a bike, who dropped her off on her first day of high school. Dad, who let Grace cry into his uniform when no one else looked like her, sunshine hair and brown freckles on brown skin. "Dad," she says, and he jerks back, surprised.

"Porter, I just want to know—"

"It's mine," she says. "All of it. My degree and whatever fucking—"

"Your language—"

"—mistakes I make, they're all mine. Whatever I decide to do, it's mine."

"Okay," Sharone cuts in. "Colonel, don't you remember being young? You didn't have everything figured out all at once, did you?"

"I did," he says firmly. "The army recruited me out of high school. It's not like I could afford college. I had no choice but to figure out what success looked like with the hand I was dealt, so I did the work to get it. Then I had a family to take care of, and I did that, too. I just want to know Porter is doing the work to get what she wants."

"I don't know what I want," Grace says, and she watches his face with a repressed sort of satisfaction. "I worked for eleven years to become a doctor because I wanted you to be proud of me."

"We agreed you would do medicine—"

"You agreed I would do medicine," she corrects, voice trembling. "And I didn't. I did something that disappointed you. I didn't get the job Professor MacMillan set up for me, and I know that disappoints you, too. But my career is mine to figure out."

Colonel sits stone-faced and unmoving. Finally, he pushes back from the table and refuses help getting up. "Then that's what you need to do," he says. "Next time, you will figure out what the best is, and you will get it. That is what Porters do."

The kitchen is quiet when he leaves. Perhaps this is where Grace figures it out. In the silent gravity of her father's home.

"That went well," she says, finally slumping down and sipping her wine. "He didn't disown me, at least."

"He would never," Sharone says. "Your father has his own shit to deal with, but never doubt he wants the best for you."

Grace nods. "I know," she says quietly. "But I don't even know what's best for me, so how the hell does he?"

"You know how he is," Sharone chides. "He thinks he knows everything."

Grace sighs and checks her phone, filled up

with messages from Agnes and Ximena in their group chat. "I should go. Want me to help with the dishes?"

"Girl, this is not my mama's house. You know I use the dishwasher." She shoos Grace away. "Want me to drive you home?"

Grace shakes her head. She feels hollowed out, her insecurities laid bare for Colonel to poke and prod. But they are hers to examine, hers to shove back into the pit of her stomach, hers to hide. "No," she decides. "I'll take a Lyft. It's fine."

"Be careful," Sharone tells her, kissing the top of Grace's head. She's tall in her heels. Grace doesn't know how she wears them all day. "Call when you get home."

"I will," Grace promises. "Love you. Thanks for not letting Colonel eat me alive."

Sharone laughs. "I love you, too," she says. "You're a good kid, Porter."

The words feel like a balm, a cold compress to the raw feeling of exposure.

Spring nights in Portland are breezy, and as Grace sits on the porch swing and waits for her car, she lets her mind wander. She is not here in a home she needs an invitation to visit. She is in the stars, bold and bright and beautiful. She is strong and unwavering, and not filled with the sour taste of failure and the weight of unknowns.

She thinks, *I'm okay, I'm okay, I'm okay,* like a mantra. She has to be okay, because there is no other option. She is okay because she must be, to muster the strength to set up more job interviews. She must be as formidable as the black, swirling universe. It keeps going, and so shall she. She has to.

The door swings open, and Sharone steps out holding a bulky envelope.

"From your mom. I didn't tell Colonel," she says. "Looks like it's been to hell and back, but it got here."

Grace opens it with careful fingers. She and Mom spoke on FaceTime two weeks ago, and she hadn't mentioned she was putting anything in the mail. She'd been in Thailand this time, and the connection was spotty.

The paper is wrinkled, the ink smeared in places like it got caught in the rain. Mom is always traveling on some spiritual retreat or holistic voyage, and Grace has become used to receiving letters and packages from all over the world.

"She'll be home soon to start doing prep for harvest season," Grace reads. "Should be ready to start up in a few months. She expects it to be a big one."

"Oh wow," Sharone says. "Running those groves sounds like so much work."

In the envelope, tucked in the bottom, are a few crumpled bills.

"For my Porter," is scrawled at the bottom.

"For my wandering star girl. Hopefully this helps you find your footing on this green earth, too. Don't get too lost in the big, vast universe."

Mom sends a little money along every few months. Grace never touches it, so the amount grows in her savings, and so does the pit in her stomach. She doesn't make a lot at the tea room. She already feels enough guilt that Colonel helps her out so much. It doesn't help that Mom does, too, from running the orange grove Grace barely finds the time to visit.

Her failed job interview leaves a sour taste on her tongue. People would kill to have the cushion of their parents' money, but it makes her anxious. They won't support her forever. They definitely won't if they find out she's been storming out of sterile, white interview rooms and leaving sterile, white interviewers gaping behind. When they find out she got drunk and happy and hitched to a girl whose name she does not know.

Sharone rubs her back. "Car's here," she says. "Go home, Porter. Everything else can wait."

Grace says, "You don't have to worry about me. Promise." Her stepmom becomes a distant shadow as the car pulls off. Grace texts the license plate and picture of the driver to her group chat and stares out the backseat window.

She picks a star and wonders if her rosebud girl can see it from her radio station in Brooklyn. *Are you listening? There are so many things I don't know how to say. Can you hear them? Is it just me out here, sending messages into the void?*

The drive is silent, but Grace listens the whole way home.

Four

This is the thing: for as lonely and solitary as Grace feels, she is not alone. She has Raj and Meera. She has Agnes. To the very marrow of her, down to the studs, she has Ximena. Raj and Meera are her family, not blood, but flesh and spirit and heart. Agnes is her best friend. Ximena is who she will grab on to when the world ends, and they will watch it burn to ash before they follow. They are two girls with their backs against the wall, and on the very good days, Grace likes their odds.

She meets Ximena for the very first time at the hospital where Colonel is recovering. Ximena wears lavender scrubs and a Dominican Republic flag pin on her name badge. They'd told Colonel just a few days before they would need to amputate above the knee. It's been years of braces and canes and gritting his teeth against the pain, *being a Porter,* and suddenly being a Porter means losing another piece of himself.

Grace knew his leg wasn't right when he came home from his last service tour overseas. He'd been gone eighteen months that time, and he came home like the shadows were waiting to engulf him. His leg buckled underneath him when he walked, and it kept him bedridden for weeks at a time. So, he sat, and he waited for the shadows to come, and eventually they did.

The doctors take his leg. They slice through it like meat for a butcher. The hospital assigns him a companion to help with his recovery. A companion is not a nurse, they say, but someone who keeps you company in the aseptic, miserable rooms. Grace visits, but she is not a companion to Colonel. She is an unwanted witness to his weakened state.

The companion's name is Ximena Martínez.

She stays with Colonel while Grace juggles working at the tea room and graduate classes. When she makes her daily appearance at the hospital, Ximena is always there, sitting at Colonel's side reading a book or texting on her phone or engrossed in a telenovela on the hospital's mounted TV. She gives Grace a smile when she comes in. Sharone is usually there, too, and they leave to let Grace and Colonel have their fifteen minutes of stunted conversation alone.

"I'll call your Mom back," Sharone murmurs quietly on her way out, squeezing Grace's shoulder. "She's been worried about you, too."

"Porter," Colonel says once they are alone. He looks more like himself each day. Grace hadn't recognized the drugged up, pain-ridden man that inhabited this hospital bed before. He says, "You know you don't have to come visit every day. I'm sure your studies keep you decently engaged."

Decently engaged, he says, like Grace doesn't spend every stolen minute at work shoving printed words into her eyeballs. Math and science and numbers and the minutiae of the universe in perfect size-twelve font for her consumption.

"It's nothing," Grace says. Sharone comes every day, and he never tests *her* resolve to visit. "Porters have a responsibility to family," she says, like a recitation.

Colonel lies back in the hospital bed and makes a satisfied noise. He glances toward the TV, still in Spanish. "That girl," he says. "I don't understand her."

"Ximena?" she asks. "She's supposed to keep you company."

"Unnecessary," Colonel says, voice bland. His hair and beard have grown out. He looks unkempt and *human.* "She keeps turning on these soap operas. I can't understand them, but she seems to find them riveting."

Grace had a roommate in undergrad who watched telenovelas religiously. She came back to the dorm between classes and found herself immersed in story lines that were universal in content, if not language.

"They're not bad," she says. He watches the drama unfold with poorly disguised interest. "Do you want me to turn it up?" She is careful to keep her amusement to herself.

Colonel looks at her. His face has never given

much away, but she sees his eye twitch. "Give me the remote, Porter," he says, "and then get out."

Grace smiles and slides the remote over. She pauses for a moment, as she does every time she leaves. Should she hug him? Should she rest her hand on the thin gown that covers him up and reassure him she'll be back tomorrow?

I love you, Dad, she pictures herself saying. *Get some rest, Dad. It'll be okay, Dad.*

She sighs and lugs her backpack over her shoulder. If she hurries, she can eat in the hospital cafeteria before class. Maybe she has time to look over her research notes. She hovers in the doorway. She will leave, and Colonel will still fight his shadows. There are no words of reassurance for that.

"Good night, Porter," he says finally, and she ducks her head and hurries out. She hears him huff and shift in the bed. "Turn this TV up, my ass," he mutters, but as Grace leaves, the volume goes up. Slowly, but it does.

She looks for a table in the cafeteria. She has work to review for class, and research for Professor MacMillan's lab, and an opening shift at the tea room tomorrow. There will likely be no sleep, so she takes solace in the quiet now. Not a substitute, but all she has come to expect.

Ximena is sitting at a corner table. She has a book on her knees, something small and worn, and she smiles at Grace when she walks over.

"Hello, army brat," she says. "You can sit down if you want. You're better company than the tech that keeps trying to touch my hair. It's like she wants to die or something."

Grace sits. Ximena is in those lavender scrubs, and she smells like sharp, chemical soap and something soft and calming, like jasmine. She wears her hair in two haphazard buns, some of the textured curls framing her face. She looks warm and kind under the constellation of freckles. Grace can see why Colonel likes her.

"Reading anything good?" Grace asks. She holds her bag across her chest like a shield.

Ximena sets the book down. "Trying to read more Afro-Dominican women authors. Gotta support my culture, you know," she says. "You speak Spanish?"

"Sorry, no," Grace says, and then, to fill the silence that makes her skin prickle, "I'm Grace, by the way. Or Porter. Whichever."

Ximena nods, but she takes her book and sits back. "I know," she says. "Colonel talks about you all the time."

Grace blinks. "He talks to you?"

Ximena shrugs, playing with her food. "Not much," she says. "But he says you're busy with school. Says you're gonna be a big-time doctor soon. I figured maybe I should shoot my shot and see if you're single and rich."

Grace huffs. "Not quite." She turns her textbook

around. "I'm getting my master's in astronomy. Then starting my doctorate in the fall." In a fit of courage, she plucks a fry from Ximena's plate. "I think he's still in the denial phase."

"That's too bad," Ximena says. "He talked you up real good. Are you at least single? I can work with a doctorate."

Grace feels her face heat up. Ximena watches her, openly teasing. "I don't have time for— *girls*." She gestures at Ximena's plate. "I barely have time to eat."

Ximena pushes her food over. "Eat, then," she says. "And maybe you can tell me about—" she tilts her head to look at Grace's notes "—vector light fields. Talk dirty to me, baby."

She lets Grace eat her cold fries and the other half of her sandwich. Grace talks astronomy to her, and Ximena listens. This is how it begins.

Ximena waits for her when she leaves Colonel's hospital room. They eat lunch or dinner at *their* table in the cafeteria. She sits on the same side as Grace and asks, "What, do you work at Starbucks or something? Why do you always smell like Canelita tea?"

They get comfortable with the weight of each other. Ximena invites Grace to her apartment after she gets out of class, and they stay up late watching straight people on Hallmark.

Ximena practices her tarot readings on Grace, her face lit up by the blue light of the TV.

"My tia taught me this," she says, carefully setting up the deck. "She's a real badass witch, like does hexes and shit." Grace watches, fascinated. "Okay, what I think it's saying is you're going to meet important people." She stares at the cards. "They're going to change you."

Grace, who is going over her notes after class as usual, fights back a smile, huddled on Ximena's ratty couch.

"Important people, huh," she says, and Ximena looks up and meets her eyes. "I could see that, yeah."

Meanwhile, Colonel's leg starts to heal. He gets fitted for a titanium contraption that he hates. He grips her hand as it sets into place, showing pain that Grace wonders if she will ever see from him again. There is sweat on his forehead, dripping down his temples, when he attempts to stand on it for the first time. Afterward, Ximena sits next to Grace until she stops shaking, and Raj comes to pick her up.

Ximena and Grace move in together, pooling their meager funds to rent a two bedroom with a shitty balcony and an ugly cactus. Grace comes home to face masks in the kitchen over cheap wine. She comes home to review her notes cross-legged on the toilet seat while Ximena soaks her aching feet in the tub and makes Grace read the passages out loud. Grace builds her own contented universe away from Colonel and Sharone and that big, quiet house.

And then, they meet Agnes.

Ximena comes home late. Her eyes are swollen and red and her arms have red scratches on them. She collapses on their ratty, terrible couch, and Grace presses close.

She says, "They put me with a new patient today. I was in the psychiatric ward." She grabs Grace's hand and one of them, maybe both of them, are shaking. "Her name is Agnes. Agnes Ivanova." She breathes out the name like it's important, like Agnes is important.

"Hey," Grace says softly, pushing into the little V-crook of Ximena's legs. "Hey, I'm here. I'm here, okay?"

"I know," Ximena says, like it's something that will always be true. Planets will form, and life will bloom and die, and stars will fold in on themselves, and Grace will be right here. "I knew it that first day we talked, you remember? You were so stressed and scared, and I just wanted to make you feel better. Like, some part of my brain said *mine*. And that was it."

Grace presses her face into Ximena's stomach. Soft and warm and trembling with each breath. "I know," she says quietly. "You're mine, too. I know. I love you so much it hurts." That's what they said to each other, because that's how it felt, the connection that blossomed.

54

"Love you so much it hurts," Ximena says, like the words were waiting. She takes a breath. "She tried to—I mean she has these—" She holds out her wrists, and Grace can imagine all the life that pulses blue underneath them. How easily it bleeds out. "I mean they're bandaged, but that doesn't mean they just go away, you know? And she has the same look on her face. The same— you *know,* Porter."

They don't talk about it. It is buried in the hollow of Grace's ribs, in the back corners of her mind, the dark, anxious pit of her stomach. Ximena doesn't ask why Grace claws at her skin, scratching until she is settled by the sting. Grace wonders, during school and work and the future-in-flux looming ahead, how long she can withstand the sting before it just—stops. How long she can burn before there's nothing left. How long a thing can be buried before it combusts.

Sometimes she hears sickly sweet voices that tell her she will never make her family proud, that she's wasted years chasing something she will never get to reach. The ones that curl and sour in her stomach when she stares at the ceiling in the middle of the night.

They ask, *Why are you here? Why do you deserve good?*

"Yeah," Grace says, finally answering Ximena. "I know."

"None of the other companions will stay with her," Ximena says. "She's mean, and she's sharp, and she knows how to make you hurt, just like she does." She looks at Grace. "She's mine, Porter. Just like you. I just *know*."

The thing is, it is Grace and Ximena against the world. Things may get very big and very dark, and they are very small in front of them. But even on the worst days, Grace likes their odds together. The way she sees it, another person, a girl with teeth and claws and hurt, can only make them stronger.

"Okay," Grace says. "Tell me about her."

Ximena does. Three is a good number against the world, it turns out.

Five

Grace can't sleep.

It's four in the morning, and she stares at the glow-in-the-dark stars on her ceiling. She wonders if somewhere else, a girl with rosebud cheeks and a trail of spell herbs clinging to her, is staring at a ceiling, too. Unsure of her place in the world but reassured, somehow, by the weight of a warm key against her chest.

There is someone, Ximena or Agnes or both, on the balcony. Grace thinks about telling them about the secret she holds. *I did more than just hang out,* she could say. *I danced under lights and swore solemn vows to a rosebud girl I don't know, but I think I want to.*

Her career and the gatekeepers she has to face fill her with dread, but these, a gold ring and a calling card she keeps under pillow, do not.

The balcony creaks, and she makes a decision. There is only so much you can hold until you are holding too much. Grace can let this go. This one thing.

She gets up.

The apartment is dark. Grace navigates it with no lights, not wanting to disturb the fragile peace. If she turns on the lights, it will all be real, and she will have to say it and not just whisper it under the quiet beam of streetlights.

She climbs out the small door. The balcony isn't really a balcony. It's a black steel contraption, just sturdy enough to hold all three of them snugly.

"Hi," she says, climbing out and seeing Agnes. "I didn't know who I was going to find out here."

"Couldn't sleep," Agnes says. She's at the edge, legs swinging against the creaky metal. "Still want some company?"

"I guess you'll do." Grace sits down. Agnes smells like smoke and chamomile, and the shadowed half-moons under her eyes speak of nightmares. "Want to talk about it?"

Agnes shrugs. "Not really? My therapist would say that's not productive, but I did actually think about sharing for a moment, so I'm counting it as a goddamn success."

Grace laughs and moves closer. "If you count it as a success, then it's a goddamn success."

They bump fists, and Agnes's face peeks out from under the comforter around her shoulders. "What about you?" she asks. "Anything you want to share with the class?"

The universe says, *This is it, places, everyone.* The universe says, *This is your time.* Grace says, "I got married in Vegas," and the world doesn't end.

Agnes blinks. "Whoa," she says. "Are we really

doing this now? Shit, I thought we were going to actually have to stage an intervention to get you to talk."

"Agnes," Grace says, staring down at the empty streets.

Agnes leans in. She is small, too-skinny. Her bleach-blond hair in its sharp, blunt cut doesn't make her look soft or approachable. She is neither, but she moves closer, and Grace takes it. She takes her edges and her sharpness and turns them into things that feel safe.

"You're being serious?"

"Do I *look* serious?"

"I can't tell if you're being serious," Agnes shoots back. "I saw the picture in your hotel room, okay? You know that. But, like, you didn't, right? You *didn't*."

Grace pulls out her necklace. The gold ring glints under the moonlight. "I got married," she says. She lets out a disbelieving, hysterical laugh. "I spent *eleven years* proving that I was the perfect daughter. I worked day and night to prove myself to everyone. Because that was my perfect, clear-cut plan. And then one night I got drunk-married in Las Vegas to a total stranger, and here I am."

Agnes stares like she is looking at an impostor. "Ximena!" she yells suddenly, and the alley cats start to scatter. The distant sound of dogs barking echoes up to them. Lights flicker on, and someone from the complex across from them raps on their window.

"You cannot scream," Grace says. "Jesus Christ."

"Had to," Agnes says. "This requires backup."

Ximena sticks her head out the sliding door. Half her face is wrinkled with sleep. "What the hell are you doing?" she asks. "You need tea?"

Agnes holds up her mug.

"Alcohol?"

Agnes pulls a flask from underneath her covers, and Ximena laughs. "Okay," she says, "so we're covered on both fronts. Why are you screaming?"

She shoves between the two of them, their solid and steady person. They lean on her, and she lets them.

"Hey," she says quietly. "Who's having the crisis?"

"For once," Agnes says, "it's not me." She sticks her tongue out at Grace. "Go ahead, Porter. Tell Mom what you did."

Grace blinks. "You know," she starts, "for someone who follows Ximena around like a lovesick, useless bisexual, you sure do have the weirdest pet names for her."

Ximena moves as if she expected Agnes to lash out, claws formed. Agnes squirms in her grip, and Ximena giggles as Grace leans away. "Calm down, Aggie," she says, voice gentle and soft and open, like it was the first few months Agnes started living with them, eyes haunted and wary. "God, I think you scratched me."

Agnes huffs. She makes a show of covering herself back up until only her ice-blue eyes are showing. She glares at Grace. "Fine," she says. "I was trying to be a supportive friend, but that's canceled now. Grace got drunk-married in Vegas."

"Asshole," Grace hisses, and Agnes grins with all her teeth.

Grace looks at Ximena. She is Grace's steady thing, her roots digging into the earth like an orange grove tree. Grace waits and Ximena's fingers tangle in her own. *I'm here,* they say. *Give me a minute, I'm here.*

Grace folds up and digs nails into her palm. "Please don't be mad. I know it was stupid."

Ximena pulls Grace in. Tucked into her tight, unrelenting grip, Grace tries to calm herself, desperate and trembling. "Hey, you're fine."

"I can't believe this," Grace gasps out. The words tumble into Ximena's pajamas. All their fear and fright embedded into cotton fabric. "I fucked up so bad. Colonel's gonna *kill* me. I'm supposed to—I'm supposed to—"

"Shut up for a second," Ximena says. She hums, this hushed, calming sound. Grace has heard it before. She hears it when she catches Ximena at work humming a tune to her last, sleeping patient. She hears it in the mornings, while Ximena peters around the kitchen, and they both pretend to ignore Agnes staring angrily at her meds before she takes them in a fit of spite.

Grace trembles and Grace shakes and Ximena hums, sings this lullaby that they have come to recognize as safe. Agnes reaches out, gently scratches at Grace's back. The sensation makes her shiver.

"You good?" Ximena asks, and Grace nods. "Positive? You don't have to be good yet." She taps a finger four times against Grace's pulse. *Love. You. So. Much. Love you so much it hurts.*

"I'm good," she croaks out, but she doesn't move from her spot. Ximena is warm; her steadiness comes with roots that are old and ancient and long. "Sorry."

"Don't apologize," Ximena says. "Just tell us how you went from drunk to married and didn't *say* anything."

It's been weeks of staring at the ceiling, counting the stars instead of sleeping. In between searching open job positions and fruitlessly closing the tabs, she memorizes the words that were written on the hotel's stationery. She memorizes them with her fingers until their ink starts to stain her own hands.

She says, "It was the girl from the bar. The girl that bought me a drink. Nobody's ever—" *Been so into me. Leaned in close, but not too close. Asked if it was okay,* like Grace could decide and not have to follow a plan for the night. "She was pretty. She was *funny*. We danced, and I was so fucking drunk, but it wasn't bad, you know?"

"She was nice," Ximena says absently, like she has the night playing out in her head, too. "She seemed nice. We tried to make sure."

"We did," Agnes murmurs. "Ximena even let me put my knife in my pocket and not my boot."

"Absolutely not the point," Ximena says. "We're listening right now."

"What about me?" Agnes whines. "What about my problems? I don't get married in Vegas, and suddenly I don't matter?"

"Are you done?"

"Yeah." Agnes sighs. "We're listening, Porter," she says, nails returning to gently scratch down Grace's spine.

Grace shrugs. "We danced. We talked. She was a little mean, but like, in a good way."

She gets lost in the memory. "There were people everywhere. Street performers and food vendors and tourists. We bought some flowers and tucked them behind our ears. We were so drunk."

Ximena and Agnes are quiet, and Grace tries to paint it, the hazy dream of it all.

"She kissed me, or maybe I kissed her. We didn't want it to end, so—we made it forever, I guess. I woke up, and it felt like I had dreamed her up."

"I believe you," Ximena says, hushed, as if she can see Grace's memories. They are fragile. Grace worries they might fade if she looks at them too long.

"Me, too," Agnes says, voice rough and low.

Grace traces the gold wedding band.

She puts her knees up and curls up small. "I've had my whole life planned out for so long. What school I was going to, what I was going to study, what job I was going to get. I feel like I don't know how to make my own choices anymore," she confesses. "But I met a girl, and I had fun, and I felt good. I *chose* that. And she chose me."

It was easy to miss someone you don't really remember. Maybe not the filled-in parts of them: their name, if they kicked in their sleep, if they really kissed you before they disappeared out of the hotel room. But, it was easy to miss the outline of them: their laughter and their sea-salt skin and the traces of magic they left.

"Fuck," Agnes says eventually. They laugh, the three of them, in disbelief and awe of the tale that has been spun. It feels like a fairy tale, a Cinderella story, but instead of a shoe, Grace has been left with a note and a radio frequency she has been too afraid to tune into. "You really don't do things by halves."

"I know," Grace says. "I'm terrible. I'm the worst. Who just gets married? Who does that?"

Ximena waves her hands. "Okay," she says.

"Okay, existential crisis later. You're *married*," she stresses, "and you have no idea who this girl is or how to get in touch with her?"

Grace moves out of their embrace. The note and business card are plucked out of her hoodie, and Agnes snatches them away and holds them between her and Ximena like a treasure map. Her mouth moves along to the words that Grace knows by heart.

"Holy shit," Agnes breathes out. "It's so romantic. I feel sick."

Ximena rereads it. "Do you have your phone, Porter?" she asks slowly.

"Yeah? Here."

Ximena's fingers tap rapidly as she reads off the front of the card.

"Wait," Grace says. "You're not really—you're not looking up her radio show?"

"Yes, I am," is the answer that comes. "I want to know everything about this girl." She puts the phone down. "How the hell haven't *you* looked her up yet?"

"I don't know," Grace says. "What if—" *What if reality is not like the champagne-pink dream? What if this, too, does not turn out how I planned? What if I am once again too brown and too gold and not the right fit?* "What if she regrets it?"

Ximena moves closer, close enough that their knees touch. "Baby," she says, playing with the coils of Grace's Bantu knots. "What if she doesn't?"

"Found her," Agnes cuts in, still curled up under her blanket. "She wasn't lying. The radio show has a dot net domain. That's downright spooky."

"Fine." Grace leans over. "Fine, let me see."

ARE YOU THERE?
brooklyn's late-night show for lonely
creatures & the supernatural.
sometimes both. 99.7 FM

There's a picture of the host. Yuki Yamamoto, it says. The sea-salt girl. The girl that left traces of bitter herbs in the hotel bed before she sneaked out. She has weird circular glasses and short black hair and a jeweled septum piercing. *Your conduit to community,* her caption reads.

"Question," Agnes says, scrolling up and down the page. "Did you marry a fucking ghost hunter? Does she, like, perform exorcisms when normal people in Brooklyn would do hip-hop yoga?"

Grace laughs. There she is: the rosebud girl.

"Slow down," Ximena complains. "How can we read if you're flying through the pages like that?"

"There's not much to look at," Agnes says. "Bio page, an *About Us*, ooh, look, past episodes."

"We can't," Grace says.

"Oh, babe," Ximena says, linking their fingers. "We totally can."

"*Yes,*" Agnes hisses. "Can we listen to one now?"

Ximena looks at Grace. "I think we should," she says carefully. "I think *you* should. But it's your wife, your life, your decision."

Agnes huffs. "Why would you read Porter her rights like that?"

Grace gives in. "Oh my God, just do it."

"Doing it." Agnes presses Play on the most recent episode.

"Are you there?"

It's Yuki's voice, as clear as Grace remembers. Not sweetened by alcohol or swallowed in a laugh. It's just her, Yuki, coming through the tinny speaker of Grace's phone.

"Are you there?" she asks. "It's me, Yuki, and for the next hour, you are not alone."

It's intimate and quiet and if Grace closes her eyes, Yuki could be right beside her.

"Tonight, I want to talk about the sea," she says. "Is that okay?" She pauses, as if waiting for someone, anyone, maybe even Grace, to answer. "Good. I want to talk about the sea and its dark depths and foaming, white tides and its swelling, hungry waves. The sea isn't inherently supernatural, or even scary. But it holds many unknowns." Her voice quiets. "Sometimes unknowns are the scariest things of all, aren't they?"

Yes, Grace thinks. *They are.*

"Tonight," Yuki continues, "I had a listener write in about sirens. So that's what I'm going to talk about. Sirens."

Somewhere in the distance, a truck rumbles by. It nears dawn, and things begin to creak awake.

"Sirens started as a Greek myth," Yuki says. "It's a woman, well, half woman, half bird. It's a creature who rested and waited and preyed upon the deep sea, whose great big lungs created sounds that lured in those who dared breach the blue. These creatures lured people under the water so sweetly they didn't even feel the burn of salt water in their chests, filling them up from the inside out.

"But this is not," she says, "just about the origins of sirens. It is about the evolution of sirens, the modern-day existence of sirens and the things used to lure us in."

She pauses, and her captive audience waits.

"I think they must be lonely," Yuki says. "I think anything that waits and sings from the very bottom, the very pit of their stomach, is a very lonely creature indeed." The dead air wouldn't work on any other radio show, but for Yuki, it becomes space to absorb her words.

"And I think," she continues, "that those who venture, traveling through the water toward their song, must be very lonely, too. I think lonely creatures ache for each other because who else

68

can understand but someone who feels the same dark, black abyss?"

Who else, Grace wonders, *can understand loneliness if not someone who sits in solitude all their own?*

"I think there must be a different song for each person. I think a siren must peer into the very soul of a lonely creature to understand what brings them closer. What song makes lonely creatures step further, toes then ankles then knees and deeper, until they are nothing but a sinking thing that a song can no longer reach?

"I have a question for all the lonely creatures out there," Yuki says near the end of her show. Grace doesn't know where the time has gone. Yuki's tale of sirens is like its own song that Grace is unable to pull away from. With her two best friends, she feels like their grip on her hands is the only thing keeping her steady.

"My question to all the lonely creatures out there is, who is your siren? Who is your fellow lonely creature who sees into the very core of you and knows which song to sing? What song do they sing for you, and do you follow? What would happen if you did?

"We are all lonely creatures in our own way," Yuki admits. "That's where I'll end tonight. I have one last thing. If you've been following along, you guys will know I'm hoping there is someone out there that's listening. Someone who glows like bee honey and has golden hair that spreads out when she's sleeping, like a halo. Someone who shares a key with me, perhaps a key to the messy, ridiculous core of me, but me, nonetheless."

Grace's breath hitches. Yuki is talking to her. She is the bee honey. She reaches a hand to the key under her shirt. Yuki is talking about Grace, *to* Grace, lonely creature to lonely creature.

"If you're out there, Honey Girl, I am singing you a song. It's a good song. It won't lure you to the depths of the ocean. It's a song that leads you just to me, I think, if you're listening. This has been *Are You There?*, and I am Yuki. Sleep tight, everyone."

Six

Before, Grace had been afraid to hope for the best about her champagne-fizz wedding. The girl who clung to her hand and kissed her gently and climbed through flower bushes to click a lock into place may not have matched her memory. But hearing Yuki's voice, hearing her call for a girl that glows like bee honey and talk so intimately about loneliness, sparks something brave and warm in Grace.

She finds herself hoping, desperately and passionately, for this to be good. For Yuki to be *good*.

She has a phone number Agnes found somehow and tries to find the courage to press Dial.

"What are you doing?" Meera asks, and Grace jolts from her thoughts.

"I'm still on break," she says. She holds her phone up to her chest, suddenly possessive. "I have, like, fifteen more minutes."

Meera blinks. "Relax," she says. "Not even Baba cares if you go over your break. You're his favorite." She squeezes into the space where Grace is hiding. "Whatcha doing?" she asks again.

Grace exhales. She still has to tell Meera and Raj. Soon. But she wants to call Yuki first.

"I have to make a phone call," she says. "It's mildly terrifying, and not for the normal 'I have to talk on the phone' reasons."

Meera frowns. "Is it for a job?"

Grace sighs. "Don't tell anyone this," she says. "But I got an email from a recruiter. He said my research seemed impressive." Grace's initial joy at the interest had quickly turned sour as she kept reading. She deleted the email as soon as she was done, but it still leaves her bitter and angry. "He also had some questions about my listed membership with the Black STEM Group and the queer group I started in the astronomy doctorate program." She shakes her head. "I'm trying not to think about jobs right now."

"You know they're full of shit, right?" Meera asks. She wraps an arm around Grace. "You deserve better than some place that doesn't want you in all your glory."

Grace turns her head so she can fully wrap herself in Meera's hug. "Thank you," she mutters into her kurti. Today the fabric is sun yellow and orange with stripes of green. It makes her look like summer. "Same goes for you. You're going to be a dope-ass psychologist one day."

"I know," Meera says, smiling. "Okay, so it's not a job that has you anxious right now." She traces the inflamed nail imprints in Grace's palms. "What is it?"

Sirens, Grace thinks. Girls who stand below

the surface to sing you a song. They have flowers behind their ears. Their eyes are dark. They know you, the deepest part of you.

She doesn't get to answer before her phone buzzes with a text.

Agnes
12:47 p.m.
did you do it

Agnes
12:47 p.m.
who am i kidding
of course you didn't

Agnes
12:48 p.m.
DO IT

"Supportive as ever," Meera says, reading the texts. She untangles herself, tidying up the errant strands loose from her braid. "I'll cover for you, okay? Do the scary phone thing."

"You don't even know what it is," Grace says. She frowns as Meera moves to leave. Maybe it would be easier with someone here, someone to hold her hand and coax the words up from the pit of her stomach.

"I have tact sometimes." Meera shrugs. "Besides, the Grace Porter I know isn't afraid of anything. I'm giving you some time to get your shit together before I bombard you with more questions. See how nice I am?"

"A saint," Grace tells her, only kidding a little. "Thanks, M."

Meera sticks her tongue out, and the kitchen door swings shut behind her.

The Grace Porter I know isn't afraid of anything.

The Grace Porter *Grace* knows is afraid of many things. She is afraid of disappointing people. She is afraid of straying from her carefully curated life plan. She is afraid of being a brown, gold, bee-honey lesbian in an academic industry all too willing to overlook the parts of her that don't make sense to them. She is afraid of hearing her rosebud girl on the other end of her phone.

But she is a Porter, and Porters do what needs to be done. She dials.

Someone answers, first with an unsure breath and then with a hesitant, "Hello?" and Grace is tongue-tied.

"Hello?" Yuki's voice turns wary and impatient and she says, "Anybody there?"

Grace takes a deep breath, like one does before jumping into the water. "Hello," she says. "This is Grace Porter."

A silence. "Hi, Grace Porter. Do I know you?"

"You do," Grace says. Her fingers clench

74

around her phone. "We, um. We got married in Las Vegas?"

"*Fuck,*" Yuki says under her breath. "Hold on, okay? Jesus, just hold on. I thought you were a fucking bill collector, and I was ready to scam my way into debt forgiveness. I'm at work. Hold on."

Grace holds on and hears the background noise of what sounds like a restaurant. There's the faint buzz of a crowd, the clink of dishes and kitchen timers that remind Grace of the ones at the tea room.

"Can you cover for me?" Yuki says to someone. "For like fifteen minutes. Yeah, I need that long, Christ." A door creaks, and there's the noise from outside. Wind and car horns and foot traffic. "New Yorkers," Yuki mutters. "You don't live here, right?"

Grace blinks. "No," she says, settling into the crook of her little corner. "I live in Portland. I don't really think it's the same."

"It sounds like a dream," Yuki says, a little laugh catching over the line. "So, Grace Porter. I'm guessing you know my name?"

Grace nods and remembers Yuki can't actually see her. "Yeah. Yes. I, um, I looked up your show. Your radio show."

Yuki whines. "That's humiliating," she says. "I left you that note and my business card like a total asshole. I don't even know why I have business cards. I think there might have been a discount."

Out front, Meera and Baba Vihaan laugh. There's the faint clank of teacups against saucers, and for a moment it's like Grace and Yuki are in the same space. They are in the same kitchen with the same plates clinking against each other.

"It was cute," she says quietly. "It was. No one's ever done that for me."

"What?" Yuki asks. "Nobody's ever made a total ass of themselves the morning after they got married to you in Vegas?"

"Nope," she says. "You're the first."

Yuki makes a satisfied little noise. "Congratulations," she says. "You married an innovator."

It's quiet. Maybe it's that word. *Married,* said aloud in an alleyway, in a deserted kitchen, between two coasts. *Married.* It makes her laugh. She laughs like she has buzzing fireflies tickling her ribs.

"What?" Yuki demands. She sounds so petulant. "What's so funny?"

Grace smiles. "Married," she says lightly. "I mean. That happened. What the fuck?"

"What the fuck?" Yuki agrees. "I came home, and it felt like—" She pauses here, and in the stillness, Grace catches dozens of words unsaid.

"What?" Grace asks, suddenly desperate to be let into Yuki's thoughts.

"It felt like a dream," Yuki confesses quietly.

"It felt like one of the stories I talk about on my show, you know? Like, there's no way I married this beautiful girl and was so fantastically happy, and it was *real*."

"It felt like that for me, too," Grace tells her, like a secret. "In my head you—"

"Tell me," Yuki presses.

"You bloomed," Grace says. "In my head you bloomed like the flowers that were stuck in my hair. You had—you had rosebuds, growing on your cheeks, you know? That's all I could think about. The girl who bloomed roses. The girl who held my hand and danced with me and—"

"Got married to you," Yuki finishes. "That was mad beautiful, Grace Porter. I almost hate to tell you the roses you're imagining were probably just the Asian flush. Not half as romantic."

Grace laughs. "That makes you more real and less like the champagne-bubble girl in my head."

"Champagne-bubble girl," Yuki says softly. "Cute. You were Honey Girl in mine. When I pictured you, it was just honey, everywhere. I woke up next to you, and I swear it was like buzzing bees. That sounds ridiculous."

"A little," Grace admits, and Yuki lets out an indignant *"Hey."* "It was just my hair," she says, separating her curls with careful fingers. "It's not blonde, not brown. It's gold," she says. "My mom used to say the sun took a liking to me."

Yuki hums, and Grace relaxes. "Sounds like

77

something moms say," she answers. "Do you think she was right?"

"About what?"

"The sun," Yuki says impatiently. "Do you think it took a liking to you?"

"No more than anyone else," Grace says.

There's shuffling and noise again, like Yuki's opened the door back to the real world. "I don't know, Grace Porter. It would be nice to be married to someone like that." Her voice goes muffled. "Yeah, yeah, I know it was longer than I said. Hold on a goddamn minute."

"Someone like what?" Grace asks, terrified suddenly that if they hang up, it will be for good.

"Chosen by the sun," Yuki says, like it's the simplest thing in the world. "Honey gold, melted sweet under the summer sun. Real poetic, you know? Oh my God, I said I'm coming."

"Yes," Grace says, listening to Yuki move farther and farther away. "That does sound nice."

"You'll do for now," Yuki tells her. "Listen, I have to get back to work. Can I—can I call you? Next time?"

Grace lets out a breath, and in it, the fear begins to dissolve.

"You can call me," she says. "We can take turns."

"Marriage is all about compromise. I gotta go."

"Okay." Grace closes her eyes. "I'll talk to you soon?"

"Isn't that what I said?" Yuki teases. "I'm hanging up now. We can't be one of those couples that banter instead of hanging up."

"We're a couple?"

"We're *married,*" Yuki says, and the word starts to sound familiar. "And I'm hanging up, Grace Porter."

"I'm hanging up, too, Yuki Yamamoto."

"That's cute," Yuki says. "Is that going to be our thing?"

"This is starting to sound like banter," Grace points out.

Yuki hangs up.

Grace saves the number in her phone.

"Come home with me," Grace says to Raj and Meera after their shift.

Ximena and Agnes are out on one of their totally not-a-date dates, so Grace has the apartment to herself. Baba Vihaan lets them go early. Raj piggybacks Meera on the walk home, and they all tumble into Grace's bed and put on the comfy clothes they keep in a drawer for nights like this.

"What's up, Gracie?" Raj asks. His hair has been put into a neat bun on top of his head, and the face mask they concocted in the kitchen cracks when he speaks. "Not that I don't *love* sleepovers with you two."

Meera curls up on Grace's lap, buried under

the covers. "I'm sensing some sarcasm there, Rajesh," she murmurs. "Some big brother you are."

Grace reaches out for both of them. They are her family, the ones she found and made and kept. "I want you to listen to something with me," she says, heart pounding too fast in her chest. "And you have to—you have to promise you won't be mad."

"I promise," Meera says immediately.

Raj squints. "Why would we be mad?"

"Raj."

He shuts his eyes and leans back against the pillows. "I'm not promising," he says. "But I will try to keep an open mind. I am filled with empathy and compassion and have never judged another person in my life. Let's hear it."

Meera pinches him, but he stays stubbornly still.

Grace sighs and glances at the time on her laptop. She felt brave when she asked them over. She felt in control. Now she feels pink-raw and vulnerable.

She exhales and watches the little audio player load on her computer. "Okay," she says. "Okay."

A pause, and then, there it is: Yuki's voice, quiet and spooky and a lonely, lost creature.

"Hello, my fellow late-nighters," she says. "I want to say hello to a special late-nighter in particular, one that I hope is listening. In fact, she is the one that inspired me for tonight's show. Are you there?"

Grace grabs Meera's hand. Raj leans closer, intrigued. Above them, Grace's glow-in-the-dark stars shine neon green and alien. Grace has counted them hundreds of times, trying to follow them to sleep, but tonight she follows them to a voice of a girl who transports her somewhere new and terrifying.

"If you're listening, Honey Girl, this is for you, okay? You said something to me. Or, actually, your mother said something to you. She said the sunlight was drawn to you. She said the sunlight loved you so much it had to infuse some of itself in you where everyone could see, and that's why your hair burns gold and melts into the bedsheets like bee honey."

Grace holds her breath. One, two, three, four. Exhale.

"I asked you," Yuki says quietly to her audience, to Grace, "I asked you if you thought it was true, and you said you didn't think the sun favored you more than anybody else. Well, I think that's bullshit. I think that maybe your mother knew the sun was watching when you were born. I think the sun saw something in you, something bright all its own, and it picked you. It dripped sunrays from the top of your scalp to the very ends of your hair, and it made you fucking glow. I saw it. I saw you glow, and I—"

Yuki pauses, her frantic, almost angry tone tumbling to a stop.

It is so quiet. Grace does not breathe. Raj and Meera do not breathe.

"I was scared," Yuki says finally. "And I'm scared now, saying this to you over a local Brooklyn airwave. But you glowed, and I was drawn to it. You were warm, like a sunrise, and it killed me to leave the bed with you in it. You are orange and pink and brown-gold, and your mother was right, and you don't even know.

"I wonder," Yuki asks quietly, "do you ever get scared like I do? Do you ever wonder how things will come together, and how things will fall apart? It seems bizarre to wonder so deeply about a stranger, but I have half of you in the ring on my finger, so I don't think you are a stranger at all. I think you are a favored child of the sun, like your mother said. I think maybe she watched as the sun sent its blessing down to you. I think maybe she saw, over the years, as the rays grew and multiplied, until you were Medusa in your own right. There were not snakes that sprouted from your head, but sunlight like fire. But gold.

"It makes me think of all the stories our parents have told us. Little magic things that we dismiss as their attempts to make us feel special. Lately, I've been thinking. What if we are special, and we just don't know? What if the stories of things bigger and bolder reaching out to claim us are true? If you are favored, touched by the sun, what does that make me? Am I a creature, or favored by something big and magnificent, too?"

Yuki laughs, and the sound echoes in Grace's ears. Her heart pounds, and her fingers tremble, and her skin pimples with gooseflesh. Meera squeezes her hand hard.

"God, I sound lovesick tonight, listeners. I met a girl, and when you meet a girl, you think too much, you know? But I hope she is listening. And I hope she knows next time is soon, and I have not forgotten that it is my turn."

The show goes on, but Grace cuts it off. The room is dark and silent. Meera does not let go, but if she did, Grace thinks she might just float up to the ceiling. Raj sits up, and Grace feels his eyes on her: inquisitive and sharp.

"Don't be mad," she says. "It's okay, it's just—you can't be mad."

"It's okay," he repeats. "Who was that girl? She was talking about you. She was talking about you like she *knew* you, like she, I don't fucking know, *fell in love with you,* Gracie."

"Okay," she cuts in, while Meera looks back and forth between them. "Stop. I—I met a girl in Vegas. We were drunk and silly and—" She taps her fingers against her arms. "She's really nice, actually. And we got married."

"Wow." Raj rubs his face, and flecks of his mask fall on the bed. "What is okay about getting drunk-married in Las Vegas? This is like that movie. That American one. What's the movie?"

"*The Hangover*," Meera says.

"*The Hangover*," Raj repeats. "This is like that. Only it's you and not a white guy I've never heard of. What did Colonel say?"

"Didn't tell him."

"Wow," he says again, falling back on the bed. He stares at the ceiling like it will provide him with answers. "Ximena and Agnes?"

"Surprisingly okay. Agnes asked me about tax benefits."

Raj turns to look at her, and she fights hard to keep her face blank. "And you?" he asks. "How are you?"

"I'm fine," she says evenly. She looks at both of them, both of their concerned faces. "I don't know what you want me to say. I've never even thought of marriage, much less to someone I don't know. But, here I am. It's—" *Nice,* is what she wants to say. *I don't want to worry about this like I have to worry about everything else.* "Okay," she says again.

"Divorce?"

"*No,*" Grace says. "So Colonel can find out? He'd probably have to pay for it. Absolutely not, no. I haven't even told my mom."

"Then, what? What's next?"

It's the question that's been circling Grace's head. It keeps her up. *What's next?* She knows, but taking that first step is terrifying. Taking your millionth step is scary. She feels like she has been taking steps for a long time.

"I can handle it," she says. She tries to smile, and Meera raises her eyebrows. "I'm a Porter. I'll figure it out. Haven't I always figured it out?"

Raj opens his mouth, but Meera cuts him off. "If you think you can handle it, then you can. We just don't want you to get hurt."

"I won't," she says. "She's still a complete stranger. Maybe I just needed to realize things don't have to be as planned out and rigid as I thought. Isn't that a good thing?"

"Okay," Meera says. "We support you."

"She supports you," Raj corrects. "Come help me wash this stuff off my face. I can't judge you properly while I'm peeling."

It doesn't have to be a big deal. It can just be a good thing for right now, the connection between two girls on opposite coasts. A siren and the one who stands ankle-deep at the shore.

It can just be a good thing, while it lasts, and then Grace will fold it up like the hotel stationery that still smells like sea-salt magic. She will gather it up and hide it in the deep cavity of her chest, camouflaged under her heartbeat. It will be a good thing, a good memory.

She has other things to worry about. Her future. Her job search. Her place in the vast, blue-black sky.

"Coming?" Meera calls from the door. "You know he only lets *you* touch his face."

"Right behind you," Grace says, and the echoes of Yuki's words come with her. *I think the sun saw something in you, something bright all on its own, and it picked you.* She lets out a trembling breath and shuts the door firmly behind her.

Late at night, when everyone is asleep, Grace crouches on the metal balcony under the moonlight.

Yuki
11:58 p.m.
Goodnight grace porter, who i rmr
shines like the sun is reaching out
from the very core of her

Grace
12:00 a.m.
goodnight yuki yamamoto, who tells
stories like they were crafted within her,
spun with magic
and sea salt

Seven

The hallways that lead to the labs and Professor MacMillan's office echo under Grace's feet. There is history in these halls. There is a younger Grace Porter, wide-eyed and determined and desperate to find a place that she carved out for herself.

It is all in us, Professor MacMillan said of the bits and pieces collected in her office. *These things, essentially small rocks and stones now, were once a part of the universe. I know many astronomers think I take a romantic approach to the science, but how can we not when presented with such grand facts? That something so small was once a part of something bigger than what our human brains can grasp?*

The younger Grace Porter tilted her head up. Up there, you see, where the stars drew a path and the comet fire lit the way? That was where she found her purpose. She fell in love with the stars, and she was going to follow where they led.

Now, she's twenty-eight years old and she's reached the comet's end. There is just Grace with a piece of paper to prove her academic merit and uncertainty eating at her insides like a black hole.

No one told her astronomers, the ones that publish research every few months and get tenured at universities and navigate programs at NASA, that those astronomers don't have sun-gold hair. They don't have sun-browned skin. Those astronomers don't have ancestors that looked at the stars as a means of escape and not in awe.

"The prodigal student returns," she hears, and the office door opens. "Grace Porter, in the flesh. It's been months. Come in."

Professor MacMillan's office is still the same. Same posters on the wall. Same plaques. Same bookshelves and encased pieces of the universe she's used in her research. She is still the same: dark blue cat-eye glasses, the way she stares at Grace as if she can see through her.

Grace is the one who has changed in the time since she's been away. She felt victorious and proud standing in front of a panel of her professors after defending her thesis. She'd worked and climbed and fought, and she made it. There was nothing, no one, that could hold her back. Not her fear, not her uncertainty and especially not thin-lipped smiles that questioned her worth.

Do you ever wonder how things fall apart? Perhaps it is here, like this, unsure of how to climb over barriers and walls and wondering, suddenly, if you should even try.

"To be honest," Professor MacMillan says, "I was wondering when I'd hear from you. I heard the interview in Seattle with Kunakin, Incorporated didn't—" her lips twist "—go well."

Grace shrugs. She spent so many hours in this room, in this chair, going over the intricacies of the observable and unobservable world. Being here shouldn't make her heart pound, her hands tremble, but it does.

"That's one way to put it," Grace says. "What did they tell you?"

Professor MacMillan tilts her head in thought. "You weren't the right fit," she says, and Grace feels a brief flare of spiteful satisfaction. "They also informed me this was in part because you walked out of the interview." She crosses her arms and stares across her desk. "I told them that didn't sound like you. What happened?"

Grace has always admired Professor MacMillan. She is one of the few women that make up this department and the astronomers that constitute the Northwest Coast. She showed Grace the stars as if she could pluck them from the sky and hold them in her hand and said, *See? You could do this, too.* It was never said that Grace would have to climb farther, higher, but Grace knew. Grace *knows.* Still, it hurts.

It hurts that Professor MacMillan thought she

could get that job. It hurts that despite the anger that pushed her to leave the interview, she still wanted to get it, just to prove she could.

"I wasn't the right fit," Grace says. "They made that clear, so I left. I don't—" She stops herself because despite her frustrations, this is her mentor, her advisor. This is a person who opened her professional network to Grace, even if some of them are rotten. "I don't want to work with anyone that makes me feel small. I'm a *good* astronomer with *good* qualifications."

Professor MacMillan frowns. "You are," she agrees. "I know that. And you already know you have a place here in my lab."

"I know," Grace says, cutting her off. She slumps in the chair. "I appreciate that, really. I just need to take a step back and figure out where I want to go. Where I want to be. I need to be the best and doing the best."

"Then take a step back," her professor says. "When you knew you wanted to be an astronomer, what did you see that made you think this was the right choice for you?" Behind her are all the plaques she's received for her work. Prestige hangs in each frame. *This could be you one day,* she told Grace once. *You could do this, too.*

"It's hard to remember," Grace says. She was young and rebelling against someone else's dream for her. Medicine was for someone else. "I saw me *here,*" she says. "I saw me becoming you one day. My own version."

"And what do you see now?" her professor asks.

Closed doors, Grace thinks. Another mountain, another fence, another endless staircase to climb. The desire to be the best and prove it to herself and Colonel and anyone who thinks she should be hindered by things she cannot and will not let them control.

"My first astronomy class," she says instead, "do you remember what you told us?"

"No," Professor MacMillan says immediately. "But I'm assuming it's the same spiel I give every year I teach that intro class. Remind me."

"You said you had romantic notions about this field," Grace says abruptly, sitting up. "You said that the universe was old, and made up of many things. You said we were old, and that the universe made us up, too." To her horror she feels her throat start to get tight. "If it is made up of me, and I am made up of *it,* I want my fair shot to see myself in it." To stand beside its chaotic, hungry voids and fill them with *her* rage and *her* joy. Her fear and her hard-won courage. "I want the chance to be Dr. Porter, the *right* fit. The *best* fit."

Grace takes a trembling breath and presses her lips together. She will not let her discouragement break her spirit in this office. She will keep her dignity and save that for home. Her fingers clench in her lap, and she struggles to look at Professor MacMillan with an even gaze. *It's not fair,* she wants to say. *I worked my ass off to be the best. I am the best you have.*

"Okay," Professor MacMillan says, like she is talking to something scared and rabid. "Okay. You're frustrated, and I get that." She leans in, voice gentling. "It can be a hard field to thrive in. More often than not I am the only woman working on a project. I am questioned and undermined despite my fair number of achievements. It can be hard, but it's rewarding work. I wouldn't put my weight behind you if I didn't think you could do it."

Grace feels her eyes sting, and she blinks furiously. She wants the validation of her mentor, someone who has passed down her knowledge and expertise and contacts. She also wants to scream because the struggles Professor MacMillan faces in this field decades into her career are compounded threefold for Grace before she even begins. She grits her teeth until they hurt.

She waits until she can say, "I know," and the words came out as words should, and not as if they had to fight a battle to get there. "I know I can do it. I just need time to figure out how. Where exactly it is I want to be."

"It can be difficult," Professor MacMillan says,

"getting that first foot in the door. You're not the first graduate to feel a little lost once they're out in the real world. But—" She shrugs, leaning back in her chair. "If anyone was going to be the next *me,* I would be honored to share this mantle with you, Dr. Porter."

"Thank you," Grace says quietly. She forces herself to meet Professor's MacMillan's eyes, as a peer and not a student. "Do you have any advice?"

Professor MacMillan grimaces. Her gray hair and crow's feet make her look tired. "Listen," she says. "I'm a researcher first, and a professor and advisor second. I don't have all the answers you might think I do."

"But you said I'm not the first."

"Of course, you're not the first. You won't be the last. I try to tell my students the same thing— be persistent, be dependable and don't back down when you know you're right. I *know* there are things that might make that harder for you. I wish I knew how to combat that."

"Me, too."

Professor MacMillan nods. "Listen, I'm not telling you anything groundbreaking, okay? You spent your undergrad, including your summers, knee-deep in astronomy. We saw kids come and go, but not you. You went straight into the master's program and finished the PhD program faster than some people finish lunch. You've spent the past eleven years racing against all our expectations and your own. And now that you've met them, you're sitting here in my office, wondering what the hell you're supposed to do now."

She pauses, and Grace waits, trying to find her conclusion.

"Grace Porter, you are one of the most hardworking people I have ever seen. Eleven years is a long time to prove yourself to anyone. If anyone asks, I'd say you've earned the right for a break. To take a step back, as you said, and figure out your next eleven."

"I feel like if I stop," Grace says, "I'll miss my chance. I have to plan it all out now, or I'll lose the opportunity I had. I won't have a second chance at getting this right."

Professor MacMillan looks at her, and Grace is certain she sees her insecurity and exhaustion and ragged determination that she feels wavering.

Maybe eleven years is a long time to focus all your energy and time on one pursuit. Maybe it is a long time proving you can reach the finish line. She is here now, and she does not feel that elation that engulfed her when she graduated. She does not feel like anyone special. She does not feel particularly favored by the sun.

"And maybe you won't," Professor MacMillan says. "If so, that doesn't make it your own personal failing. It's not yours to take on. We'll be losing a damn good astronomer if they refuse to make room for you. But you want to know something I've learned?"

Grace nods.

Professor MacMillan crosses her arms. "You are made up of stars and the black glittering universe," she says quietly. "It may be too romantic for most of the people in this field, but it's true. But you are still just a human. Just a small thing that has to find its way like everyone else in this enormous world. It will not be simple, Grace Porter, and it will not be easy. You may have to make a lot of noise, and the universe's silence can be oppressive and thick. But you want them to hear you, and they will. So do not, not even for one second, stop making noise."

"And if they don't listen?"

Professor MacMillan shrugs. "Don't give them that choice."

Grace
7:39 p.m.
having an existential crisis.
lol text it.

Yuki
7:45 p.m.
[fuckboi voice] wow . . . without me?? 😉

Grace
7:46 p.m.
lmao
i am tired and frustrated and anxious
about work and i have no one
to take it out on you married
a real winner

Yuki
7:49 p.m.
i married the sun's favorite girl. who else
can say that?

Yuki
7:54 p.m.
weird question but are you okay

Grace
7:56 p.m.
i'm okay
i can handle it

Yuki
7:58 p.m.
totally believable. nailed it

Grace
8:03 p.m.
i have no choice but to handle it
do you ever feel like that?

sorry i know you have your
show soon

Yuki
8:04 p.m.
um excuse me this is what wives
are for. in my gay fantasies growing
up i always wanted my wife to
text me late at night then we'd run
away together and join like
a circus

Yuki
8:05 p.m.
is that what's happening here

Grace
8:07 p.m.
joining the gay circus? no.

Yuki
8:09 p.m.
we went from kill your gays to kill your
gay circus

Grace
8:10 p.m.
#progress
go do your show sorry
i'm going back to staring at my ceiling

Yuki
8:14 p.m.
anything good up there?

Grace pauses. Yuki doesn't know this part of her. She doesn't know Grace spends her nights staring up at the sky. She doesn't know about the hours spent in a lab, hunched over samples of asteroids and space dust and computer data— not just for her studies, but to feel connected and seen by something bigger.

Grace
8:17 p.m.
stars. i have glow in the dark stars
all over my ceiling.

Yuki
8:19 p.m.
omg you're a space nerd

Grace
8:20 p.m.
space doctor actually. i got my phd
back in january

Yuki
8:22 p.m.
holy shit. and you married a waitress
who spends her free time telling stories

Grace
8:24 p.m.
i like your stories. they make me
feel like i am not alone
they remind me of that

Yuki
8:28 p.m.
you're not
alone, i mean
it's my turn, right?

Grace
8:29 p.m.
for what?

Yuki
8:31 p.m.
to call. i said next time was my turn

Grace
8:32 p.m.
you don't have to. i promise
i'm fine

Yuki
8:34 p.m.
i can't hear you i'm dialing

. . .

was it this scary? calling me?

Grace
8:36 p.m.
terrifying. you really don't have to

Incoming call from: Yuki Yamamoto

"Hello?"

Yuki lets out an audible, relieved breath. "Grace Porter? That you?"

Grace laughs softly, unwilling to ruin their quiet, hushed atmosphere. "Who else would it be?"

In the background, there is the noise of a city that never sleeps. "A clone," she answers. "Technology is very advanced these days."

Grace closes her eyes. She imagines the soft drunken blush on Yuki's cheeks. She can smell the sea and crushed herbs. "How long have you been walking?" she asks. "Why are you walking? It's almost midnight your time, and doesn't the city have, like, a million subways?"

Yuki scoffs. "You're vastly overestimating New York City's subway system."

"But there *are* subways," Grace argues. "Why are you walking at night?"

There's a startled silence. "Are you white-knighting me right now? And to answer your question, I got off the subway when you texted that you were fine. I'm walking the rest of the way."

"Yuki," Grace sputters, sitting up in bed. "It's so dangerous. Are you crazy?"

"Probably," Yuki says, sounding bored. "Only assholes have whole conversations on the train. I got off like a normal human being so I could call you."

"I could have waited."

Somehow, *somehow,* Grace knows Yuki is shrugging. "Maybe I didn't want you to," she says. "Plus, I have mace and a Taser. I have the power to zap someone's nuts off if they get too close to me."

"Reassuring," Grace says, collapsing back on her pillows. "You really didn't have to, though."

Yuki *hmph*s and Grace turns her head to hide a smile in the blankets. "Wanted to. Don't mention it," is all she says.

"My lips are sealed," Grace says through a yawn. Turned away from the ceiling, she has nothing to focus on but Yuki's quiet breathing and the faint, rhythmic thud of her shoes against pavement. "Will you tell me about your show tonight?"

"Nope, I want you to listen," Yuki says. "I hear you yawning. Nip that shit in the bud. Drink some coffee."

"It's too late for coffee."

"Live fast, die young," Yuki says. "You should stay up and listen," she adds, more sincerely. "I was undecided between two topics, but I know which one I'll do now."

Grace goes warm. "So, it's about me," she guesses.

"I have the right to remain silent," Yuki says brightly. There's the sound of keys jangling, and Grace hears, "Hey, Jarrell, just me. Yeah, I'll lock up. Night." Yuki's voice comes back clearer. "I'm here, by the way, at the studio. Are you going to listen?"

Grace is exhausted. She feels like she could melt into her mattress and never see daylight again. It would be a comfortable way to go. Yuki's voice is calm and luring, and Grace could follow it to sleep and away from the heavy weight of worries.

"Grace?"

"I'll listen," she says. "No coffee, but pure will."

"Pinky promise," Yuki demands, "that you won't fall asleep."

"You can't see my pinky."

"Your verbal pinky," Yuki argues. "Your metaphorical pinky."

"Oh my God." She holds her pinky up, as if anyone else can see. "Okay, I'm pinky promising."

When Yuki speaks again, she sounds far away, like the phone's been put on speaker. "No crossed fingers, no take-backs. Bye, Grace Porter."

"Wait, what—" But the call ends. "I'm married to her," Grace whispers with an air of disbelief. "I'm married to this weird girl, and I like it." *I like it so much.*

With her earbuds in, it is just Grace and the dark as she watches the loading circle on her phone and waits.

Finally, the player loads, and Yuki's voice comes through.

"Hello, lonely creatures," she says quietly, sounding so much different than the out-of-breath girl Grace just talked to. "Are you there? I hope you've had a good day, and if you haven't, maybe being with other lonely people tonight will help you. Hopefully, I can help you.

"I struggled with what to talk about tonight. But recently I've found some good in a person, and hopefully they found a little bit of good in me. Tonight's show is about the origin of lonely humans. It is from Plato, from a dialogue composed in his work *The Symposium.*"

Grace closes her eyes and gets comfortable.

"In the beginning of the world," Yuki says into the mic, "humans looked very different. We had two heads, four arms, and four legs. We had heads with two faces, to see all the things around us."

"We were powerful," she says. "The earth trembled beneath us, and we grew so arrogant in our feats that we dared to test the gods. We dared to wage war against them."

Her voice spins the tale like it's a spider's silky web, and Grace finds herself intertwined. She is not in her bed in Portland. Yuki transports her to ancient Greece, surrounded by wine and ripe grapes and gods that walked the earth.

"The gods," she continues, "beat us down, of course. We were not as powerful as we thought, and we faced a terrible fate." Her voice trembles. "The gods, in their wrath, decided to split us, right down the middle. They decided to halve us as punishment. We became just one. One human with two arms and two legs and two feet. Weak."

She laughs, a brittle sound. "It would explain a lot, wouldn't it? It would explain the longing you get, out of nowhere sometimes, for a person you cannot see. It would explain the ache we get in the hollow space between our ribs, and the uneasy thoughts at night in our beds, hoping that maybe someone, somewhere, is thinking of us, too.

"So, we were halved. Broken into pieces. According to Plato, and echoed through Aristophanes, it does explain that feeling. It explains why humans sometimes spend their whole lives looking for their other halves, and why we try so hard to fuse ourselves into one. Perhaps it is because we once were exactly that. One."

Grace grips her phone. The feeling that Yuki

stirs, the hollow feeling like the pit of a peach, weighs heavy in her belly. It is what she feels, sitting in a sterile room, sitting in front of her mentor, reading through recruiter emails, begging for someone to *see* her. To not water her down or pity her. It is perhaps what pushed her toward Yuki, that hot night in Las Vegas. It is perhaps what's pushing her toward Yuki now, toward a girl that hears Grace's "I'm okay" and sees, really *sees,* the ugly truth of it.

Grace blinks until her eyes stay closed. Darkness, the good kind, the deep sleep kind, begins to cloak her. And like that, with a voice in her ear, she falls asleep.

Grace doesn't know that Yuki continues to talk, a siren song leading her thoughts and dreams into the blue-green saltwater deep. Yuki says, "Maybe there is not a specific half destined for us. Maybe we have to keep trying to fit ourselves together, until we find the pieces that fit."

Asleep, Grace does not hear Yuki's careful voice as she weaves her tale into the night. She does not hear, "Maybe pieces come when we least expect it. Maybe you find yours in the dry desert, and they are like bee honey, sweet enough to keep your throat from needing water. Maybe you pledge yourself to them, your promise held in a metal lock, and you do not know it yet, but you will dream of the flowers in their hair for weeks afterward. You will dream in golds and

105

yellows and browns, and you will be scared, the good kind.

"Maybe Plato knew something we didn't. Or maybe the gods did, when they split us in half and left us to reclaim our missing fragments."

Eight

The base where Colonel works always smells medicinal and clean. Everyone walks around in their uniforms, moving with purpose. So determined to get from one destination to the next.

Grace embraced that for a long time, still does, though now it feels heavy and difficult and tiring.

It's no different today. Grace leans against the front desk and waits for Miss Debbie to check her ID and sign her in, as if she didn't practically grow up on this base.

"Do you think today you'll finally prove I'm an impostor?" Grace asks, when for the third time Miss Debbie holds up her license and squints at it. "Has this all been a sixteen-year-long con?"

Miss Debbie narrows her eyes and slaps Grace's ID down on the desk. She has pointy, sharp-angled glasses with a chain attached. Even sitting down, Miss Debbie will find a way to make you feel small.

"It's you, all right," she says. "Nobody else comes in here with a mouth like that."

Grace smiles with all her teeth, a terrible habit picked up from Agnes. "Can you buzz me in, please, Miss Debbie?"

She mutters something under her breath that

Grace can't hear. Grace's mouth has gotten her in trouble here more times than she can remember; she's given up counting.

"I'll walk you to Colonel's office," Miss Debbie says, locking up her desk and computer before heading toward the big vault-like door that separates them from the people working inside. "I'd hate for you to get lost."

"I know where I'm going," Grace says, annoyed. She sighs, following behind Miss Debbie's office-regulated black heels and her tightly-wound bun.

There was a time Miss Debbie tried to embrace Grace as her willing and malleable pupil. Grace remembers coming here when they first moved. Her clothes still smelled like citrus. Her palms still had scratches from climbing grove trees too high. She remembers Colonel standing here at Miss Debbie's same desk, a firm hand on her shoulder.

"This is my daughter, Porter," he said, mouth curving up into what Sharone calls his *people smile*. "This is Miss Debbie. She runs this place with an iron fist." Then he winked, like the three of them were in on some joke.

Miss Debbie stood up and reached a hand across. "Hello, Porter. Aren't you a beautiful thing? Everyone calls me Miss Debbie."

Grace was angry and lost. Her parents were divorced, and Colonel had moved her across the country. She looked up for orange groves and only found towering, terrifying redwoods. She could climb those forever and never reach the top.

She kept her hands by her side, she remembers. Colonel's hand tightened on her shoulder, and Grace liked it. She liked the feeling of provoking him, of causing that downturn of his mouth. No more *people smile*.

"My name is Grace," she said, with all the force she could muster, "and I am not a thing."

The impression was lasting and brutal. Grace Porter made a lifelong enemy out of Miss Debbie that day.

They walk. The office is full of people but still hushed, like even the conversations in the little kitchenette are confidential. It's mostly white men with the same haircut, suits and ties buttoned up so tight their necks bulge. No one bats an eye at Grace. Her gold hair and her amber-brown, freckled skin and her mismatched parents are no longer worth gossip. *That's just Porter,* they probably think, while they engage in global warfare at their computer screens like it's a game of *Tetris. Just Colonel's daughter, nothing special.*

The door to Colonel's office is closed. Miss Debbie knocks and waits. Grace peers into the office and waves through the glass wall. Colonel holds his finger up, gesturing toward the phone.

Miss Debbie glares, huffing at she turns away. She points at the row of seats outside the office until Grace picks one and sits. "You will wait there," she says sternly. "Very important things happen in this office, Grace Porter, and I will not be responsible for you interrupting your father and jeopardizing security."

Grace crosses her legs and smiles. "Yes, Miss Debbie," she says. "The nation's enemies won't hear a word from me. God bless America."

Miss Debbie starts to walk away. She pauses in front of Grace, leaning down just enough to ensure her voice won't carry. "Your father had such high hopes for you," she says softly. "It's a shame."

Grace looks up and meets her eyes. "A shame, indeed," she says, and Miss Debbie leaves. Grace lets her shoulders drop like she's shedding heavy armor.

"Porter?" Colonel calls, sticking his head out of his door. It takes everything in Grace not to feel like she's picking all that armor back up, heading into the battlefield of Colonel's office. "What are you doing here? Is everything okay?"

"I'm okay," she says. She sees his desk is pulled up to a standing position, and try as he might, he can't hide the stiff way he limps as he walks toward her.

It's better now with the metal leg. He might stiffen up, but the thing doesn't buckle underneath him or make him immobile. Even still, she can tell it's one of his Pain Days.

Colonel gestures toward one of the chairs. Grace sits and folds her legs up in it. He stays standing in front of his computer, pushing his glasses to the top of his head to stare her down.

Finally, he clears his throat. "I'm glad you're here."

"You are?"

"I've been talking to Sharone," he says, "about what you said to us at dinner. She made me realize—" He looks at Grace. She doesn't know what he sees. "You know I love you, right?"

She freezes. She sits up straight, suddenly self-conscious of her ripped jeans and ratty sweatshirt she stole from Raj. "Yes, sir," she says, wiping her hands on her pants. "Yes."

Colonel gives her a wry smile. "Good," he says. "Sharone said maybe I'm too hard on you. That I expect too much."

Grace remembers being a kid in Florida. She remembers running through the orange groves and getting caught up under people's feet and climbing too high. She remembers falling.

She remembers the blood that dripped from her palms. Mom fretted, considered driving into town to the hospital. Colonel, stoic and calm, knelt in front of her as she wept. He could still kneel then, and he did, right down to her line of sight and grabbed her hands.

"Porter," he said. "Hey. *Hey.* Look at me."

She looked at him. When Colonel said jump, you jumped. When he said look, you looked.

"You're a Porter," he said. "Porters fall, they get back up. Porters bleed, they don't cry. They bandage themselves, and they get back up. That's what we do."

Grace sniffled. "But it hurts."

"That's life," he said. "But I expect you to be able to handle it. Do you know why?"

Grace, tearful and bleeding, knew. Of course, she knew. "Because I'm a Porter."

"Because you're a Porter," Colonel reiterates. "So, hold your hands out, and I'll bandage them, and it'll be done."

Grace thinks back to that day while she sits in her father's office. He says, "Maybe I expect too much," and Grace, still remembering the hurt in her hand, says, "I'm a Porter," the way she knows she should. "There's no such thing."

He nods. "That's what I told Sharone. I said I didn't know what she was talking about."

"You don't expect too much from me," she says. "I just—"

"You want to be the best," Colonel says. "It's normal to need to think about how to get there."

"That's not what you said at dinner," she mutters. Louder she says, "I'll figure it out."

He raises his eyebrows. "I know you will. Is that what you came to talk about?"

Grace stares at her knees. "I talked to Professor MacMillan," she says quietly. "We talked about how I've been doing this for so long."

"This?"

"School," she clarifies. "Studying. Pursuing this goal. Research. Working."

Colonel makes a small, questioning noise. "You're committed. You create goals, and you reach them. That's how I raised you." *You're a Porter. That's what Porters do.*

"Yeah." Grace sighs. "But did you ever think that maybe one person isn't meant to go so hard for that long? That maybe—" She looks down and steels herself. "Maybe I need time now because I never had a chance to do anything else but my studies. *Be* anything else."

"Porter—"

"Listen," she demands. Her knuckles go tense around the arms of the chair. "I've been fighting for this since I was eighteen. I'm turning twenty-nine this year, and I've never taken a damn day off. Not even on weekends."

"Okay," he cuts in, hand up. "Let's try to keep this civil. Now, let me see if I can break this down."

She opens her mouth to argue, and Colonel raises an eyebrow. "Didn't I let you talk?" She shuts her mouth. "You chose a course of study. You pursued that course of study as you were expected. You became a doctor in the field. How am I doing so far?"

Grace blows out a breath through her nose. She stays quiet.

"You didn't want to do medicine, so you didn't do medicine. The only expectation I had was that you see astronomy through to the end of its course and find a stable career in that field. It seems our expectations are no longer aligned. So, explain it to me. You'd like a vacation instead of a job?"

Grace can feel her entire body pull taut and tense, like a rubber band stretched to its limit. One wrong move, and it turns into a stinging weapon. "I didn't say anything about a vacation. I just think maybe I could use a break. I know it'll be a fight to get in the door. I just want some time to breathe before then."

"You knew this when you decided to pursue astronomy, yes?"

She bites her tongue hard. "Yes, sir."

Colonel runs a hand over his face. He turns his back to her and stares out his huge window. There's nothing out there that will give him any answers, but he turns away regardless. "You know," he says quietly, "I think there was a part of me that always knew this would happen."

"There's nothing happening." She feels frustration simmer like heat in the pit of her stomach. "I'm not doing anything wrong. It's just hard and frustrating and—"

"I knew this would happen," he repeats. He

turns back around, and he looks at Grace like she is a stranger. "Things get hard, and you want to give up. You want to flee. There is more of your mother in you than you know, Porter."

It hurts like a punch in the gut. He says it with such shame, such disappointment.

"Is it so terrible to be like Mom in some ways?" She stares up at Colonel, eyes burning. She lifts her chin in defiance, like a stubborn, jutting coastal cliff. "Is it so terrible to be like someone you loved once?"

Another standoff. She refuses to break, refuses to cave, refuses to give in. Colonel deflates. It's nothing noticeable, but Grace has seen the proud stature of his shoulders enough to know when they come back down to earth.

"What do you want me to say?" he asks wearily. He rubs his leg, aching again, and he looks older and more tired than Grace has ever seen. He looks like a Black man who has been going and going for a long time and never, ever stopped. Someone who never wavered from the path they were put on.

"Mom sent me some money," she says suddenly. "Maybe I could—" She falters, trying to find the words. "Maybe I could visit her for a little bit." Colonel barks out a dry, disbelieving laugh. Grace flinches and has to catch herself. "It's been a while since I—"

"I know how long it's been," he cuts in. His

arms come free of their crossed grip. "Is she even in Florida? Or is she doing some candle retreat in Tibet again? Or was that sheep farming in Iceland?"

Grace shakes her head. "I think she's home," she says. "I could stay until harvest season. Maybe help her with the groves and recharge and clear my head. It's honest work."

Colonel nods, as if things he already foresaw are being confirmed. He walks across the office, leg held stiff and his teeth gritted. He opens his office door, a clear dismissal.

"It is honest work," he says, his voice as quiet as Grace has ever heard it. "But, it's not your work. Dismissed, Porter."

"Yes, sir." She walks out, flicking her scrunchie against her wrist. The sting of this distracts from the one in her father's words.

Colonel closes his door. She slinks through the aisles of the office, and no one gives her a second glance. Not even Miss Debbie.

"And then he said, 'It's not your work' and it was so goddamn condescending. I just sat there and let him say that to me." Grace groans, turning her head into Ximena's lap. "I know it's not my work, but *my* work is keeping me up at night."

Ximena hums. It's nearing 10 p.m. and the hospital, this part of it anyway, is quiet. Ximena's in her lavender scrubs and ugly, comfortable shoes, and she's the best person for a good hug. "He's your dad," she says simply. "Parents are weird. Our parents were taught that they couldn't stop. If they worked hard enough, twice as hard even, things would work out. It's hard to fight them on that, you know? They think they're right, and we think we're right."

Grace relaxes at Ximena's reassuring smile. They're out of the way, tucked in a corner of one of the waiting rooms. It's empty except for them and an old woman who's sleeping with her chin tucked into her chest. She looks like she's been here for hours.

"I'm not keeping you from work, right?" she asks again. "I can leave." Grace really, really wants to stay.

Ximena snorts, but she doesn't move. "We both know you wouldn't leave. You would mope around until Agnes came, and then you'd be griping at her."

"Yeah, so?"

She flicks Grace on the forehead. "You're not keeping me from work," she says for the third time. "Room 542 told me I was 'in too good of a mood' and sent me away, so I'm free for another eight minutes."

"Good," Grace sighs. "That means you have eight minutes to commiserate about how Colonel was wrong. Let's get to it."

Ximena is silent, and Grace looks up to see the hesitation on her face.

"Ximena," she says. "I'm waiting."

Ximena blows out a breath. She checks her watch, because she's responsible and efficient and wears a watch, and glances down at Grace. "I know you and Colonel have your issues," she starts slowly, "and normally you know I would say he's being too much."

"And how is this different?"

Ximena shoves her curls behind her ear in frustration. This close, Grace can make out the brown freckles that splatter over her nose and cheeks and brown skin. "He was wrong to dismiss you for needing a break," she says. "Because it's true, Porter, you need a fucking break. You think we all can't see that?"

Grace tenses, and Ximena smooths a hand down her back. "I don't *need* a break," Grace insists. "I just think having one would help clear my head. Anyway."

"Anyway," Ximena says, "I think maybe you should think about where he's coming from. He's always worked so hard, and he taught you to do the same. Maybe he sees you staying in Florida with your mom for a while as running away from the problem."

"But it's *not* running away."

"It's not," Ximena agrees. "I'm not saying he's right, Porter. I'm just saying maybe you need to make him see your perspective. Maybe get your mom to help. You don't have to do it by yourself."

Grace squeezes her eyes shut.

"Not right now," she says to Ximena. "I feel like I'm falling apart as it is."

"Okay," Ximena says. Her voice is calm and even. "I'll drop it." She looks at her watch again. "I should probably go anyway. I have a new patient. Apparently, she has grabby hands."

"Really?" Grace asks. "I mean, I couldn't blame her. I have one of the hottest best friends in town."

Ximena shakes her head with a small, teasing smile pulling at her mouth. "Maybe it'll be a welcome change from those horny-ass teenagers who ask me to read them porn. Like, fuck off, Timothy."

That startles a laugh out of Grace, loud, cackling and inappropriate in a hospital waiting room. It frees up some of the black sludge in her chest.

"There you are," Ximena says softly. "There's my girl."

"Here I am."

They maneuver up, and Ximena leaves her with one last kiss, buried in her hair. "Agnes should be around soon. You know she likes terrorizing the staff while she waits for me to get off work."

"That sounds right," Grace says. "She was a menace when she was stuck in here."

119

Ximena huffs. "She's a menace now. Don't leave before you see her, okay? Promise."

She holds out a pinky that Grace takes easily. "I promise. Love you so much it hurts."

"Love you, Star Girl."

Ximena walks away. The nurses leave Grace be because she's familiar enough to them now. She closes her eyes and envisions a timeline where it succeeded, the compromises she made to keep Mom and Colonel and herself happy. Where following her dreams didn't feel like so much endless, uncertain work.

She comes back to herself when Agnes slinks into the waiting room. It's late, and it looks like she's been asleep since she got off work nearly six hours ago. Her scarlet beret is impossible to miss, as is the relieved groan she lets out when she sees Grace.

"God, I thought you were on the fourth floor, not the fifth. I was looking for you for, like, ten minutes."

Grace gives her a weak smile. She's tired. She tries anyway.

Agnes plops down on the seat next to her. "Shit," she says. "What is it? Are you in trouble? I've got us covered." She rummages around in her pockets, and then her holographic fanny pack.

Grace reaches for her. "I'm not in trouble," she reassures. "Agnes, *Agnes,* what are you looking for?"

Agnes looks up. In her hands she's holding a small pocketknife and eight quarters.

Grace sighs. "I guess I can understand the knife? But why the quarters?"

"Pay phone," Agnes says. "Duh."

"Right, of course. But I'm good."

Agnes shoves her knife and all her change back in her fanny pack. "So, you look like shit," she observes. "Wanna talk about it or do that thing where we pretend feelings are stupid and don't exist? I love that one."

"The second, please," Grace says. She pulls her phone out of her pocket and stares at the screen. Her home screen, the one she looks at now, is a picture of an orange grove. Her orange grove. She took it the last time she was there, last summer, before she needed to put her head down and finish her doctorate program. She misses it terribly.

It'll look the same when you come back, Mom told Grace. *Everything stays the same around here.*

But Grace is not the same. Instead of the familiar fight to make room for herself in classes and labs, she finds herself in the unfamiliar terrain of the working world. And for the first time in eleven years, she finds herself weary and hesitant and wondering, *Why did the universe choose me, if it knew I would have to fight tooth and nail?* Grace has been *busy,* and now she

121

would like to slow down. She would like to stop for a moment.

"You're hurting yourself," Agnes says suddenly. She grabs Grace where she's digging red, painful half-moons into her arm. "You know what, let's get some air. This place makes me remember when I was stuck here and crazy. Crazier. C'mon." She tries to pull Grace up, but Grace makes herself heavy and unmoving, like the roots of a tree.

"Porter," Agnes says, voice sharp. "Let's go outside."

Grace shakes her head, exhaustion hitting her all at once. Maybe it was the conversation with Colonel and rehashing it with Ximena. Maybe it is deciding, for once, to put her own needs first. "I want to call my mom," she says. "I think I want to go away for a little bit. Visit the groves and have some space to *breathe*."

Agnes narrows her eyes, fingers still working to uncurl Grace's nails from her skin. "Not that it's any of my business, but do you need to call right now? It's ten at night and even later there. Maybe get some sleep first."

"My mom is an insomniac like me. She'll be up," Grace says. She looks at Agnes. Her beret and sleep-mussed hair and moon-shadowed eyes. "I am tired," she admits out loud. It becomes real, like that. "Maybe it'll help to see what she thinks."

Agnes closes her eyes. "Twenty minutes," she says. "If you're not back by then, I'm sending Ximena after you."

Grace nods. "I'll be okay," she says, the thought buzzing in circles around her brain. *I just want to slow down. I just want to stop.*

"Okay," Agnes says. "Get your hands to stop shaking before you call."

"I'm fine," she says, disappearing out of the waiting room. "I'm okay."

She picks a back stairway where the walls and concrete steps don't echo too much. It's cold and dusty and dark, and she crouches low on the steps, back against the painted wall. She presses Call and listens to the line ring until the voice mail clicks on.

"Figures," she mutters. "Jesus fucking Christ. Just pick up." Frustration boils over. This hallway has heard worse, if not from Grace then from someone else, frustrated or grieving or hiding.

One more time.

"Hey, Porter," Mom says when she answers. Her voice is light, like perpetual summer. "I thought we were having a FaceTime call later this week? I'm in Germany."

Grace sighs. Of course, another trip. "Sorry," she says. "Is this costing you money?"

"The hostel has Wi-Fi," Mom says. A deep voice comes from the other line, muffled and distorted. "Kelly says hi."

123

Kelly is Mom's fiancé that Grace has never met in person. He wasn't around when she visited last summer. Grace has only met him informally through grainy video connections. "Hi, Kelly," she says flatly.

"He just woke up," Mom says. "Lightest sleeper I've ever seen. But nothing like your father. A yawn could wake Colonel up. Is he still like that?"

Colonel had awful nightmares when she was younger. She would wake up to get water and would find Colonel sitting in the dark, his hand in the shape of a gun pointed at an invisible enemy.

His hand never wavered, never trembled in its grip, even in his sleep.

"I don't know," she says truthfully. Sharone would never say. "Listen, do you have a few minutes to talk?"

"How long do you need? We're heading out once we're dressed for the day, and then I'll lose the Wi-Fi. I'm all yours until then, Star Girl."

Grace squares her shoulders in this empty stairway. A soldier's posture. "I want to come visit you at the groves," she says, willing her voice firm. "Things have been a little—a little difficult, and I just need some time away." She pauses. "What do you think?"

"You want to come visit?" Mom asks. "I thought you'd be busy heading up teams to research distant moons by now."

"Well, I'm not," Grace snaps, short-tempered. "I could help you get ready for the harvest season," she says. "I would work. I'm not asking for a handout from you."

"Where is this coming from?"

"Mom—"

"Listen for a minute, Grace Adrian Porter," Mom says. "I'm just asking you to tell me what's going on. You don't sound good. What's wrong? Is it Colonel?"

Grace leans her head against the wall. "No," she says. "It's not Colonel, Mom. It's me. I just need—I *want* to get away for a while. Everything moved so fast for so long, and now I just—I just want a break." She inhales a shaky, uneven breath and wipes her eyes. She lowers her voice, so not even her echo will hear her beg. "Please."

Mom clears her throat. "Tell me what happened," she says. "You don't sound like yourself."

"It's nothing I can't handle," she says. "It's been taking more out of me than I realized, finding a position. The *people* have been taking more out of me. I want some time to decide where I want to go next with my career. Professor MacMillan thought it sounded like a good idea, too." She squeezes her eyes shut. "I'm just tired, that's all. Maybe getting away would help."

"I bet Colonel was thrilled to hear that," Mom

says, and Grace racks out a wet, broken laugh. "Can I tell you something?" Mom asks.

Grace sighs. "Yeah," she says. "Sure."

"I want you to know you can always come visit. Southbury is your home, same as Portland. But, baby, *getting* away won't make the things *go* away, you hear me?" Mom's voice is soft. "It took me a long time to learn that. But your father is a fighter, and he raised you to be a fighter because he knew what kind of world we're living in. Don't let it break your spirit or wring you out dry. Okay?"

Grace swallows hard, tasting salt water. "Yeah," she croaks out. "I hear you."

"Jesus, Porter, don't cry. I can hear you. Don't cry."

"I know." She wipes her stinging eyes. "Porters don't cry. I know."

Mom sniffs. "I used to hate hearing you say that," she says. "But you've always listened to Colonel like he was God."

"Well, I didn't know any better," Grace says.

"That's a lie if I ever heard one," Mom says, voice fierce. "I know neither me or Colonel are always right, but we always want the best for you. If you think coming to stay in Southbury for a while is the best thing for you, then I won't say no."

"But?" Grace asks.

"But it'll be hard whether you're in Portland

or Florida or the North damn Pole. I don't want you to stop because it's hard. I know that's real easy for me to say, but it's true. Stop if you need a break, honey, but don't stop because they want you to. You got too much potential."

It breaks something in Grace, the simple honesty in her words. It breaks something, to acknowledge out loud that it will not be easy, no matter where she looks. She mourns for the optimism she felt right after graduation, when she thought, *I have come this far, and I will go even farther, and no one can stop me.* She grieves for that feeling because even if Porters don't cry, Grace does. Grace cries, in a hospital stairwell that's heard worse.

"My Star Girl," Mom says. "Please stop crying. It's breaking my heart."

Grace tries, she really tries, but the tears don't stop and neither does the hollow black abyss spreading right under her ribs. It used to be filled with research and classes and exams, the dream of what lay ahead. Now there's just nothing.

She cries, and all that nothing eats her up. The stairwell echoes with it.

She stays there until eventually someone wraps their arms around her and holds her tight.

"Let me go," she says, choking on her voice as she struggles in the grip. "Let me *go*."

"No," Agnes says. "I'm not letting you go."

She sounds scared, voice shaky. "You're hurting yourself. Look. *Look*."

Grace looks. There are long, red scratches on her knuckles, on her wrists and arms.

"Hello?" Agnes says, picking up Grace's dropped phone. "Hi, Ms. Mel, this is Agnes . . . Yeah, I'm gonna get her home, I promise . . . Yes. Yes, I promise. I have to go now . . . Okay. Yes. Bye."

She hangs up, still wrapped around Grace. "You never sound that polite," Grace says, enough of her energy gone that she goes limp. Agnes takes her weight.

"Yeah," Agnes grunts, shifting so they don't fall. "Well, you never scare the shit out of me like this," she mutters. "Twenty minutes, I said. Twenty minutes."

"Did you tell Ximena?"

"You already know the answer to that." She holds Grace tight. "She called Raj to pick us up. Fuck if I'm dragging you on a train or into an Uber like this."

Grace sighs, closing her eyes. "Aggie," she says quietly. Her throat and her eyes ache. Her heart aches. "I'm so tired."

"I know, dummy," Agnes says. "But you're not allowed to hurt yourself. I don't care how tired you are."

Grace nods. "Sorry."

"It's okay," Agnes says quickly. Grace can't

see her, but she hears the salt water in her voice, and her stomach lurches. "Just don't scare me like that." She clutches Grace's hands, her palms, her wrists, where on Agnes's there are moon craters. The terra firma skin there has been brutalized and torn up and scarred over. "Don't hurt yourself."

"I won't," Grace mumbles clumsily. She grips Agnes's hands back, tight as she can. "Just tired."

"Okay," Agnes says. "Okay, Porter. We're gonna go home, okay?"

Time passes in a blur. There is Agnes, ever-present Agnes who doesn't let go of Grace's hands. There is Ximena on Grace's other side, who holds her up. There is Raj, who curses and helps Grace into the car. He looks into her eyes, kisses her forehead and says, "Hey, little sis. You good?" He presses quick, insistent kisses on her face.

There is a long, quiet ride. Agnes doesn't buckle up. She sits as close to Grace as possible, so close she might as well be in her lap. As the trees and roads and buildings race past, Grace hears Ximena and Raj talking in whispers up front.

He carries her, bridal-style up to Ximena's bed.

"We're having a sleepover," Ximena says. "That sound good, babe?"

All four of them squish together in the bed. They hold Grace together, hold her bursting seams closed. Eventually she tumbles into a weary, dizzy sleep.

Nine

It is as if the first mournful tears shed serve as permission from the vast, black, formidable universe for Grace Porter to feel all that she has been pushing down, folding up, holding back. All the frustration, all the spitting anger, all the bitterness at relying on the goodwill of networks that were never created with her in mind. If she wants to be her own version of Professor MacMillan, she will have to meet her own people, find her own right fit.

Raj tells Baba Vihaan she's sick. *She's sick, Baba, don't worry. She'll be fine soon.* She says she's sick for almost a week before the guilt churns like a real sickness and despite all of them telling her to stay home, she makes the trek alone to the tea room.

Baba Vihaan is a stern, sweet man. His eyebrows are dark and furrowed, but when he smiles, it warms you from the inside.

He waits for her in the doorway to his office, keen eyes on the way Meera clings to Grace and doesn't want to let go. Eventually, they have to part, even though Meera almost refuses to go. She walks Grace the few feet to the office and tilts her chin up.

"Grace doesn't feel good," she says to her baba. "Be nice to her."

"And you go be nice to our customers," he says, pushing her away. "Come in, Grace. Rajesh said you've been ill."

She shrugs, slumping into a chair. Feeling ill would be good. Feeling ill would mean she could take some medicine, drink some soup and sleep it off. Instead, Grace feels bone-tired. She feels like she is drifting in space, calling back to command, *Houston, do you copy?* and there is a purposeful silence.

"Yeah," she says. "That's actually what I wanted to talk about, Baba Vihaan."

She sees a flash of fear on his face and immediately feels guilty for causing it.

She remembers Meera and Raj's mom. Mama Niya was a kind, beautiful woman, draped in gold bangles and bright scarves and glittering designs. She didn't say much, couldn't say much, because the oxygen tank that trailed behind her took up all her energy. She had a commanding presence that not even the cardiomyopathy could take. She could bring Raj down with just a look, one Meera is still trying to perfect.

When she died, the tea room closed for two weeks. Raj and Meera and Baba Vihaan stayed home. Grace received occasional texts and one sobbing, hysterical phone call from Meera, hiding in the bathtub away from her family and whispering her grief to Grace through a staticky phone line.

"I'm not sick," she says hurriedly. "I think everything just sort of caught up with me at once." *Things are not going my way, and I dealt with that by getting married in Vegas.* "I put my head down and grit my teeth for a long time, and I never stopped to consider if it was good for me. If—if things would be different now if I had been honest with myself from the start about what I would need and how I would get it. I haven't been—" She starts to pinch her skin and catches herself. "I haven't thought about myself or taken care of myself for a while now."

"You worked hard for a very long time," Baba Vihaan says. "Meera admires you so much for it. My Niya was like that, a hard worker, never taking enough time for herself." He sits back and stares at Grace. "I wish you could have known her better. You are a lot like her. Meera and Rajesh, they are like me. But you, I see her in you, like you really did come from us. Working too hard, thinking all the time." He taps his temple. "You get lost up there. She did it all the time."

"I'm not *lost,*" she says. "I'm—I just need time to—shit." She grimaces. "Sorry."

He laughs a low, gentle chuckle. "You get it from Meera and your white girl. The one skinny like a bird," he says. "Terrible mouths, those two."

Grace smiles. She always feels comfortable with Baba Vihaan. She doesn't want to leave and face the real world. She wants to sit in this office and listen to him talk.

"I bet you wouldn't say that to Meera's face," she says.

He shrugs. "Maybe not. I like my peace." He pauses. "She said life after graduation has been hard for you."

Grace shrugs back. "Harder than I thought it would be," she says. "Now I have too much time to think, like you said." She looks up at the ceiling, like she can reach up and pluck the words from the tiles. "Everyone says I need a break, Baba." It is easier, somehow, to say the words now. "Maybe it's true. I think maybe I do."

One hand moves to the top drawer of his desk, which stays locked. "You need money?" he asks.

Grace laughs and ignores how it makes her eyes water. "No," she insists. "Thank you, but no. Mom sends me some, you know that. And Colonel takes care of me." She takes a deep breath. "I think maybe I need to leave Portland for a little while."

"The rain doesn't make you feel better?" he asks wryly. "These cold, gray skies?"

"Somehow, no," Grace says. "I'm sorry. I should have given you some notice."

"Gracie," he says, disapproval heavy in his tone. "I treat you like one of my own. You *are* one of my own," he says, "Rajesh and Meera and Gracie. My kids, you know that."

He reaches across the desk, and she meets him halfway. Both of his hands wrap around hers.

"I'll miss the tea room while I'm gone," she says. "I'm a snob now. I don't want to get my tea anywhere else. You taught me well."

"Then don't stay away too long," Baba Vihaan says. "I have only the wisdom of my own life to share with you. And my life has taught me to take care of myself, so that I can take care of everything else. You'll figure out how to do that."

She spends the next few days lounging around the apartment. There is a foil-covered plate on the counter. There's a note chicken-scratched on the fridge that says "Eat" and also "Will check on you later."

Grace heads for her room. She hasn't slept there in days, but she aches for the comfort of her own bed. Her weighted covers envelope her in warmth and darkness when she crawls underneath them completely. Suddenly, Grace feels happy to have locked her door. She might think too much, get lost in her head, but sometimes she just needs to be alone with her own thoughts.

Her phone buzzes. She sighs, mentally typing out the *I'm fine* to appease her friends. It could be Mom's now daily text, checking in to see if Grace is still planning on heading to Southbury soon.

The text is not from any of them.

Yuki
12:23 p.m.
feel free to ignore in case this
is weird but it's been quiet for
a little bit so i just wanted to ask
are you dead? if yes, did you
get a chance to add me to
your will

Grace lets out a small, hiccupy laugh. In her world beneath her covers, she's allowed to focus only on this and not the rest of the big, wide world. She's allowed to smile at the stupid ring emoji she put next to Yuki's name. She's allowed to cry a little at how good it feels to have someone talk to her like she is not broken.

Grace
12:25 p.m.
would you cause a scene at my
funeral?

Yuki
12:26 p.m.
10/10 would real housewives that shit.
maybe throw a prosthetic leg or two

Grace
12:26 p.m.
your own or someone else's

Yuki
12:28 p.m.
why not both, grace porter?
also if you hadn't understood the
prosthetic leg ref i would
have filed for divorce

Grace
12:29 p.m.
you know we're probably going to
hell for this

Yuki
12:33 p.m.
i'm already a lesbian. you can't go
to jail for two things

Grace
12:35 p.m.
you definitely can, yuki

Yuki
12:36 p.m.
i grew up watching law and
order svu, i'm basically a
lawyer mostly bc i had a huge
crush on olivia benson
but if my parents ask it was for
bd wong
#asianrep

Grace
12:37 p.m.
am i allowed to laugh at that

Yuki
12:41 p.m.
thank you for asking for permission
to laugh at my niche asian jokes
and yes you can, it was funny
also me asking if you were dead
was code only cowards ask their wives
if they're okay after days of silence

Grace
12:42 p.m.
yes i'm fine

Yuki
12:43 p.m.
and i watched law and order svu
for bd wong
wanna try again or you want
me to drop it

Grace sighs and stares at her phone. It's hard to explain that you are tired, bone-deep, rib-deep, belly-deep tired. It's hard to explain that someone held their hand out to the stars and said all of these can be yours, and you believed it. You believed the climb and the barrier and the gate would not break you. You spent eleven years ignoring that your mind and body said, *Stop, breathe, be kind to yourself,* and you punished yourself for even thinking it.

Yuki
12:45 p.m.
that was pushy right
tell me to go away
put me out of my misery
you are legally obligated
but you can tell me
omg i can't stop talking

Dialing Yuki . . .

"Grace Porter," Yuki answers, out of breath. "I was doing that thing where you text something embarrassing and then throw your phone across the room, only it kept buzzing. Because you were calling me."

Grace curls up under her blanket world. Yuki doesn't sound gentle or soft or hesitant. She doesn't know Grace has been falling apart and doesn't treat her like she has. It's freeing.

"Hello?" Yuki says. "God, you didn't really call me on your death bed, did you? That's gross."

Grace closes her eyes so tight that fireworks burst behind her eyelids. "No, just my regular bed." Her thoughts are still racing, and she plucks one out. "Did you ever hear about the Opportunity Mars Rover?"

There's a weighted silence. "Is that your kind of science? Mars rovers?"

"Not me," Grace says. "I still think it's fascinating." She pauses. "Do you want to hear about it? The Mars Rover?"

"Tell me," Yuki says.

"They named it *Opportunity*. It was only supposed to survive for ninety days," Grace says, like a quiet eulogy. "But it stayed and did its mission for fifteen years. Because it had a plan, you know. And when you have a plan, you don't fuck it up. You keep going."

Yuki clears her throat softly. "That sounds like a lot of pressure."

"It is," Grace murmurs. "It had like arthritis, you know? I mean, not really, it's a robot but—"

"I get it," Yuki says. There's shuffling and creaking and then Yuki's voice, low and muffled like she, too, has entered her own blanket world. "Tell me some more about it."

"It started forgetting stuff," Grace says. "Like, information it was supposed to send back to the command center. I'm sure it was hard. It's hard when you have a plan. Plans are so goddamn hard."

Yuki doesn't say anything, so Grace keeps going. Her words trip over one another. "There was a dust storm," she says. "And then the temperature dropped. And it couldn't—sometimes you fight so hard to follow what you're supposed to do, but it's hard and you *can't*."

"Yeah," Yuki says. "Life is shit like that." There's more shuffling, and Yuki's voice drops to almost a whisper. "What happened to it?"

"Died, as much as rovers can." Grace sniffles. "The last message it sent to Earth was about its measurements of power production and the atmospheric opacity. Both were critical."

"I'm a waitress," Yuki murmurs. "I have no idea what any of that means."

"God, sorry." She clutches her blankets tight. "The team behind the rover simplified its message, you know. It's kind of ridiculous, that we anthropomorphized this machine so much, but I can tell you what they translated it to if you want."

"I want."

" 'My battery is low, and it's getting dark,' " Grace says quietly. "Those were the last words of a Mars Rover that was only supposed to survive for ninety days. It followed its plan until it couldn't anymore." Grace wipes her eyes. Little hiccups of grief come for plans followed and plans dismantled and in need of repair.

"Hey," Yuki says. "Can I tell you something?"

"Yeah."

"I feel like that little fucking robot sometimes, I think. I feel like I'm sending my last message out into the universe, and I'm hoping that someone is listening. I think that's why I started my radio show. So I could talk about all the things that lurk in the dark that reminded me of *me,* and I would know that someone, even one person, was listening."

Grace swallows hard and pulls the covers up even more to hide the smallest rays of the afternoon sun.

"Grace Porter," Yuki says. "Are you there?"

Are you there? It's the question that starts every session of Yuki's radio show.

When Grace first listened, it felt directed at her. *Hello, lonely creatures. Are you there?*

Now it is.

"Yuki Yamamoto," Grace says, voice scratchy and stuffy.

"Yeah?"

"My battery is low," she confesses, and the hurt of it unveils like a thorned flower. "And it's getting so dark."

She tells Yuki she had a plan, a *good* plan, and when she got to the end, there was no trophy with her name etched on it. There was no welcome committee thanking her for all that she had sacrificed to get here. There were no offers waiting for her. There is just Grace Porter with a piece of paper that says *doctor* and another that says *married.*

She stays curled up through all of it. She stays

folded in, protecting the soft, vulnerable parts of herself from the world and her unrelenting brain. She stays with the phone low on speaker and her knees pulled up to her chest. Yuki stays with her.

"That sounds really hard," Yuki says, like it's a fact and not pity. It makes Grace relax. "It must be scary, right, getting to the end and realizing how much more work there is to do."

"Everyone tells me what I need, what I should do," Grace says, "but I don't even know. The responsible thing would be to keep pushing. To keep applying for jobs and promoting my research and forcing them to see me, to hear me. That's the responsible thing, right?"

"Okay, so not to sound like another person trying to fix your problems with a hammer," Yuki says slowly, "but who said you had to be responsible? I mean, you have a doctorate, and you're—" She pauses. "Shit, how old are you?"

Grace lets out a laugh. "I'm turning twenty-nine in August."

"Well, almost-twenty-nine-year-old Grace," she says, "it sounds like you've spent a really long time being responsible."

Grace exhales. "I knew I married you for a reason," she says, and Yuki laughs. Here, she doesn't have to be exhausted. She doesn't have to be burnt out or in need of a break. She doesn't have to be grieving. She doesn't have to be responsible. It feels like relief.

Yuki is quiet on the line, waiting.

"Yuki," she says, heart thumping in her ears. "I want to ask you something that might sound a little crazy."

Yuki scoffs. "Grace Porter, we got drunk and married in Las Vegas. We have wedding rings I can't remember getting, and there's a picture of me looking at you like you hung the goddamn moon. Like, somehow, I knew you were connected to all those millions and billions of stars up there. There's nothing crazier than that."

"Billion trillion," Grace says, biting her lip hard enough to hurt. "Assuming there are about ten billion galaxies, right, and that there are one hundred billion stars in each galaxy. It's a billion trillion."

Yuki sighs. "Honey Girl," she says. "Ask me."

Grace feels her throat constrict as she tries to formulate the words. She doesn't know Yuki, not really, but Yuki sees the things relegated to the shadows. She sees the things that are lonely and feared and misjudged. Grace feels seen in Yuki's stories, and in the way Yuki seems to understand her in ways Grace doesn't have to articulate. Yuki said she was singing her a song, and Grace can hear it. She wants to follow it, without one of her perfect plans, and see where it leads. She wants to follow this good thing, this *girl,* she found in the desert. This girl that does not feel like the oppressive work that Grace wants to escape. This girl that feels like new, mutual work that benefits both of them.

Yuki tells her to ask. Grace decides, for once, to tell the little voice in her head that demands she keep going until she has nothing left to *shut up*.

She asks.

Ten

Grace has never been to New York.

Yuki offered to meet her at the airport. "We can make it a cheesy Hallmark movie," she said the night before, voice faint through the phone as she painted her nails. "Or, we can make it gay and awkward. Visitor's choice."

Grace told her she could do it. She was already imposing on Yuki's hospitality. She could figure out this part by herself.

Grace
10:35 a.m.
i landed

She waits.

Yuki
10:39 a.m.
do you feel like a new woman?
inhale that nyc air

Grace
10:40 a.m.
remember when i said i could figure
out how to get to the train station
i changed my mind

146

new york is big and scary and
i haven't even left the airport yet

Yuki
10:42 a.m.
oh yeah i totally knew you would fuck
that up you had no idea what you were
talking about it was cute i thought i'd let
you have your fantasy

Grace
10:43 a.m.
a girl laughed at me because i asked if i
was in manhattan

Yuki
10:44 a.m.
of course she did
why would you be in manhattan
laguardia is in queens

Yuki
10:45 a.m.
go outside omg
i'm laughing but i'll help you
are you outside

Grace
10:48 a.m.
i am outside

i can't tell if this is better
or worse

Yuki
10:49 a.m.
it's laguardia
outside is better

Grace makes her way outside, already feeling
the heat from early summer.

Yuki
10:51 a.m.
the easiest thing to do is to take a car of
your choosing
idk your ethics on uber or lyft
or maybe you are a yellow taxicab
kind of girl

Grace
10:52 a.m.
it's so expensive

She has the money from Mom in her savings
account, but she still feels afraid to spend it. The
sooner she spends it, the sooner she has to make
her way back home.

Yuki
10:54 a.m.

i got good tips last night
split the fare with me

Grace
10:55 a.m.
absolutely not

Yuki
10:57 a.m.
marriage is about compromise
welcome to new york grace porter

"I can't believe you let me do this," she whispers into her phone while the driver turns the music up. "This is a mistake," she says. "What was I thinking?"

"What?" Ximena asks. She sounds way too chipper for it to be so early. "Why do you sound like that? Were you stuck next to a baby the entire flight?"

"My seatmate was actually very nice. We exchanged a few pleasantries while boarding and didn't speak or make eye contact for the rest of the flight."

"Sounds wonderful. Why so glum?"

"I'm in *New York City,*" Grace says. "I'm in New York City to meet a girl I married in Las Vegas."

Ximena makes a thoughtful noise. "Yes, I thought we already knew this."

"Colonel will kill me if he finds out," Grace hisses. "I told my parents I'd found a summer research opportunity. I'm not just derailing the plan I've had for over a decade, but I'm making shit up about it now. In the contest for World's Worst Daughter, I'm top two, and I'm not number two." Her breath hitches, and she covers her eyes with a free hand. She'll *die* if she cries in this Toyota Prius.

"Calm down," Ximena says softly. "Don't cry, you know it stresses me out." She lets out a deep exhale, and Grace can almost hear her mind whirring. "Okay, do you need me to tell you again why this isn't a terrible idea?"

Grace sniffles and hides a smile in her sleeve. It's too hot for her tie-dye hoodie, but she's wearing another one she's taken from Raj, and she pretends she can still smell his cologne in the fabric. It's comforting to have this reminder of her family. "Yes, please. Love you."

"So much it hurts," Ximena says. "Now, we decided—*you* decided—it was okay to need a break, right?"

Grace shrugs. "I guess," she mumbles. "I probably should have taken a break in Florida."

She hears an exaggerated "oh my God" in the background. "Is that Grace Porter?" Agnes asks. "I thought we already convinced her it was okay to enjoy being married to a cute girl? Summer in NYC. It's like a movie!"

150

Grace's eye twitches.

"Go away, Ag," Ximena tells her. "Go eat before you leave to terrorize the working world. There's mangú and huevos fritos and aguacate."

"I want mangú," Grace sulks. She's starving after a five-and-a-half-hour flight, and it mixes with the apprehension and anxiety churning in her belly. The tops of her wrists are sore. Where the skin is thicker and sturdier, and she pinched and released and pinched and released while she waited at baggage claim.

"You," Ximena says. "*You* need to just relax. I promise it's okay." She lowers her voice, so it is just her and Grace the words fall between. "I know we think we have to be on all the time. But, Porter?" she asks, voice quiet. "It's okay for us to just *be,* too. Enjoy this, okay? Enjoy getting to know Yuki, and don't overthink this like your ridiculous Virgo brain tells you to do."

"But—"

"Go meet your wife. Fall in *loooove.*" She yawns, a little squeaky thing that makes Grace homesick. "I worked a late shift last night. I'm heading back to bed."

"But, *Ximena—*"

"Text me later! Love you!"

The call ends, and Grace lets out a muted scream through clenched teeth. She hides under her hood and stares out the car window.

"Okay, Grace Porter," she mutters. She squares

her shoulders. "You married this girl. Now, go get her."

The car pulls up in front of a redbrick building. Her heart skips because this is it. She's a Porter, and Porters are strong and fearless. But she is also Grace, and Grace is nervous and scared. Her hands tremble as she gets out of the car and grabs her bags.

Up ahead, a girl sits on a stoop with a bouquet of yellow and orange flowers next to her.

"Yuki?" Grace calls, and the girl jolts, standing up jerkily. "Yuki Yamamoto?"

She decides to be brave about this. She dumps her duffel bag on a dirty New York City sidewalk and throws herself into Yuki's arms. Yuki catches her. There is a solid body against hers, and the world goes quiet. She squeezes her arms around this girl's soft waist, *her* girl's soft waist.

"Grace Porter," Yuki murmurs. "In the flesh, at last."

Grace leans back. "Were you afraid I was a figment of your imagination or something?" She reaches out, hands hovering over Yuki's hair. It's shorter, she's positive, hanging just over the tops of her ears. Feathered, too-long bangs fall into her eyes. Her undercut is neatly buzzed. "Did you cut your hair just for me?"

Yuki steps away, head down so all that shows is her septum piercing and the curve of her mouth. "Yes to both things," she says. When she talks, it's different from her radio voice and less distorted than how she sounds on the phone. She sounds like a real person with a real body and real fingers that grip a bouquet of yellow and orange flowers tight enough that they start to droop.

"Here," she says, holding them out.

Grace takes the flowers gently and buries her face in them, inhaling. "You got me flowers," she says, her voice held tight with wonder.

Yuki scratches behind her ear. She tilts her head up, just enough that one eye peeks out from underneath her fringe. "If you hate them, then it wasn't my idea," she says quickly. "If you like them, then they reminded me of you. The yellow and the orange. As close to gold as I could find."

"Yeah," Grace breathes out. "I like them. They're beautiful."

Yuki squints at her. "Good," she says. "Then it was my idea."

Grace rolls her eyes, feeling light and silly. "Thank you."

Yuki looks up fully. Grace can take in all of her: her scrunched nose and her sharp eyes and her dimpled cheeks and the quarter moon light that glints off her ears from all her piercings. "You're welcome," she says back, like a challenge. She steps back and holds out her arms. "Welcome to Harlem."

Grace turns and just from here she can see

153

copper-brick row homes and small apartment buildings and cramped little food spots. There's soul food and West African carryouts at two opposite corners and a buffet farther up that smells like Maw Maw's at Thanksgiving, the table filled with mac and cheese, and greens, and yams with the syrup dripping from them like grease.

"You hungry?" Yuki asks. "We can have leftovers for lunch if my roommates haven't eaten them all."

Grace cranes her head to take it all in. "You haven't told me about your roommates," she says distractedly. Somewhere in the distance, she can pick out the familiar smell of hair grease and burning curling irons. Maw Maw always did her hair when she was younger, always told her to *hold your ear* and *that's just the steam, girl, calm down*. Portland is many things, but it tucks away all the things that remind Grace of herself in secret corners and shadows.

"Are you listening to me?" Yuki asks, and Grace turns.

"No," she says honestly, and Yuki sticks her tongue out. "I was having some culture feelings, sorry. Wasn't expecting it."

"Ah," Yuki says, following her line of sight. "Is this your hashtag Asian rep moment, Grace Porter?"

"Maybe," she confesses. She turns to Yuki,

who's staring back at her. "Okay, quick. Tell me about your roommates before I meet them."

Yuki leans against the stoop railing. "They're a little weird," she says. "My weird, queer family I made myself. I thought it would be too much, living with three guys, but we make it work."

Grace blinks. "You live with three guys?" she asks.

Yuki shrugs, a small, shy smile on her face. "We make it work," she says. "And they're not assholes, I swear." She scrunches her nose up as she thinks that over. "Not unbearable assholes. I would have smothered them in their sleep otherwise."

She turns toward the front door, and Grace takes in the apartment building in full. It's crumbling in places, but there are flower boxes hanging from every window, little pink and purple blossoms that bloom in hello. From the flagpole hangs a rainbow flag with the black and brown stripes. There's a sign taped to the first-floor window that says "God welcomes all, regardless of color or creed." There's a welcome mat on the front porch that says "All love welcome here."

Yuki pinks up. She looks embarrassed. "Our landlady is a little much," she says quietly. "But we got really lucky with her."

"She seems pretty fucking cool," Grace says. "How long have you lived here?"

Yuki ushers them inside and up the stairs.

"Long enough that Auntie Anna Mae—that's our landlady—knows way too much of my business." They stop in front of apartment 206. "This is me," she says, looking nervous. "I'm not responsible for anything my roommates say or do. You're not allowed to divorce me if you hate them."

Grace frowns, feeling her edges to see if the gel is still holding her baby hairs down. "What if they hate *me?*" she asks, her mind racing with worst-case scenarios. Maybe they'll take one look at her and know Yuki made a terrible mistake.

Yuki waits for silent permission before she runs soft, gentle fingers through the ends of Grace's gold-honey strands. "All this hair," she says softly. "It's all I could remember for so long. All this gold hair. The sun *did* want you to stand out."

Grace groans, pushing her hands away. "I should have never told you that. It's such mom bullshit."

Someone raps on the door from the inside. "You told us to make sure we were all home, and now you're gonna make us wait while you stare into each other's eyes like a Harlequin novel?" There's muffled curses and a muted *thump*. "I've been silenced," the voice calls out. "Oppression wins again."

Yuki shuts her eyes tight. "They're all awful," she confesses. "I lied. They're all total assholes." She opens the door.

Three people are spread out. There's a white

guy sitting cross-legged on the floor, glitter in his long shaggy hair as he folds paper hearts.

There's a dark-skinned Black guy sitting on their kitchen counter. It's not so much a kitchen as much as the insides of a kitchen pushed against the wall. But there he sits, alternating between eating out of a huge mixing bowl between his legs and throwing glitter at the guy with the hearts. Little mini paper hearts are tucked in the strands of his dreads like flowers.

In the very front of it all, hands on hips, is a guy with his chin tipped up in defiance. His right eye is bruised and black, and his long shiny black hair hangs in a thick braid on his shoulder. Somehow, he is completely free of glitter and hearts. His only decorations are the pinkish-red indents in his deep brown skin from his chest binder.

"I cut my MMA training short for this," he huffs, eyes flicking over Grace. "And," he says, thumb pointing back at the glitter and hearts behind him, "I've had to supervise arts and crafts time. So many hearts! It's not even Valentine's Day! It's June!"

"You sound bitter," Heart Guy says. "Plus, I like hearts. Hearts are love and all that shit I have to teach to my first-graders." He looks up and gives Grace a salute with his scissors. "Are you the wifey?"

Grace shoots Yuki a look. "I think so? Most

people just call me Grace. Or Porter. I answer to both, I guess."

"But which one do you like?" he asks. "Which one feels like you?"

"Jesus," the guy on the counter says. Another clump of glitter goes flying through the air. "She just got here. At least let her sit down before you make her question her entire existence."

Yuki dumps Grace's duffel bag on the floor. "Before this devolves any more," she says, "let me introduce you. That's Dhorian." She points to the guy on the counter. "You probably won't see him much today because he'll be cleaning up all this goddamn glitter. That," she says, pointing to the guy meticulously cutting out hearts, "is our token white boy, Fletcher. We love him but will kill him first when the revolution starts."

Fletcher shrugs, holding a pink heart up to his face. "I've accepted my place in this household."

Yuki moves to wrap her arms around the guy with the swollen black eye. She pinches his cheek. "And this absolute looker is Sani. Don't let the black eye scare you. He almost always has one. Happens when you're a big ol' softie in the boxing ring."

She ducks, cackling as Sani whips around to grab at her. "Behave," she screeches, slung over his shoulder. "We have company. Grace, this is my commune. Commune, say hi."

"Hi, Grace," they intone out of sync. "Or

Porter," Fletcher adds, not even flinching as more glitter gets thrown at him.

Sani puts Yuki down. "So," he says. "You're the girl that got Yuki drunk and married in Vegas."

"Relax." Yuki frowns. "Technically, I think I got her drunk."

"You did," Grace says, fidgeting with the straps of her backpack. "And I can't remember it, but from the picture, the wedding seemed really nice," she admits.

Yuki makes a surprised noise. "You kept it?"

"Yeah." She shrugs. "It makes me happy when I look at it."

The room is silent, and she stares down at her feet.

"Did you bring the picture?" Dhorian asks. He shakes a spoonful of cookie dough at her. "You can share this with me if you say yes."

"Yes," Grace says. "Why?"

He lets out a shriek. One of their neighbors beats on the wall. "Yuki refuses to let us see it," he says. He lifts his mixing bowl like an offering. "Today, girls and gays, we feast on drunk love." He jumps down off the counter. "I think I have vodka stashed somewhere. Reconvene in fifteen. Hut hut!"

"Hut hut!" Sani and Fletcher yell.

They scatter, and Yuki grabs Grace's hand and pulls her down a hallway. The grip has started to feel familiar, as does the way Yuki sends shy glances at Grace out of the corner of her eye, like she's checking to make sure Grace is still there.

Are you there?

"I'm here," she says quietly. She feels an unhindered sense of acceptance. She can just *be* here, without any heavy, weighed down expectations.

She says it now, standing in the middle of Yuki's room. She is surrounded by posters and old radios and a little altar, as Grace suspected, with crystals and herbs and vials of sea salt.

Yuki looks at Grace to check that she is really there, and yes, she is.

The first lesson Grace learns about Yuki Yamamoto is that she's a blanket hog.

It would bother Grace, if she was someone who slept much. Instead, she climbs out of the full-size bed and the memory foam topper Yuki splurged on. The apartment doesn't have a balcony like Grace's back in Portland, so she makes do with cracking the window open. Yuki doesn't wake.

She has to be careful with the windows because Yuki has little statues lined up along the sill. They go in between burned down incense, and Grace leans down to smell the lingering remains. She finds herself wondering, sleepy and alone under moonlight, what Yuki was thinking when she lit these. If she was thinking about the stars or work or the lonely creatures in the dark. If maybe she lit these once and thought of Grace, and watched the incense burn down to its stumps.

"Honey Girl?" Yuki murmurs, voice hoarse with sleep. The half-moons under her eyes are part of their own galaxy. "What are you doing?" She doesn't lift her head off the pillow, so her hair falls in her eyes and covers them up. "Sleepy."

"Sorry," Grace whispers back, carefully closing the window and tiptoeing back toward the bed. Her body sinks into the mattress as she crawls back in. "Insomniac."

Her hair falls around her in streaks. Yuki reaches out hesitantly, watching Grace's face as her fingers start to twirl in the sleep-flattened curls. She hadn't said anything when Grace changed out her pillowcase for a silk one. Had only rolled toward it and said it smelled like jasmine.

Now she tugs lightly at Grace's hair, the strands meandering over the sheets. "This is what I remember," she croaks out. "It never really got dark that night in Vegas, and you were passed out on the bed. All the lights hit your hair. Honey gold," she tells Grace. "A girl with hair from the sun."

Grace sighs. She closes her eyes, cocooning herself in the quiet intimacy. "That's not me," she says.

Yuki makes a soft noise and shifts closer. "It's a good story," she says.

"It's *just* a story."

She feels Yuki's gaze on her, sharpening by the second. "Can I tell you something I've learned from stories, Grace Porter?"

In a fit of spiteful bravery, she tugs half the covers away from Yuki. "Yes," she says finally, burrowed underneath. "What have you learned?"

Yuki takes her half of the covers and burrows under, too. The two of them are underneath, a hidden fortress for whispering secrets. "People may not believe the stories," she says, pink mouth cracking open with a yawn, "but that doesn't mean they aren't real."

Grace spends the rest of the night staring up at Yuki's ceiling, wishing for her own plastic, glow-in-the-dark stars. She spends the rest of the night breathing through the feeling of her chest aching, her heart *breaking,* wishing she could believe the stories as simply as Yuki does. In the real world, people do not easily accept the things on the fringes, the things with teeth and claws and wants and dreams. Stories do not change that.

Grace gets up at eight while Yuki is snoring away next to her. She sleeps in, Grace will learn, until about noon, then wakes up angry to be alive until she's had her toast with jam.

Grace meanders into the living space.

No one is cooking breakfast, but Dhorian is slinking in the door with a hoodie pulled on over his hospital scrubs. He waves a tired hand at Grace before he collapses against the kitchen counter and sighs longingly at their cheap coffee maker.

"I need coffee," he says, "but I'm too tired to make coffee."

She hesitates. "Do you want me to—" she starts to ask, voice breaking in the middle. "Do you want me to make your coffee?"

He tilts his head. "Porter," he says quietly, "if you make the machine do the thing, I will fly to Vegas and marry you, too."

She laughs quietly, coming out of the shadows. She waggles her fingers until her gold band is visible. "I think I did okay the first time around." The coffee machine gurgles. "How was work?" she asks, anxious to fill the space with words that aren't about her drunken night with desert flowers and forever vows.

Dhorian groans. He instructs Grace on how to work the machine between yawns. "Night shift in the ED. Sorry, the emergency department. It's—what's a nicer phrase for 'absolutely fucking ghoulish'?"

"I think that works."

"Okay." He looks like he could fall asleep right here on the counter. "Then, it was absolutely fucking ghoulish. Kid came in with a broken arm and a suspected case of negligence. Probably child abuse. The paperwork alone is enough to kill you," he says, "but it's really fucked up when you gotta send the kid home. Sugar and cream, please."

She gets the sugar and cream.

"What made you choose that field?" she asks him. "You're a resident, right?"

He nods. Watchful, sleepy eyes follow her progress. "Mom's a pediatrician. Dad's a pediatrician. Sister's finishing up her pediatric residency," he says ruefully. He stands up to stretch. "What's a rebel without a cause, huh?" He grabs his mug with both hands and shuffles down the hall to the room he shares with Fletcher. "Next time you see me, remind me to ask you about your work, okay? Thank you, Porter," he says, before his bedroom door shuts behind him.

If Grace has anything to say about it, she won't remind him. She doesn't even want to think about it herself.

Instead, she wanders around the apartment, careful of creaking floorboards. She runs her hand along all the exposed brick, and the rough scratchy surface reminds her of the asteroid particles back in the MacMillan lab. Their little living room is exploding with pictures and magazines and a film of glitter. There's a fish tank in the corner of the room filled with neon-bright fish. They are the same color as Grace's stick-on ceiling stars, the ones that hear all her hopes and dreams and fears and worries.

She crouches down in front of the tank and

wonders if these fish, innocuous and quiet, have heard the same from the people in this apartment. She presses a finger to the glass and taps lightly. One darts toward the sound.

"Hello," she says quietly, watching it flick from side to side. She taps again, and it follows. "Hello, bright little thing."

The fish swims away, back into its little coven of neon friends. They are mesmerizing to watch, content as they are to swim in their little group in their little tank in their little world.

"What do you think about?" she asks the fish in the tank. "Do you ever think about the big, wide ocean, and how you would feel if you could swim in it?" She taps the glass again, and another, or maybe the same fish, darts forward. "I thought I wanted to be out of my tank," she confesses with a whisper. "But the ocean is big, you know, and I am very, very small." The fish follows her finger. "I don't know that I like it," she says, so softly she can barely hear it herself. "I don't know that I like feeling this small at all."

Eleven

On the nights Yuki doesn't close up the restaurant and come home with aching feet and meager tips, she does the radio show. Grace watches her undo her work-sanctioned white button-down and black tie, and turn soft and pink and relaxed after a shower. She only wears comfy clothes to the radio station, and tonight she tumbles out of her steamy bathroom in black leggings and oversize lesbian flannel and settles on the couch.

Fletcher has been trying to teach Sani and Grace how to play Egyptian Rat Screw for the past hour, still in his suit jacket and tie from school. His hands are covered in paint.

The end of the school year is bullshit, he said when he came in. *I just let them finger-paint.*

Now he says, "Seriously, how have you guys never played this?" He deals the cards evenly. "Every day at recess I used to wipe the floor with those uppity punks who tried to out-slap me."

Fletcher is from Queens.

Sani wrinkles his nose and stares warily at the cards being thrown in front of him. His long hair hangs in his face. "I don't know," he says, collecting his pile. "There are other things to do when you grow up on a reservation. Egyptian Rat Screw was not one of them. Blame your government for not giving us access to your weird-ass settler card games."

He looks up when silence falls. "What? Too deep?"

Fletcher sighs. "No. Go on, do you want to give Porter the speech? She's never heard it."

Sani sniffs, offended. He's like a cat, all long, stretchy limbs and wary affection.

"What's the speech?" Grace asks. "I didn't know you grew up on a reservation."

"Well, I did," he says. He cuts his eye at Grace. "Are you going to ask me what it was like?"

"I'm only half-white," she argues. "Give me some credit for sensitivity."

Sani lets out a surprised laugh, leaning into Grace's shoulder. "You're not so bad," he says, resting his head there. He looks at Fletcher. "Teach us how to play this game. We're going to kick your ass."

"No kicking any ass," Yuki says suddenly, looking up from her phone. "I won't be here to supervise."

"Can I come with you?" Grace asks, feeling courageous. She wants to see Yuki work. She wants to watch the stories come to life as they move through radio airwaves.

Yuki blinks. "You want to? You're actually asking to come?"

Grace stares. "Why do you sound surprised? I like hanging out with you."

"Oh," Yuki says. "I think I'm having an emotion." She disappears into her room.

"Rain check on Egyptian Rat Screw?" Grace asks, the three of them staring at Yuki's closed door.

Sani waves her off. "Go, go," he says. He throws the cards behind him. "We," he tells Fletcher grandly, "are going to play Uno to the death."

Grace leaves them. She knocks carefully on Yuki's door. There's no answer, so she lets herself in slowly.

Yuki sits on a small pillow in front of her altar. She has two little crystals in her hand, quartz and another one Grace doesn't recognize. The room smells like the ocean, like Yuki, like her basil and herbs and little green flowers she lets grow wild on a sacred tabletop.

"Hey," Grace says softly. She sits down, careful of the crystals and the plants and the magic and reverence that seem to hover here. "Talk to me?"

"I'm sorry," Yuki says. "I don't know what's wrong with me. It was a rough day at work, and I realized I just wanted to come home and—"

"And what?"

"You make it feel easy," Yuki says, "and it terrifies me a little. I had a rough day at work, and I wanted to come home and see you. I wanted to kiss you, and touch you, and, I don't know, maybe even fuck you if the mood was right. I wanted to let you *in*." She presses the two crystals tight into her palms. "I almost wish you would stop making it feel so easy."

Grace bites her lip. The words warm the pit of her stomach and make her throat dry. She did not just leave Portland because she wanted time, perspective, a *breath*. She also wanted a girl singing a song that drew her in. "I think it's a good thing."

"Do you?" Yuki asks.

"I was scared to come to New York," Grace admits. "Terrified. But from the first time I heard your voice on the radio, I knew you were a good thing."

Yuki lets out a long, slow breath. Her flannel shirt hangs off her shoulder. Her hair sticks to her forehead. She is a prickly cactus flourishing in desert heat. "Terrified to come here," she starts, turning to look at Grace, "but not terrified of me, right?"

Grace folds herself up, knees to chest. Yuki has all sorts of quartz on her little altar. Rutilated quartz and pink quartz and smoky quartz. Quartz is supposed to be a healing crystal. She doesn't know if all the quartz in the world could heal two lonely creatures in the dark. She hasn't kissed Yuki yet, not here, because she feels too much like the things in the shadows. Like she could draw blood without trying. She hasn't kissed Yuki because she is still learning how to be this lonely creature.

"I don't know yet," Grace says. This close, Yuki's eyes are black, glittering pools. Her arms, like armor, guard her heart and her ribs and her soft parts, like she is scared, too. Grace doesn't want either of them to be scared. "But I wasn't scared of you in the desert when we put flowers in each other's hair. I wasn't scared when a man in a fucking glitter suit asked if I wanted you as my lawfully wedded wife. I wasn't scared when I said *yes*."

Grace reaches out, hoping desperately that Yuki will reach back, and she does. She *does*. Yuki opens her palm, and Grace takes one of her crystals. "I don't want to be scared of you, Yuki Yamamoto."

"Then don't be," Yuki says, voice quiet and low and reverent. "I looked it up, you know. I looked up how to get an annulment. Printed out the paperwork and everything. Even filled it out and signed my name. But then you *called* me, and I ripped them up." She places her crystal on the altar like an intention. "I don't want to be scared of you, either, Grace Porter."

Grace lets out a small laugh. "We're kind of a mess."

Yuki shakes her head. "On my show I asked 'Are you there?' All the lonely creatures that were listening said *yes,* and it turns out you were one of them," she says. "Us lonely creatures have to stick together." She taps at the matching band on Grace's ring finger. She reaches up to touch a glinting key, the one nestled against Grace's chest that feels so a part of her that it thumps in time with her pulse. "You're my mess now, and I'm yours. No take-backs."

Grace told her parents she was coming to New York for research. It was a once-in-a-lifetime opportunity, she said. Maybe that part wasn't a lie. "Then can I come with you to do your show?" she asks. *Let me in,* she thinks. *I will try to be your good thing, too.*

Yuki smiles. Her eyes are dark and her teeth are sharp. She is a lonely creature of the dark. Grace doesn't want to be scared. "Yes," she says.

This part is easy.

Yuki's radio station is an unassuming building. The guard at the front desk hands Yuki a key.

"Need me to lock up?" she asks. "You know I love having so much power, Jarrell."

The guy, Jarrell, rolls his eyes. "Babysitter fell through. I'll owe you one."

Yuki waves him away. "Go be a responsible parent," she says. "Is Little Jay still working on that history paper?"

Jarrell nods. "He says Tudor England is, and I quote, 'a white people soap opera,' like I got any idea what he's talking about. They ain't teach no damn Tudor England when I got my GED."

Yuki laughs, leaning against the desk. "Tell him to text me, and we can talk it through."

Jarrell glares at Yuki as he leaves. "Don't let me find out you're turning my son into a history major like you."

"He'll thank me when he's in debt up to his eyeballs all for a useless degree," she says. "Night."

"Night," Jarrell calls, "to you and your friend."

He turns the light off and waits until Yuki locks the door behind him. "I didn't know you were a history major," Grace says quietly. "You never told me that."

Yuki leads them down a long dark hallway, until they get to a door hanging ajar. "Like I said," she starts breezily, "completely useless for the real world. My classes taught me some of the first stories I used for the show, though. Yay for secondary education."

Grace follows her inside. There's a brown-skinned girl with headphones on and her feet up on a small desk. She gives them a peace sign and keeps tapping at her phone.

"That's Blue," Yuki says, flicking the girl on the forehead. "She makes the magic happen."

Blue takes one headphone out. "She means that literally. After two years, she still has no idea how any of the controls work."

"Host," Yuki says, pointing at herself. "I don't

need to know those things. Also, this is Grace. We're married. It's complicated."

Blue lets out a low whistle. She looks Grace up and down. "This is why all your stories have turned so romantic lately, huh?"

Yuki screeches, embarrassed and flushed. "Can you go set up, please? Do that magic stuff you claim to do?"

Blue puts her hands up. She flips her cornrows and beads and disappears to the other side of the studio. "Whatever you say, boss."

Yuki stares up at the ceiling when she leaves, refusing to make eye contact with Grace. "What do you do when you hate all your friends?"

"Kill them," Grace says. She settles into a chair in front of a whole switchboard of lights and commands. "Can I ask you something?" she says carefully, her mind on a different conversation.

"What?" Yuki starts taking notebooks out of her backpack. "You gotta ask Blue if you want to know how any of this shit works."

"Not that," Grace says hesitantly. She turns around, watching Yuki. "Why didn't you pursue history? And I know," she cuts in, when Yuki opens her mouth, "it's totally hypocritical of me to ask. I studied astronomy for eleven years, and I feel more disconnected from it than ever. So, I get it. But, why didn't you?"

Yuki keeps her head down. "Do you think I have a sob story, Grace Porter? I don't look up at the stars and wonder if Asada Goryu is thinking about me in the afterlife or anything."

"Impressive name-drop, but ouch," Grace says. She leans an elbow on the desk, careful of the switches.

Yuki's mouth twitches in amusement. She spins around to match Grace's rhythm. "I paid for college myself," she admits. "My parents wanted me to do something practical, you know? Like, business or law. If they were gonna pay for it, it had to be something worthwhile, you know? They're first-gen immigrants, so they think the American dream is something that actually exists. They weren't going to let me follow my dreams and study medieval history or, like, fucking astronomy." She glances at Grace. "No offense."

Grace smiles, wry and bitter. "My father wanted me to study medicine. He ended up helping me pay for my undergrad and master's programs, but I was on my own for my doctorate. Then he walked out of my graduation ceremony, so I think he still made his opinion of my degree quite clear."

"A fellow family disappointment," Yuki says. "I took out a bunch of loans I keep deferring, and now I'm a waitress with a radio show." She grabs her notebook and turns away, making small notes in the margins. "No sob story, I told you."

Grace watches her, her fellow lonely creature. Whereas Grace looked up and thought, *This is where I belong,* Yuki looked into the past and thought the same thing. Now they're both sitting in an old radio station, reaching out into the unknown dark.

"Now, I have a show to start," Yuki says, firmly closing the subject. "Are you ready?"

Grace leans forward. Yuki's handwriting is atrocious. "What are you talking about tonight?"

"You'll see," Yuki says. She pushes the sleeves of her flannel shirt back to reveal the tattoos that run up her wrists. Blooming flowers wind around her forearms like ivy around an old, haunted house. She has one behind her ear, too, a small cluster of petals that reminds Grace of the first signs of life after winter. Little buds peeking through thawing dirt and melting snow. She puts her headphones on, and it gets covered up. "I need to have some secrets."

Blue raps on the window and gives Yuki a thumbs-up. She presses a button, and the control panel turns orange and green and yellow.

It is like magic, and Grace feels goose bumps.

"Good night to my fellow lonely creatures out there, waiting patiently in the dark. My name is Yuki. Are you there? I hope you're listening."

Grace holds her breath.

"I've talked a lot about loneliness," Yuki says. "We are lonely creatures in a big, big world." She tucks her hair behind her ears, and though she speaks of loneliness, she is on display here in her little, dark studio, an open book. "Loneliness stems from a lot of things—uncertainty, self-preservation, fear. But what about loneliness that stems from something different? What about the creatures relegated to the dark because of deviation?" Grace curls up in her chair and watches as Yuki weaves her dark tale.

"I've told you there are a lot of monsters that lurk in Japanese culture," she says. "When we used to visit home during the summer, my grandmother always told me stories. She told me once about the Yamauba. They were old women pushed to the very edges of society and forced to live in the mountains.

"Even as a child, I wondered why so many of the bad things, the scary things, were women. I asked my grandmother once, and she told me it was the way of the world. Sometimes monsters became women, because women who deviated were monsters. I didn't understand that until later.

"But the Yamauba, these were horrifying monsters in the shape of women. They were old and childless. They lured young pregnant girls up to their little shackled homes, promising safety and warmth, and then they ate their babies. They saw these crying, red, screaming creatures that stormed into the world, these things the Yamauba could never create themselves, and they ate them."

Grace leans forward, mesmerized. Yuki is able to find humanity in monsters, or maybe she gives monsters their humanity back. She says here is a terrible, horrifying thing, and holds it up like a mirror to anyone listening.

"There were more stories. The Yamauba would sneak down from their homes and eat children in the village when their mothers were gone. It is strange that the Yamauba, old and barren and childless, seemed so enamored with children. It is strange that one whose belly has never stretched is still so eager to make it full.

"But this is not just a story about women and their expectations. This is not just a story about monsters, born from being unable to contort and fit into the small box we have given them and suddenly are afraid of what they have become.

"This is a story about how deviation from the norm can create scary, monstrous things. What my grandmother didn't know was that years later, society would still create Yamauba. We would still be seen as dark, terrible things simply for refusing to fit a particular narrative. Perhaps the truly terrifying thing is to step away from what you're supposed to do and what you have planned. Perhaps you, the monster that you are, find yourself feeding on what you could not bear yourself.

"Perhaps Yamauba were created because we did not want to name something we brought forth with our own hands," Yuki says. "Perhaps flesh-eating monsters are simply people who break their molds and their boxes, and find themselves demanding all they have been denied."

Yuki motions at Blue and Grace blinks, eyes aching, like she is waking from a terrible and deep sleep.

"My name is Yuki," she hears. "Good night, my lonely creatures. Are you listening? Are you there?"

I am here, says the darkness inside Grace. *I am listening.* It takes shape. With each rejection, each uncertain move, each deviation from how she is supposed to fit inside the plan that has been made for her, it twists and contorts. It consumes itself.

It has become very ugly, indeed.

"Are you there?" Yuki asks as she signs off.

I am here, the darkness says. Its voice sounds eerily like Grace.

Twelve

Some nights, Grace falls asleep to the sound of Agnes and Ximena murmuring in her ear. Those are usually the nights Yuki has to work late, so it is just Grace in the room that smells like burnt embers and luck oil. Yuki's roommates have odd, disjointed schedules, so she never knows who might be home or out in the city. Sometimes, she prefers the solitude. She hides under Yuki's covers and listens to her friends talk.

Some nights it's Raj and Meera. They tell her about the customers at the tea room, about how it is not the same without her. There is still space being left for her in Portland, and she feels it through the phone, even though they are miles apart.

"We miss you, Space Girl," Ximena says, and the sentiment echoes from the other voices with her. Grace sticks her head out of Yuki's window and looks at the moon and thinks, *It is the same one. We are all under the same one.* "Love you," and the words echo again.

"So much it hurts," Grace tells them. When Grace needs it again, the words and the feelings from home, they will be there.

Most mornings, she wakes up in Yuki's bed to sunlight and the smell of pressed petals. Yuki lies next to her, and when Grace reaches out, she can touch. The girl in the bed is tangible. Grace traces the blooming flower behind her ear as she sleeps.

This morning, Yuki is still asleep while Grace reads her email. The "Dear Applicant, your application for the position of DATA SCIENTIST at the GIDEON SCIENCE INSTITUTE has been reviewed. You were a highly qualified candidate, but unfortunately we have—" lights up the screen. She does not read on to see why her high qualifications do nothing to even get her in for an interview.

She swipes it away angrily, and it disappears from her inbox. Good riddance.

She knew the Gideon Science Institute by reputation. They were one of the few in the field that prided themselves on diversity in science. They had a mentoring partnership with two of their local public schools. The vice president was the first Latina woman in a leadership position. They had women astronomers of color with long lists of achievements in conjunction with the institute's work. They were a *good* company.

They employed one Black astronomer and had no Black people on their executive board. Grace almost wishes she could swipe the email to hell again.

Instead, she sets her phone to the side. She has an idea, better than giving more energy to this new rejection, and this idea requires Yuki be awake. Yuki's body goes squished and soft when she curls up in her sleep. Grace's eyes roam over the hills and valleys and wonders how long it would take to explore all of its terrain. Longer than the summer? Months beyond? Years?

"You're staring at me," Yuki murmurs, opening one eye. "Like what you see?"

Yes, Grace thinks. *I want to look at you. I want to touch you. I want to kiss you, my good thing. I want to replace the bitter taste of rejection on my tongue with your acceptance.*

"Can I kiss you?" Grace asks, propping up on one elbow. "You're just—"

Yuki smirks, closing her eyes again. "I'm just what, Grace Porter? Don't be shy."

Her teasing words are warm. "Shut up," Grace says. "You know you're hot."

"Oh, I'm hot, huh?" Yuki stretches, all of that skin beneath her T-shirt and sleep shorts on display. "You should probably kiss me, then, before I get scooped up by someone else that wants to marry me after a few drinks."

"Probably," Grace says. She leans over Yuki, feels her body heat and heaving chest. Her face is bare and wrinkled with sleep. Grace's honey curls tumble between them, reaching out like tendrils.

Grace kisses her. She is afraid, terrified, but she is also a Porter. So, she kisses Yuki, who tastes like sleep and salt thrumming heat. Grace's fingers skim over Yuki's ribs, her dimpled thighs, her soft dough belly. It is their first kiss since that night in the desert, and Grace sinks to the bottom of the ocean with her siren, and the water does not burn her throat.

When they pull back, Grace reaches for her phone again. "I have an idea," she says. "Well, Meera had an idea. Have you ever been here?" She shows Yuki the screen.

"The Rose Center for Earth and Space," she reads. "I've never been there. You want to go?"

Grace looks down. She picks at the skin on her wrist, little starbursts of pink and red that ground her and distract from her vulnerability. "I want to go with *you*," she says. "You have your radio show. I have—" she gestures broadly "—this."

"Okay, Sun Girl," Yuki says, rolling to her feet. "Let's go, then."

On the train, Yuki situates herself behind Grace. "What are you—" she starts to ask, but then there's Yuki's warm hands at her waist, Yuki's nervous, uneven breath in her ear, all while she tries to keep them steady.

"Is this okay?" Yuki asks, and though no one in this crowded train car is paying them any attention, Grace feels like they have a blinking sign over them. Look Here, it says.

Grace nods, voice caught. She keeps her eyes on the window, and in the reflection, she can see Yuki's short black hair, her glittering eyes, her chin resting in the dip of Grace's shoulder. She watches Grace and holds her when she jerks at a sudden lurch. She catches her, like one could catch a falling star if they stood in just the right spot.

"Got you," Yuki says, and she leads Grace to their destination.

The Rose Center for Earth and Space is a joy. Grace holds Yuki's hand tight and leads her down their Cosmic Pathway and the Hall of the Universe. They sit in the Hayden Planetarium, and Yuki leans across the chairs to settle in Grace's lap. Grace finds herself rambling in awe about the Digital Universe Atlas, whispering about the star clusters and nebulae and hungry galaxies.

She looks down to find Yuki staring at her, eyes wide. Suddenly, Grace wishes she hadn't pulled the front of her hair up. She feels open and raw, exposed like a live wire. Is this how Yuki must have felt, letting Grace into her innermost sanctum of the radio station? *This* is Grace's domain, at home amid the things that venture into the endless abyss, and this is her letting Yuki in. Letting her see.

"Too much?" she asks. "You can tell me to stop. I forget not everyone cares about this stuff like I do."

"No," Yuki says, wriggling into a more comfortable position. "You're good at this."

"Good at what?"

"Teaching." Yuki gestures around them. "Making me interested in the faraway things."

Grace narrows her eyes in thought. "You think so?" she asks. Professor MacMillan wasn't initially a teacher. She didn't have a passion for it. She was a researcher at heart. She wanted to open things up and understand the writhing pulse of the cosmos. She did not want to be constrained to teaching its basics in a lecture hall. "My mentor always said astronomy was romantic, and I think I agree. I can't help but want other people to see that what may seem out of reach and untouchable is actually—" She cuts herself off. "Am I rambling?"

"It's actually what?" Yuki prods. One of the little barrettes in her hair has gone crooked, and Grace reaches down to straighten it. They are blissful and giddy and entangled. Yuki's denim overalls scratch rough against Grace's bare thighs. Her little upturned nose is blush pink.

Grace married a very cute girl.

She blinks down at Yuki. "It's everywhere," Grace says. "It's in our skin and our hair, and it turns our midnight blue blood to rust red." She presses fingers to the dotted freckles across her cheeks. "We are birthed from its dust and ashes the same as those hulking masses in the sky." Her words rush together, embattled on her tongue. Yuki listening so earnestly makes her loose and flushed and impassioned. It makes her want to tell Yuki all the ridiculous notions of the universe she keeps tucked under her breastbone, out of sight but thumping just as steadily as her beating heart. "How can anyone think we are not evidence of the thumbprint of the galaxy?"

"Holy shit," Yuki says. She laughs, bright and loud. Loud enough that some of the people turn to look, and Grace glares at them. "Grace Porter, you are magnificent," she says. "You are the best astronomer there has ever been."

Grace rolls her eyes. "Too bad I can't use you as a professional reference." She thinks of the email she swiped angrily into her trash file this morning.

"Why can't wives be references?" Yuki asks. "I would tell them that you, Dr. Grace Porter, are the best Black, lesbian astronomer they will ever have the pleasure of meeting. It is *their* honor to be in the same field as you." She wrinkles that pink upturned nose. "And fuck them, also."

Grace laughs, shoulders relaxing. She laughs, and the screen in front of them flickers. The short film is about to start, but she can't look away from the glinting, sharp girl in her lap. "I think that would be an excellent reference, actually." She looks away for a moment. "I would say the same about you, you know," she says, quieting her voice. Yuki meets her eyes. "I don't know that I've ever called anyone *magnificent,* but if

185

I did, it would be my Japanese wife, who is one of the smartest people I know. History is lucky to have you as its orator."

"It's my turn now," Yuki says. "You showed me your big, bad cosmos. Next, I want to take you on a monster hunt. We can make it a group trip."

"I'll hunt monsters with you," Grace says. "I bet Porters are great at monster hunting."

The big screen in front of them turns on, and the opening credits for the documentary start to roll. Grace doesn't see them, though, because she decides that this day will not be about studying the cosmos. This day will be about how the sun feels against her skin. About how Yuki is soft and malleable to the touch. About how she tastes like berries and melon and the red wine they sneaked in, and her lips are stained with it, too.

Grace tastes the universe bursting on Yuki's tongue, and it is—magnificent.

It takes nearly five hours to drive to Lake Champlain. Five and a half, if you count the coffee pit stops and the pee breaks and the way they have to pull over and combine all the change from their wallets to get through the toll, because no one carries cash.

Grace spends most of it smushed in the backseat, legs entangled with Sani. Dhorian spreads across both their laps, and Sani pretends like he's not stroking his neck and his back and his shoulders while he sleeps.

"Cis men take up so much space," he says huffily, tracing Dhorian's little gold hoop earrings. There's a matching gold ring in his nose, and it makes him look a little otherworldly. "Does he think he can sleep like this for five fucking hours?" He scoots a little, probably trying to get feeling back in his legs, and his mouth comes right next to Grace's ear. "Porter," he says quietly, "at the next stop we're tricking Fletch into letting me drive."

"Hey," Fletcher says, eyes up in the rearview mirror. "I hear plotting. I thought we agreed you are not allowed to drive my dad's car. You ran straight through a red light last time."

"Maybe the red light ran straight through me," Sani snipes, digging out his headphones. He shuts his eyes. "Wake me up when we get there, or the world decides it's time to eat the rich. I'm not picky."

Yuki turns around. "You holding up back there?"

"Seems that way," Grace says. "I still can't believe we're going to look for a monster. What kind is it anyway? Loch Ness?"

Yuki makes a face. "Hey, Genius Girl," she says. "That thing is supposedly in Scotland. We're going to the border of New York and Vermont. Wanna see?" She holds out a map with circled areas of interest. "These are all the places where the thing, they call it Champ, has been spotted. We're going to hit up the spots closest to this side of the state border."

"Why not go into Vermont?" Grace asks, staring at the meticulously marked map.

"Too many white people," Yuki and Sani say together, though Sani keeps his eyes stubbornly closed. "I'm not here, carry on with the monster mash."

"Seriously?" Fletcher says incredulously. "You know the 'Monster Mash' from *American* fucking *Bandstand* but not Egyptian Rat Screw?"

"I'm asleep," is the only reply he gets.

Yuki rolls her eyes and shoves the map toward Grace again. "We're gonna split up around here, I think. Me and you, then Fletch, Sani and Dhorian if he ever decides to wake the fuck up. Why is he so tired?"

"Twelve-hour shift in the ED, then he took an Ambien," Fletcher says. "I don't think he factored lake monsters into his plan for today, so he might just stay in the car and get eaten."

"If anyone's getting eaten by a lake monster," Yuki says, "it's going to be me. Are we there yet?"

They are there according to the signs as they near the lake area. The trees are thick and green and lush, and the ground is sprouting with weeds and flowers. Fletcher parks his dad's car a little way back, and they sit, staring out the windows.

"There is nothing here but undiscovered bodies and maybe, like, some water pollution," Fletcher says doubtfully. "What will your radio listeners think about the scariest monster of them all— humans contributing to climate change?"

Yuki elbows him sharply and gets out of the car. Grace follows, eyes immediately tracing the long line of trees up and up and up, reminding her of being a kid and looking up at orange grove trees.

"There you go," Yuki says quietly. Grace has heard her voice often enough to know when there's fondness in it. "You're always up in the clouds, Grace Porter." She tilts her head back, too, hand shielding her eyes from the sun. "What do you see up there?"

Grace squints. "They remind me of home, I guess," she says. She inhales, and the air smells like lake water and grass and sand and wood.

Behind them, Sani is trying to wake Dhorian up, keeping his voice low as he apologizes for the early hour. "It's the boss's fault," he says. "She wanted a lake monster, so we gotta see a lake monster, babe."

Dhorian groans, loud enough that the sound carries. "Do you think the lake monster will let me nap? Do you think it will take pity on me?"

Yuki snorts. She bumps her shoulder against Grace's. "These trees must have nothing on the ones you have back home," she says. "Those big Oregon redwoods—"

"Not those," Grace says thoughtfully. "I grew up in Florida," she explains, "in a little hippie town called Southbury. My mom's family owns an orange grove there."

She feels Yuki's eyes on her, but she is looking up again. She's been looking up her whole life, it seems, at one thing or another. "I used to climb the trees," she says, like recounting a dream on the verge of being lost to morning. "You weren't supposed to, and Colonel had my hide every time I got caught. But the best oranges were the ones at the top." If she closes her eyes, she can feel branches scraping at her palms and arms, wounds to deal with later. But they were worth it, to find that perfect fruit, to hide in the trees that were big and strong enough to hold her.

She opens her eyes and clears her throat, swallowing down her most vulnerable memories. "Are we ready to monster hunt?"

"Born ready," Sani says. They turn around, and Dhorian has pulled himself up, and with sleepy eyes and languid hands is braiding Sani's hair into a high bun.

Fletcher tosses Sani items from the truck. "Three waters, Fletch."

He wrinkles his nose. "You know the amount of plastic—"

"Normally," Sani cuts in, "I would let you do

this. I promise I would. But it's 7 a.m., and if you want me to stay awake to Scooby-Doo this shit, I need to be hydrated. Dhorian, do you agree?" He turns his head a little, and Dhorian makes a little annoyed noise.

"Fletch, I get it. Climate change, polar caps melting, plastic in the oceans." He yawns, hiding it in Sani's neck. "But I'm very thirsty. I promise to recycle it. Or compost it. Or whatever it is you hipster Brooklyn yuppies do."

"I'm from Queens," Fletcher says, but he does throw three water bottles at Dhorian's head.

"I really worry about them," Yuki says absently. "They're so weird."

"What does that say about you, then, ringleader?" Sani asks sulkily. "Give me the map so I know where we're going. God knows these two can't read it."

"I can read a map," Fletcher says, but shrinks under the gaze. "On my phone. To be fair, you didn't specify."

Sani turns away from them. "I am filled with regret."

"You," Fletcher argues, "do not get to be filled with regret." He bends down and nods toward Dhorian. "Get on before I change my mind," he says, and Dhorian climbs onto his back, happily burying his face in that long hair.

Yuki hands one of the maps to Sani, who looks it over with a keen eye. "You want us to hunker down on the other side of the lake?" he asks. "The green circle?"

Yuki reaches up and tucks an errant strand behind his ear. He glares at her, but allows it. He reminds Grace so much of Agnes, it hurts. "Yes, please," Yuki says. She turns to Fletcher and Dhorian and kisses the side of their heads. A soft, little thing that passes between them like a thank-you. "Sorry you're tired," she says, "but you know. Lake monsters."

Dhorian gives a sleepy little cheer before they follow Sani along a diverging path. "Lake monsters! *Fuck*—Fletch, don't run me into goddamn branches."

Grace watches them, Yuki's own little orbiting universe. "How long do you think Fletcher will carry him?"

Yuki pulls a ball cap out of her backpack and slips it on. "Whole time," she says. "We're codependent like that. You need a hat? I have Yankees and my college alma mater." She holds out a white-and-blue hat with BARNARD printed along the front. "That's, like, letterman jacket material right there," she tells Grace.

"Oh, well, if it's that serious." Grace slips it on and strikes a pose. "Do I look ready to face the supernatural?"

Yuki holds out her hand, and Grace grabs it. "Born ready. Now, c'mon, I wanna see how murky the water is from the docks."

It smells out here, like nature, like earth. Their shoes leave imprints in the ground as they make their way to the water.

"How did you find out about this monster?" she asks.

Yuki looks away from her map. She leads them down a rocky, gravelly path, getting closer to one side of the lake. "Sometimes listeners will write in," she says. "Like, if they've heard of something local or have seen something themselves and want me to check it out."

"And you do?" Grace asks, fingers firmly intertwined with Yuki's as they stumble over rocks and fallen branches. "What if it's a hoax? What if it's dangerous?"

They break through the trees. There's more sand than dirt here, like a little beach with sprouting, grassy weeds. She can feel the grit start to sift into her shoes as they make their way to one rickety dock out of many.

Yuki takes her shoes off and nods for Grace to do the same. The wood is summer-warm under the soles of her feet. They settle at the end, legs dangling over dark blue-green water.

"Grace Porter," Yuki says, as if minutes haven't passed since they last spoke a word. "Are you doubting my ability to spot supernatural bullshit?"

Grace sputters. There is nothing to indicate that anything beyond pollution-mutated fish and wiggling seaweed lives here. Maybe that is what someone saw, sitting on this same dock. Some shadows and fish moving in the water.

"I don't doubt you," she says finally. "I just don't get it, I guess. You don't know what's out there. You don't know if anything is out there. All you have is the word of someone who listens to your show."

"Just some weird, lonely insomniac with delusions of grandeur, right?" Yuki shoots back, her voice dry as she stares at the water and not Grace.

"I didn't say that," Grace says. The sun reflects off the water, off Grace's hair. "I just don't get it," she repeats. "The other stories I've heard you tell on your show, they sound like stories. I mean, they sound like stories that have been around for a while, you know? This," she says, waving a hand at the vastness of the lake, "is different. There's nothing mythic here. It's just a—a campfire story, right?"

Yuki is quiet for a long moment. They both stare out at the water, at the little island way out, like there they will find all the answers they're looking for. Her feet dangle over the side of the dock and hit the edge on the way back. *Thump, thump, thump,* she goes. Like a beating heart. *Thump, thump, thump.*

"What about the stuff up there?" Yuki asks, voice low. "The stories people tell about the stars and the moon and constellations. What's the difference?"

Grace leans back. "The stars and the moon and the constellations are real things," she says. "Physical and observable things. Things made of mass and matter and energy. *Real* things."

"They are," Yuki agrees. "And then people create mythos from them, *for* them. They create stories as a way to understand something that is so much bigger and blacker and more expansive than we can comprehend." She wrinkles her nose. "Do I believe that sirens lure men into the sea to watch them drown?" she asks. "Do I believe there was a time where I had four arms and four legs and two heads, and that I was cut in half as a punishment?"

"Yuki—" Grace interrupts, fingers gripping the edge of the dock tight enough her knuckles bulge.

"I don't know," Yuki says abruptly. She looks at Grace. Her fingers reach out, stopping just shy of Grace's hair, frizzy under the cap from the humidity. A small lake breeze blows, and the strands blow, too, as if completing what Yuki does not. "Do I believe the sun favored you enough to turn your hair that shade of honey? I don't know, Grace Porter. Maybe it's just a story, or maybe I think it's true."

"I didn't mean—"

"The story is," Yuki barrels on, "there's a

monster in this lake. People have said it looks like a reptile. They don't know, maybe a serpent. There's a guy that wrote a book about the thing. Says it resembles something prehistoric, and maybe this thing has been lurking under the waves for millennia, waiting."

"Waiting for what?" Grace asks before she can stop herself. She feels foolish for questioning any of it, because isn't she here because she followed her own creature, her own siren?

Yuki shrugs. "I don't know. They call the fucking thing Champ. Maybe it's waiting for someone to find a better name."

Grace breathes out, shoulders slumping. "So, people have seen it?"

"The guy that emailed me said he saw it," Yuki says. "Said he couldn't sleep, which—" She throws a wry look at Grace. "That's kind of the point, you know? So, he couldn't sleep, and he's just driving. He said he just drove, until he ended up here. Didn't know where he was driving to when he started." Yuki kicks at the wood dock, where it begins to buckle from age.

"I've always wondered about that," she says quietly. "I've had a few listeners say that's how they found my show. Can't sleep, get in the car and drive. Fuck around with the radio until somehow, they land on me. When I can't sleep, I've ridden the train before. It's stupid, riding it alone late at night, but. Sorry," she says suddenly, to Grace. "None of this is what you asked me."

"Tell me," she says, her voice rough. Her hands claw into the warm planks beneath her thighs. "I'm listening."

Yuki looks down at the water beneath them. It shimmers blue-green and dark. The water is a swamp-like mystery, and Yuki stares at it like she can see straight through.

"The walls blur so fast, you don't notice that when it's rush hour and the train is packed. Sometimes it's just me in an empty car, and it goes by so fast, I can't even recognize my own reflection." She shakes her head, and the fringe under her ball cap shifts into her eyes. "I wonder if it's the same when you're driving. So tired that you can feel it, like, like a cloak or something." She looks at Grace. "Have you ever felt like that?"

When Grace can't sleep, she counts. She counts tiles and stars and the number of cars that pass once she relegates herself out to the balcony. When Grace can't sleep, time does not blur so much as stand still. It is frozen, as Grace is. Her eyes prickle and her chest aches and sleep hovers just out of reach, just like the stars that meander across the sky.

"Yeah," she says simply, blinking fast. "I think I get it."

Yuki nods, and maybe she can hear how much Grace does truly get it. Maybe lonely creatures can hear it in other lonely creatures. That thing in their voices that says, *I am like you.*

"So, he was driving, and he ended up here," Yuki finishes with a shrug. "Says he sat on a dock and stared out into the water and something stared back. Something else was awake and hiding in the dark. I don't know," she says again. "It's just a story he told me. But I wanted to see. I wanted—I wanted him to know that I was listening and believed him, so here we are."

That's all Yuki says for the rest of the time they sit there. The sun beams steadily, and they sit, and they wait, and they watch. Yuki stares resolutely out into the water, her fingers tapping an incessant, infrequent beat.

Grace finds herself wanting to tell Yuki stories about the moons orbiting Jupiter, named after the god's lovers. She wants to tell Yuki about vain Cassiopeia, condemned to the sky, and the eagle Aquila, who threw thunderbolts in Zeus's name. Maybe she can see it now, the thin line that connects fact to a story passed down.

She extends her hand in the space between them and hopes that a tentative touch serves as a story of its own. She waits, and Yuki reaches out, too, their fingers tangled together over warm wood and under a vast sky.

"Find anything?" Yuki asks when they get back to the car.

Sani shakes his head, lifting his sunglasses to reveal a bruise from training that seems extra dark in the sunshine. "It seems as if our monster was quiet today," he says. "Fickle little things, aren't they?"

"Aren't we all?" Yuki sighs, lugging her and Grace's backpacks into the trunk.

"This was the most peaceful and relaxing monster hunt we have ever done," Dhorian says, rubbing his eyes. "Let's do more like these."

"What?" Fletcher starts, rolling over carefully so he hovers over Dhorian, teasing. His long hair has been braided, little leaves and flowers tucked in the strands. "You didn't like breaking into funeral homes like that one time?"

"Something touched me," Dhorian whines, and Sani laughs, jumping off the top of the car. "There were cold spots all over that place, and something touched my leg. I'm Black, I don't do ghosts."

"You felt a presence?" Grace asks, curious as she leans against the car. "You really felt something?"

Yuki raises her eyebrows, a satisfied smirk pulling at the edges of her mouth. "You sound intrigued," she points out. "Maybe there's more to these stories than you thought, huh?"

The ride back is sleepy and hushed. Yuki hunches over her phone as she tries to format a script for the next episode of her show. Dhorian goes back to sleep, pillowed once more in Sani's lap, his hoodie under his head.

Sani and Grace watch slime videos on his phone. "I watch these after a match," he says quietly. "Too much adrenaline gets in my system, so this weird shit helps me calm down. I tried ASMR, but I don't like strangers whispering in my ear, you know?"

Grace smiles, eyes locked on lime-green slime that gets molded and folded and poked and prodded. "Yuki says you're good," she says, "at the MMA fighting thing."

He shrugs, but his eyes crinkle, pleased. "I found this trans-inclusive gym in Brooklyn," he says. "It's been good. You should come watch me fight. Sometimes you just need to punch shit out, you know?"

"Seems healthy," Grace says. But she thinks she sees the appeal. She can't punch the uncertainty or the guilt or the fear folded inside her. But she would like to. *God,* would she like to. "But yeah, I want to come."

Sani makes a satisfied noise and looks back at his screen. "Good."

She goes quiet, working up the courage to ask the question that's been growing in her.

"Do you think," she starts, voice low to ride under the sound of the car and the radio, "Yuki really believes in this stuff?"

Sani turns his head to squint at her. "Believe what?"

She makes a frustrated noise. "This. The show, the—we drove five hours in the middle of the night to watch a lake. There's no—even if there *was,* it wouldn't come out if it knew we were watching, right?"

"Ah." He nods. "You asked her, didn't you?"

"Asked her what?"

With one foot he kicks the back of Fletcher's seat, and the car lurches. "Turn the music up," he demands. "We're trying to have a private conversation back here."

"We genuinely could have died," Fletcher says, but he hovers over the radio. "Any requests?"

Sani passes his phone up. "Turn on NAO," Sani says. "The *Saturn* album, in honor of our very own space girl."

Fletcher grumbles but obeys, and music plays through the speakers. Sani waits until it's loud enough that they can whisper without the threat of being overheard. In the front seat, Yuki remains engrossed in her show draft. "You asked her if she really believes in this shit."

Grace shrugs. "I didn't think she'd get so—"

His eyebrows rise. "She read you the riot act, huh?"

"She made me feel very ridiculous for asking, yes."

"Poor baby. Listen," he says, "I'm going to

201

tell you something about our feral leader, okay? And it's weird and disgusting, so don't think any differently of her for it, okay?"

Grace sits up, alarmed. "Maybe this is something I should be hearing from—"

"Nope," Sani says somberly. "I've let it go on long enough without stepping in and saying something." He inhales and leans close. "Yuki," he says, "she cares about people." There's a pause as he watches Grace. "I'm sorry you had to find out this way."

There's a moment where Grace's brain goes off-line, before she elbows Sani hard enough that he falls onto a sleeping Dhorian. "I thought you were being serious," she hisses.

He cackles, hands covering his face. "Shit, I'm sorry, I couldn't help it. You looked so distressed. God. Okay."

"Can you be serious now?"

"I am, I am," he says, laughter fading into a wide, but sincere smile. "I am. Really. She believes in people. That's what this whole thing is really about. She'll never say that, though, but you learn a lot being friends with someone for as long as we have."

"But what does that mean?" Grace asks, frustration boiling over. "What does that have to do with sitting on a lake dock for hours?"

Sani shrugs. "I don't know how to explain it, exactly. It's just—there are people who write into her show with bullshit. She knows it. But sometimes there are ones that—" He looks out the window, eyebrows furrowing. "I think the people who find comfort in her show, real comfort, are just really, really lonely. Have you ever felt loneliness like that?" he asks. "When more than anything, you want someone to hear, really hear, what you're saying? Even if it's a stranger on the radio?"

Yes, Grace thinks. *I'm that lonely now, stuck inside my own head. This fading image of my future, folding in on itself from too much weight. Do you hear that? Do you hear me?*

Grace wonders at the girl in the front seat. *Have you ever been that lonely? Have you ever been so lonely you ask every show if someone is there, if they're listening?*

"Someone wrote in to say there was a monster at the bottom of that lake," Sani continues. "It doesn't matter to Yuki if it's there or not. What matters is she walked through the same woods they did, and sat on the same dock they did. The same sand under her feet. The same seaweed creeping up from under the water, you know?" He grabs one of her hands with rare, genuine solemnity on his face. "*Are You There?* isn't about monsters. It never has been, don't you get it? It's about people. Every episode is about people."

Later, days later, episodes later, Yuki talks about Champ, the monster of Lake Champlain.

Yuki
11:34 p.m.
listen to the show tonight
blue says hi

Grace reads the text at the apartment as she and Fletcher watch a marathon of *Love It or List It*. She turns the radio show on and puts the volume up, and Yuki's voice filters through the apartment, fills up all the space between the walls.

"Hello, lonely creatures," she says into the mic. "Are you there?"

Grace, warm from wine and the open windows and Fletcher squished next to her, thinks, *Yes*.

"Tonight, I want to talk about what causes us to believe in monsters. I've been thinking a lot about it. I've been thinking about if we have to believe, or if maybe just *wanting to,* is enough. Someone made me think about this recently, and made me question why it is that this lonely creature created this show, and why lonely creatures listen to it when they could be sleeping."

Grace listens.

"I think believing in monsters is not what this show is about. It's not what I think about when I come here to talk to you all. What I think about is, what makes me any different from this terrible thing? What makes me the same? At the end of the night, I do not find myself asking if I truly believe in the sea monster that lies waiting in the body of a lake. At the end of the night, when I pack up and shut off the lights I think, is that me? Am I that monster? In what ways am I the terrible, frightening thing?"

She pauses for a moment, and the dead air only adds to the tension of her question. "Lonely creatures, what makes us so different from the stories we tell in the dark?"

Fletcher sighs, handing the wine bottle back to Grace. "Deep," he says. They pass a joint back and forth and cuddle underneath a heavy blanket. "That's some deep shit, bro. Yuki is so deep."

Grace takes out her phone and thinks about a girl that smells like sea salt and herbs and lingering incense. Her phone illuminates the room like something otherworldly.

Grace
12:20 a.m.
i'm listening

She pauses, and then her fingers type out another message.

Grace
12:21 a.m.
idk if i believe in all the stories
but i believe in you
hi blue

Thirteen

Grace is trying to come to terms with her loneliness. It is not as clear-cut as being alone. She is *not* alone. But she finds herself missing the familiarity of Portland. She finds herself missing the rigidity of her academic schedule, the coziness of the White Pearl Tea Room. She misses the people that do not know Grace Porter taking a break and figuring things out, but Grace Porter in control, always in motion.

But she *is* taking a break, and she finds herself in NYC surrounded by people that do not judge her for it, no matter how much blame she aims at herself.

They're in Sani's bedroom. He's icing bruised knuckles and trying to psych himself up to swallow down three ibuprofens.

"You just throw 'em back," Yuki says. "We go through this every time!"

"And every time it's traumatic!" he shouts back. "You'd think the billion-dollar pharmaceutical industry could make smaller pills. Some of us have delicate throats."

Yuki makes a face at Grace, who's trying not to laugh over her late-night onigiri. "Bet that makes you a hit in bed," Yuki mutters.

Sani glares. "More than you," he says, voice

silky-smooth and dangerous. "Who exactly are you fingering with those ridiculous *claws?*"

Grace chokes. Yuki lets out an inhuman screech and launches herself across the room. She lands on top of Sani and they go crashing to the floor, while Grace watches from the bed.

"Is everybody okay?" Grace asks. "That sounded painful."

Yuki sits up and lets out a long, anguished groan. "He started it."

"Well," Sani says huffily, not even bothering to get up, "you knocked over my pills and my water. Now I have to start that process all over again. It's a very psychological experience for me."

"I have no sympathy for you," Yuki says, sending him a nasty glance. She checks over her newly painted pink nails. "I'm a femme who likes long nails, and I am very valid, thank you."

"Hey, Yuki?" Fletcher calls suddenly. "There's a guy at the door."

"Does he live here?" Yuki calls back. "A lot of guys live here, maybe it's one of them."

There is just Fletcher's pointed silence.

"No," he says. "He does not live here."

"Does he want to live here?" Sani yells. "Is he at least cute?"

"Can you assholes just—" Fletcher cuts himself off, murmuring low to whomever it is. "He says he's here for Porter."

Yuki and Sani look at her, and Grace looks back with wide eyes.

When she gets to the door, there is a guy waiting for her. A guy that smiles when he sees her, who has seen Grace at her very worst, snotty and bawling and angry. He smells like Portland redwoods and mamri tea.

"Raj," she breathes out. She barrels into his solid frame and waiting arms. "What are you doing here? How did you even know where here was?" She burrows into his rain jacket and overflowing hair.

"You sent the address to everyone before you left, remember?" His fingers grip tight around Grace's waist. "Just in case anything happened. The great Grace Porter, always prepared. Baba has the address printed out and tacked on the board in his office."

She hides a smile in his neck. If she could get herself any closer, she would. Instead, she sniffs and clings and tries not to pinch herself in case this is a dream.

"Well, nothing's happened to her yet," Yuki says dryly. It hits Grace that all of them are in the living room watching. "Sorry you wasted a perfectly good trip."

Grace pulls away when she feels Raj stiffen. Yuki stands like a small, angry dog, all puffed up and indignant.

"Yuki," she says, unwilling to let go of Raj yet.

208

One hand finds its way into his pocket, and she would try to fit herself in there if she could. "This is Raj. The one I told you is kind of like my—" She looks at Raj for help.

He pulls back his shoulders. Wet from the rain outside and challenging. "I'm her brother," he says flatly. "Hi."

"Hi," Fletcher says, moving forward to shake Raj's hand. "Shit, like, come in, man. Sorry for all the questioning."

Grace pulls him inside. "Come in," she says. "Sit down. Tell me everything. Why are you here?"

They sit on the couch. Yuki stands against the exposed brick and crosses her arms, and Fletcher pushes Sani out of the room. "The tension," he whispers loudly. "Let's go be bad people and text Dhorian about it while he's at work."

Grace grabs Raj's hands as they leave. She can't believe he's here. She can't believe a piece of her Portland galaxy navigated its way to New York.

"Why are you here?" she repeats. "*How* are you here?"

He shrugs. "I'm not really here," he admits. "If Baba finds out I made a pit stop in New York on the way to my meeting, he won't let me use his flier miles again."

"What meeting?"

"It's probably nothing," he says, ducking his

head. "But it's to discuss opening another White Pearl Tea Room in Boston. So. I'm going to that. But for tonight, here I am."

Her eyes grow big. Baba Vihaan has put his blood, sweat and tears into that tea room. Even when he was shrouded in grief after his wife died, Grace never doubted his dedication to his work.

"Holy shit," she says. "You have to tell me everything."

He laughs, a thing that's mostly a shaky exhale. "Can we do it over a drink?" he asks. "I have to catch my next flight tomorrow morning, and I could really, *really,* use a drink with my favorite sister before I have to leave."

"You know I'm telling Meera, right?"

He scoffs. "You think I didn't tell her? You take me for a coward, Gracie?"

The banter hits her right in the chest. She is home, just for a little, with Raj here. She sees home in his wild hair and his dark eyes and his calloused hands. "Jesus," she whispers, blinking fast. "I missed you. Yes," she says. "Let's get drinks. Let's get drunk." She gets up from the couch and looks back. "Don't move, okay? I don't wanna come back and you're gone."

"Little sister," he says softly. "When have I ever left you?"

She nods, disappearing down the hall to change and grab her wallet. She hears Yuki's soft bare feet behind her, little thumps that have become as familiar as the other sounds of the city. Grace drops on the bed and tries to untangle all the knotted feelings that have curled up in her chest. How strange it feels to have part of her orbit back in its place again.

Yuki leans in the doorway. "So," she starts, and Grace looks up at her tone. "Going out?"

Grace blinks. "You should come," she says. "Raj was just being protective. You'll like him, I promise."

Yuki crosses her arms. She's in her pajamas: the same thin, white T-shirt Grace has, with BRIDE printed across the front and these frilly, yellow shorts that barely cover her ass. She looks dimpled and a little angry. She could make Grace do just about anything like this.

"Did I do something?" Yuki asks. Grace sits up straight and waits, curious. "Did your friends really have to come and check on you? Did you ask them to?"

"Yuki Yamamoto," Grace says carefully. She studies the girl in front of her. "What are you asking me?"

Yuki huffs, pushing flyaway strands away from her face. "I know I don't know you like they do," she says, a little bit of a bite in her voice. "God knows half the time I don't even feel like I *get* you, Grace Porter. But I've been trying. I've been—I've been trying, you know?"

"Trying to what?" Grace asks slowly.

"To take care of you!" she says, shutting the door. "I've been doing a terrible job. Go on, tell me."

She stares, and she waits for Grace to tear her down. Terrible, scary Yuki. Soft, trembling Yuki. Yuki sprouting thorns and velvet petals.

"Okay," Grace says. "Can you sit down?"

"Absolutely not," Yuki says, covering her face. "Just send me a text message about it like a normal maladjusted person in this millennium."

Grace smiles. "I'm not going to text you when you're right in front of me," she says. "But, Yuki, I don't—" She shakes her head, as if that will help the words fall into place. "Being here with you is a good thing." She takes a deep breath to steel herself. "You're a good thing."

"Okay." Yuki blinks. "You're. You know. Good, too, or whatever." She grits her teeth and stares at her ceiling. No stars. Nothing to count and keep yourself grounded with. "It's just that we're married, and I'm selfish. I've had enough therapy that I can admit to that." She looks down and gives Grace a small smile. "I want to take care of you, Grace Porter."

"You do," Grace says. Her fingers curl into the covers. "My friends know that. Everyone knows that."

"And I want you to take care of me, too," Yuki adds, like a challenge. "Isn't that what married

212

people do? I mean, you have people that fly across the country just to make sure you're okay, and maybe I feel—"

"You feel what?"

"Lonely right in front of you." Yuki's laugh is dry. "I went to Las Vegas and got married in the middle of the desert to you. And I know this is—coming here is a break, a breather for you. I get that. But I want to—I don't know, feel like a home for you, too. One day. Maybe."

She's breathing heavy by the end of it, chest heaving with the weight of what she's just said.

"Yuki," Grace says. That's all that comes. *Yuki,* she thinks. *I'm right here.*

"Please don't," she says quietly. "I feel stupid, and you know as an Aquarius I can't deal with that like a regular human being."

"Stop joking," Grace says. *I'm right here,* she says, in the silence. *Don't you see me? Don't you hear me? Didn't you say lonely creatures recognize other lonely creatures?* "I didn't just come here for myself. I came here because I wanted to meet you and know you and—" She takes a deep breath. "I'm listening to you. I *see* you."

"I don't want you to," Yuki argues, "because this is ridiculous, and I don't even know why I said it." She flops on the bed. She is not a hazy champagne-bubble dream. She is real person, a girl, a mess just like Grace. "I'm sorry."

"Please don't apologize." Grace's hand hovers over her warm body. The creases and curves and bends.

Yuki lets out a breath. "Aren't you supposed to be getting changed? This is New York, but I still think people will judge you for going to a bar in your pajamas."

She looks down at her flannel pants and her NASA tank. "Be honest, would this be the craziest outfit I'd see tonight?"

Yuki's mouth widens with a smile she tries to force back. "Probably not," she admits. "You could say you're making a political statement."

"I could." Her hand makes contact with Yuki's. "Come with me. I want you to meet Raj."

Yuki shakes her head. "I have plans to lie in the dark and try to disappear from earth," she says. "Very busy, very booked." She moves slowly, very slowly toward Grace and holds her pinky out. "You won't disappear on me now that I've revealed this terrible side of me, will you? Pinky promise."

"Yuki—"

"It was in our vows," she says somberly. "I wrote it in. I have the right to invoke the pinky promise at any time."

"I promise," Grace says, wondering how she can find a way to keep it. She hooks their pinkies together and wonders if the universe will allow her to keep both: the galaxies and this girl born of their glittering dust. "Pinky promise."

Grace finds a bar with cheap drinks and low music and a table for two. They order shots and stare each other down.

"Are you going to explain yourself now?" she asks. "Why didn't you tell me you were coming to New York? Plus, another tea room opening on the East Coast? I mean, what gives? How did you get Meera to keep this from me? Usually she can't hold water."

Raj runs his hands over his face, peeking through his fingers. "You're asking me so many things right now, and I'm way too sober."

"Well, answer one," she presses. "Answer half of one. Why do you need to be drunk to answer my questions?"

"Because," he says, "I'm jet-lagged as fuck, and I haven't texted Meera or any of our friends yet to tell them I made it here. I need to be drunk for that, too. Where are our shots?"

"Relax," she says. "So, was this, like, meant to be a surprise? You coming here? God, Meera must be pissed. You know she's wanted to come to New York for forever."

Raj shrugs. The bar's poor lighting emphasizes the circles under his eyes, the lines in his face, etched in deep. "She's giving me the silent treatment," he admits. "Like it's my fault she's taking that summer class. What's it in again?"

"Neuroethics," Grace says. "I told her it seemed a bit much, but she's—"

"Stubborn," they say together.

"Plus, she has to cover the shop with Baba while I'm gone. She knows all of this, she's just being difficult." He sighs. "She knows how much I have to deal with, so I don't know why she can't just—"

"Hey," Grace cuts in, leaning back as four tequila shots appear on their table. "She's your sister. You know she has your back. Take a shot, please. You're stressing *me* out."

He does, taking them one after the other. He grimaces and turns toward the bar. "What do we want next? I'm trying to leave this astral plane."

Grace grabs his hand when he signals for more. "Okay, let's chat a little before we get blackout drunk, okay? You had your shots, now spill."

In the moment, Raj looks way older than thirty-three. He looks tired and worn-out. Grace wonders how she forgot that other people could wither away from stress and anxiety and the weight of the world, too.

"Hardball, huh?" he asks. "Okay, well I'm here. Surprise. I told everyone, but I didn't know if I could make it happen until the last minute, so I asked them to keep their mouths shut. I'm honestly shocked they all did."

"Okay," Grace says. "So, it was a surprise. I'm surprised. Tell me about the other tea room." She leans back, squinting. "Why aren't you more excited about this?"

He crosses his arms. "It's nothing. I'm just a terrible son, I hate my life and I'm sacrificing my millennial dream of hitting the lotto and fucking off to travel the world in order to run my father's tea room." Four more glasses are set on the table. Raj downs one almost viciously. "Maybe I'll even run two now. Fucking congrats to me."

Grace blinks. "Okay," she says carefully. "That's a lot to unpack, but I see now why you wanted alcohol to do it."

Raj gives a bitter smile. "Maybe you were onto something, Gracie," he says softly, eyes hooded. "Maybe there's something to running off when things get too hard."

"Ouch." She takes another shot, and both the words and tequila sting. "Tell me how you really feel."

"You asked. Maybe I should fuck off to a new city and leave my friends to deal with all their shit, too. *Ughhh.*" He rubs his eyes hard and stares into an empty glass. "That tequila is gonna hit so hard."

"You're drinking too fast," Grace says. "Also, are you, like, mad at me, or does drinking just make you point out my less than stellar coping mechanisms?"

Raj shakes his hair out of his eyes. "Mad? I'm not mad at you. Maybe I envy you. Did you ever think of that?"

She glares. "Do I even want to know what *that* means?"

"Did I ever tell you what I wanted to study?" he asks abruptly. "Did I ever tell you that?"

Grace is starting to get a headache. The bar starts to feel warm and too bright and too loud. "You have a business degree," she says indulgently. "Maybe no more shots for you."

He nods and wobbles in his chair. "That's what I did study," he says. "But not what I *wanted* to study."

Grace waits.

"Medicine," Raj says. He stares at her. He looks like the man who was wary of her when she first started working at the tea room. The one that hovered as she learned the different types of tea leaves and how to steep them and how to win over Meera. He looks less like the brother she has come to know, the one who is protective and safe and giving.

"I wanted to study medicine. Mama told me—" He inhales deeply. "She said Baba would understand in time. It was my dream, you know? Become a doctor, make my family proud, tell Baba he would never have to worry about that fucking tea shop again because I was going to take care of him. I'm the oldest, right? I have to take care of my family."

Grace carefully places her hands across the table, close but not touching.

"You remember how fast Mama got sick," he says, eyes distant. Raj Bhamra, both here and in the past. "It was like one day she was here, and the next we were barricaded in that house for two weeks."

"Raj—" she starts.

"I never told anyone," he admits. "Never said I was a coward who couldn't look his baba straight in the eye, because I wasn't sure I could keep the resentment off my face. *Resentment,* Gracie." He grabs her hands too tight, like he's anchoring himself. She lets him. "I resented him. Because I knew I couldn't tell him I wanted to be a doctor when that fucking tea room was the only thing keeping him going. It was the only thing keeping him going, with us, after she died. You remember."

She remembers. She remembers the stillness. She remembers how sometimes Baba Vihaan wouldn't come out of his office at all, the whole day. It would just be Grace and Raj, struggling to keep up appearances so Meera wouldn't burst into tears. So she wouldn't start sobbing at the register over someone's cup and have to apologize—*Sorry, my mama just died. Here's your ginger root tea.*

"I hate that tea room," Raj confesses. He smiles

219

at Grace. "You should see how horrified you look right now." He takes another shot and gags. "Fuck, that burns."

"I didn't know that," she says quietly. "I thought—I guess I *never* thought about it. I just always knew the tea room was Baba Vihaan's and one day it would be yours. I thought that's what you wanted."

"Nobody wants to inherit a tea room. But who else is gonna do it? Meera?"

Grace presses her lips together, quiet.

"The worst part is if I told her, she would. If I said, 'Hey, M, I really, really don't wanna run this place,' she'd stop studying psychology. She'd fast-track a business degree, and she'd do it. And I'd win big brother of the year, right?"

"But it's not fair—" Grace says, and he slams his glass down hard enough that it rattles.

"That's the point," he says. "It's not fair, but that's what people have to do. It's life. Sometimes you don't want to run a goddamn tea room, and in the end maybe you have to run two. We all have *responsibilities,* and we don't just get to drop everything when they blow up in our faces."

"Hey," she snaps. "This isn't my fault, okay? You don't get to take your shit out on me. It's not like I have it fucking easy—"

"How long are you going to do this?" he asks, eyes flashing with rare anger and upset. "*You* decided to study astronomy. *You* decided to get a fucking doctorate. You knew it would be hard, and now that it is, you want to leave us all behind and run away with some girl you don't even know."

Grace jerks back. The words come like a tangible slap across the face. "Okay," she says, and it is a trembling, shaking breath. "Okay."

"Shit," Raj murmurs. "Shit, I didn't mean that."

She takes a shot. It burns in her chest, but no more than the burn behind her eyes or on her cheeks, incensed at what he apparently thinks of her.

Raj grabs her hands again. Soft this time. Gentle this time. She can't look at him.

"Gracie," he says. "This tequila is hitting at the absolute worst time. Listen. I'm an ass. I'm jealous and upset, but I didn't mean that. Okay?"

"Okay," Grace says carefully. "Then, what did you mean?" She snatches her hands away and puts them in her lap. Humiliation burns in her gut, and she finds herself digging painful grooves across her knuckles. "Is that why you're so upset? Because I had the chance to study medicine like you wanted, and I didn't? Because I left the tea room, and put my own dream on hold? Because I don't know what I want or who I am or where the *fuck* I'm supposed to be? Because I'm realizing *I* don't fucking fit?"

"No," he breathes out. The room is so hot, and

it starts to spin. "I shouldn't have—"

"Because it's not just hard, Raj. That job, the one my mentor told me had my name written all over it? They questioned every piece of my research. They insinuated that it was Professor MacMillan who had done the work and *graciously* allowed my name to be included. One of them wondered if my professional memberships with the Black STEM Group and Black LGBTQ Science were advocating division, and they made sure to mention division was not a part of their *culture*." She closes her eyes, trying to get a handle on her emotions. "I've spent months fielding rejections, Raj, for all the various reasons that they deem wrong with me. I don't expect to just be handed things, but why the hell not? I spent eleven years doing nothing else but chasing this. Sacrificing so much and running myself into the ground for this. Why shouldn't it be handed to me now? Why should I have to fight? Haven't I proved myself enough?"

Her tongue tastes sour from the tequila. "So," she spits out. "What did you mean?"

He scrubs his hands through his hair. "I wasn't trying to be the bad guy here."

"Is that your explanation?"

"No, *Porter*," he snaps. "It isn't. My point is that this was never about you. You buried yourself in your work and your research just to prove Colonel wrong. Everything else, everyone else, came second to that. So, I'm sorry you didn't get the job. I'm sorry they don't see you for all the work you've done, because it's *good* work. You're a *good* goddam astronomer, just like you wanted to be, and it fucking sucks that it's so hard. But, was it worth it? Was it the big fuck-you you wanted it to be? Or not, since everything else has always been less of a priority than breaking your back to prove you're the best?"

It seems so absurd, but when you've known people so long, you know how to love them, and you know how to hurt them. You know all the soft spots where your claws dig in and press.

"Or was the fuck-you running off with a stranger you drunk-married in Vegas? You left us behind like we don't have our own things that are hard. Like we haven't spent years holding each other up, because that's what we *do*. I can't help you, I can't support you, and you can't support me, when you just leave." He swallows hard, looking away. "Why do you always think you have to get through everything alone? It doesn't have to be hard *alone*."

Grace grits her teeth so hard, her jaw starts to ache. They shouldn't be drinking. In the morning, or even in a few hours after he's gotten sick, Raj will apologize. He'll call Grace *little sister,* and they'll hug it out. Now, though, he's drunk, and his claws dig deep at the soft parts she forgot she had to protect. His words reveal a truth she's

223

tried hard to bury: Grace Porter is not as strong as she thought she was, and instead is the lonely, terrified creature she has yet to embrace.

"This is the fuck-you," she says, throwing her next shot at Raj.

Tequila drips down his face and shirt. It seeps into his hair and his eyes, and she knows it must burn. He waves away someone when they come over to check if things are okay.

This is me, says the monster from the deep. *Here I am.*

They're silent. She stares hard at the table, her fingernail digging into the grout.

"Well," he says finally. "Since we're drunk and getting things off our chests—is there anything else you'd like to share with the class?"

She can't help it—she laughs. These tight giggles that offset the way she wants to cry. They laugh, and they're going to feel this, all of this, in the morning.

"I miss you," Grace says once they quiet down again. "I miss you and Meera and Ximena and Agnes so much, I can hardly stand it. I'm *not* alone here, but I am lonely. I don't know how to be this Grace Porter that isn't chasing something. I don't know how to deal with my big, grand plan falling apart."

Raj listens.

She takes a deep breath.

"I don't know why I started studying

astronomy," she says quietly. The room sways. "Jesus—maybe it was a fuck-you to Colonel. Maybe I wanted to show him I could do something for me and still be the best. That first year after switching my major, everything just clicked. I was so certain it was what I wanted to do for the rest of my life. And now I have to figure out how to make that happen, and it fucking sucks, okay?"

"I'm sorry," he murmurs. "I didn't mean to—to diminish your shit just to talk about my shit. If I could, I'd make it better. I'd fix it."

"I know." She blinks down at her hands. "I have no idea how to fix it or make it better. I don't know exactly what I want anymore. I just know that it includes Yuki. So, I'm here, and I'm trying not to think about the rest of it yet."

Raj laughs softly. "She seemed a little vicious."

"She is!" Grace exclaims. "She's vicious and a little mean and kind and weird and patient and I—I got married to her. I want her, I know that. I just don't know how to keep her and the rest of it. Eventually I'll figure out where I need to be, and I don't know how she fits into that. But I want her to fit. I want to keep her. I want to have one thing that's just easy. That I don't have to fight for."

Raj holds his glass up. "Then we'll drink to it," he says. "To deserving things that are easy."

They clink their glasses together like it is an

intention. Grace closes her eyes and wishes for it like kids wish on stars.

Cheers.

Yuki wakes her up with toothpaste kisses all over her face.

Grace's mouth tastes like cotton, tongue thick and swollen and a little sore. She blinks awake, and a sleepy Yuki hovers over her, black fringe in her eyes, metal piercings glinting, eyebrows raised.

"You cling like an octopus when you're drunk," she says. "And you smell like tequila, get up."

Grace buries her face in the covers. "I don't even remember getting home."

Yuki narrows her eyes. "I had to come pick you up," she says. "You and your brother owe me big-time. Why did you get that drunk?"

Grace sighs, the night coming back in pieces. "Sibling bonding."

"Never been happier to be an only child. Now, get up." Yuki shoves her lightly. "I'll make you something to eat if you drink some water and take some painkillers."

She moves to get off the bed, and Grace grabs her wrists and feels the small, delicate bones there. "Thank you," she murmurs. "For taking care of me and getting me home."

Yuki ducks her head. A rose flush blooms on her cheeks. "Anytime, Grace Porter."

Grace follows her into the living room to find

Raj buried under the covers on the small couch. All of Yuki's roommates seem to be asleep or out, so Grace doesn't feel subconscious pulling her hoodie up and hiding.

"Big brother," she says, shaking him. "If you don't get up, I'm telling Meera you can't hold your liquor."

An arm shoots out from under a thin blanket. It grabs Grace's hand and squeezes.

"You wouldn't dare," he wheezes. "I'll tell her about that time you smoked bad weed and spent the rest of the night trying to tightrope around the toilet seat."

She shrieks and jumps on top of him, ignoring the way her stomach lurches. "You swore we would never speak of that again," she hisses. "I'll tell her about the night you finally got the nerve to ask Ximena out, but you were so drunk you ended up giving your whole speech to a mannequin instead."

A sharp elbow knocks into her chest. "What about the time you accidentally took molly because the girl who offered it was *so nice?*" he counters. "You thought it was ibuprofen, and ended up getting stitches because you fell off a four-inch curb."

He emerges from the blankets. Wild morning hair and bleary eyes glare at her. Grace says, "Like you would ever turn down a politely given pain reliever. Working in the lab gave me back pain, I thought it was obvious!" She shoves him, and he lets out a small *oof.* "Remember when you showed up to work drunk and Baba Vihaan thought you had a fever from how bad you were sweating?"

"I'm a lightweight," he says. "Is it a crime? Is it an offense against humanity?"

"Wow," Yuki says, and they turn. She looks unimpressed. "Is this what it's like having a sibling?"

Grace collapses on top of Raj, ignoring his long, pained groan. "No judging," she says. "I'm weak and hungover. Can't take it."

Yuki rolls her eyes and makes her way to the kitchen. She's changed into a long T-shirt that says Some Girls Eat Girls. Grace feels unstoppered adoration flow through her.

"Do you two hungover people want breakfast?" she asks. "We have—" She peers into the fridge. "Rice and leftover pizza, but I'd put my money on the rice. I can make toast, too."

"Riiiice," Raj moans. He holds one hand over the top of the couch. "High five for the staple dish of the Asian diaspora."

Yuki snorts, but she gives him a corny, terrible air high five, and Grace watches in wonder as her ears and neck flush pink, before she turns back around. "I always burn toast," Yuki says. "So, look forward to that."

"Let me do it," Grace says. She shoves Raj

again and gets up. "I grew up in a 'no burnt toast allowed' household. I got this." She hip-checks Yuki out of the way and pauses. "Hey," she says softly, and waits until Yuki turns to face her. "I'm going to kiss you, okay?"

Yuki makes a face. "You don't have to announce it, Honey Girl."

Grace crosses her arms. "Why not? Consent is sexy!"

"Um, yes," Yuki says, "but if you make this a habit, I'm going to scream and probably, like, implode? So, I feel like maybe we can just assume unless I say otherwise."

"That's fair," Grace says. She puts careful hands around Yuki's waist and just—kisses her. *Good morning, hi, I want to keep you.*

Yuki curls her fingers around Grace's neck, or rather, around Grace's hoodie. She probably looks terrible right now: exhausted and bleary and a little sick, but Yuki keeps kissing her anyway. She pushes her hood back so she can see more of Grace, can see the bags under her eyes and her chapped lips and limp hair, free from its myriad of products.

"Rice," Raj calls as they pull away. "Toast. I have a flight to catch, and I can't show up to the airport like this. It'll really ruin my whole vibe for the trip, which is already not great."

At the reminder of last night's drunken confessions, Grace feels herself tense. It's ridiculous because they were both drunk and mean and bitter, but she still feels the words burn like the tequila did, right at the center of her chest.

"I'll do the toast," she says quietly, and slips out of Yuki's hold. She hears a sigh behind her, before the microwave opens and starts to hum with warming rice. She turns to the toaster. This one simple thing, she can do.

She remembers making toast after Colonel's surgery. He was aching and ill-tempered and snappy. He couldn't move and with his meds couldn't really eat, so Grace got up every morning before work and made toast with jam. The meds made his stomach upset, and the pain made *him* upset, and she remembers, too many times, the bread and plates that went flying.

Jesus, Porter, it's burnt, while Grace got on her knees and picked up slices and crumbs and wiped at stains. *I got one goddamn leg and a daughter burning my toast. Get off the damn floor, Porter. Just leave it, I said. I'll have Sharone order something.*

So, Grace knows how to make toast. Perfect toast.

She stands guard at the toaster because you can't leave it too quick or too long, or the whole thing will be ruined.

"You're watching it like it's going to eat you," Yuki says. "Or like it's going to up and

230

disappear."

Grace leans on her elbows. "Habit," she says.

The microwave dings, and Yuki pulls plates down out of the cabinets. Raj drags himself in and settles on the floor. "We're eating here," he decides. "This is where I deserve to eat right now."

So, they eat rice and toast on the floor. Yuki can only find one clean fork. She and Grace share it, passing it back and forth between bites, and Raj digs in with his hands.

"Just like home," he mumbles through a mouthful. "Meera says it's 'uncouth' now, but that's only because the white kids at her college told her it was weird."

"Fuck white people," Grace and Yuki say together.

"True that."

Soon enough, he has to leave. Grace follows Raj down the steps, and they stand in the warm summer breeze waiting for his Uber.

"So," he says, arms crossed. "Wild night, huh?"

Grace *hmm*s. "Threw up twice this morning, but sure. Wild. Not disgusting at all."

"Ha, I'm at three, probably more after airplane turbulence." He raises his eyebrows at her. "I win."

She crosses her arms, too. The little moving car on his screen says four minutes until his ride arrives. "What do you win?"

He doesn't look at her. He's held Grace up more

times than she can count. Figures eventually he'd knock her down at least once, too.

"Maybe forgiveness?" he says. "For being a total and complete ass last night? Tequila really doesn't agree with me."

Grace turns to him. Her head is pounding; her throat is still dry. Somewhere, in the cavernous hollow cave that is her chest, drunk, angry words sit embedded in a perfect target. "You weren't all wrong," she admits. "I didn't just spend eleven years sacrificing my own things. I also sacrificed so much time with you all. Being there for you. Drunk words equal sober thoughts, right?"

"Okay, first," he says, "that sounds like a Pinterest quote. Never say that to me again. Second—" He takes a deep breath. "It's in the big brother handbook to call you out on your shit. But your shit isn't just *hard,* it's a bunch of systemic bullshit. I know that. I was wrong to suggest otherwise. So, thanks for calling me out, too. Maybe little sisters know what they're talking about, sometimes."

Grace smiles, even though it hurts. The sun is too bright and the city is too loud and everything is too much. Everything has been too much for far too long.

She sniffles, and Raj freezes up. His hands hover somewhere around her shoulders, like he has no idea what to do. She wipes her eyes as she laughs at the absurdity. "I'm telling Meera you said that, too."

They look at each other, hesitating like they never have before.

"Just hug it out!" Yuki yells from the window. "Who knew earth signs were so goddamn emotionally incompetent?"

"How do you know I'm an earth sign?" Raj asks.

"Broke into your phone while you were in the bathroom and added you on that astrology app," she says, disappearing inside. "Your passcode is whack!"

He looks back at Grace. "You really picked one."

She looks up at the window. "Yeah," she sighs, unable to keep the affection from her face. "I really like her."

"I like her, too," he says. "She's good." He opens his mouth and takes a moment before speaking. "I really am sorry."

Grace holds her arms out. He leans in, and she inhales his familiar scent. "I'm sorry," she breathes out. "I'm sorry I didn't know. I'm sorry I never *asked*. I would have—I don't know what I would have done. But I could have tried."

He laughs quietly. "I know you would, dummy. I'm sorry I never told you. I'm sorry I got mad that you're trying to figure out your own shit, and I can't figure out mine."

"Not your fault," she says firmly. "I love you."

"Love you, Space Girl." He pulls away. A gray Honda pulls up to the curb. "My chariot awaits. Next time you talk to me, I may be in the market for a new employee in Boston. Right up your alley."

"I'm there," she says.

"You ready?" the driver asks.

Raj nods, taking a deep breath. "Wish me luck?"

"Good luck, I guess. I'm conflicted about it."

"Well, as long as you're conflicted," he says, climbing into the car. "Don't miss me too much."

"Impossible," she whispers, and the car zooms off, into the busy streets of New York.

Later, while *Clueless* plays on Yuki's laptop, and Grace nurses her second cup of hojicha, her phone vibrates.

She groans. Raj already texted that he arrived in Boston safe and sound. Ximena sent her photos of the therapy dogs in the hospital today, golden retrievers and German shepherds and little Yorkies with bows in their hair. Agnes sent a string of skull emojis, but she also had group therapy tonight, so it checks out.

Meera, the display says.

"Shit."

Yuki makes a questioning noise, half asleep from half a bottle of wine. "Me or you?"

"Me," Grace answers, rolling off the bed. She snatches the phone up and says, "Give me a second," before she presses it to her chest. "Gotta take this. I'll be right back."

Yuki nods, rolling into the warm spot Grace has left. "Want me to pause?"

Grace shakes her head. "I've seen this movie like a hundred times. Please."

She tiptoes out the room. Dhorian is in the living room, case studies and paperwork laid out in front of him on the coffee table. He's in comfy clothes, sweats and a long-sleeved shirt that says Black by Popular Demand. He gives Grace a little salute when he hears the bedroom door shut.

"Is that Porter?" Sani calls. "Tell her and Yuki we're having a *Crash Bandicoot* tournament once you're done trying to save the world."

She waves her phone, and Dhorian nods. "She's busy," he says. "Must be important, because who the fuck talks on the phone anymore?"

Grace shuts herself into the bathroom. She gets in the tub and pulls the curtain for extra privacy.

"Hello?" Meera sighs impatiently.

"Hi, Meera."

"Finally," she says. "It took you forever to say hello. What if it was an emergency? What if I was on that game show where you have to phone a friend? I would have lost."

"Are you talking about *Who Wants to Be a Millionaire*? Is that what you're talking about? Why would you be on that?"

"Have you ever heard of hypotheticals?" she

asks. "Like, hypothetically, my brother is driving me crazy with his weird guilt over whatever went down with you two while he was in New York. So, spill. What did he do?"

Grace glares at the shower tile. Trust Raj to leave it up to her to fend off Meera. "It was nothing," she lies. "We were just drunk."

"He said he crossed some lines," Meera says. "You know I'll let him have it if he said something wrong. Love my brother, but he can be—well, my brother."

"Seriously, M, it's fine. He was just nervous about the meeting. The pressure was getting to him."

She knows she said too much when Meera turns from protective to worried. "Pressured about what? Did Baba say something to him? I swear he lets that man guilt him into anything. I'm gonna call him back—"

Grace curses. "It wasn't like that," she says soothingly, voice quiet. "He just wants to do well. You know how much he loves the tea room. He wants to make a good impression. That was it. I probably shouldn't have let him get so drunk the night before."

It's quiet for a moment before Meera speaks again, sounding small and scared, like a little girl. "You promise? You'd tell me if he said it was getting to be too much for him, right?"

If I told Meera I didn't want to run the tea

room, she'd drop everything, and she'd do it.

"Promise," Grace says, the lie settling in with the rest of the sludge in her chest. "If he said anything like that, I'd tell you."

Meera sniffs a little, but Grace hears the relief in the silence. "It's good he has you," she says. "He still thinks he has to protect me, but I'm glad he can be honest with you."

"Me, too," Grace croaks out. "But enough about that. Tell me about you. How's that class?"

"Oh my God," Meera says. "It's seriously the best decision I've ever made. I love it. I can't imagine doing anything but psychology. It just feels right, you know?"

She'd give up everything if I said I didn't want to do it.

"That sounds so great, M," Grace says. "You have time to talk? I wanna hear all about it."

When they're done, she creeps back into the bedroom.

Yuki's eyes blink open, bleary and swollen, as Grace scoots closer. "There she is," she says quietly. "The favored girl of the sun." She reaches out and pulls Grace in. "Honey Girl."

"Are you drunk?" Grace asks. "Or just sleepy?"

Yuki burrows into the covers. "Both. Are you done talking on the phone like it's 1999?"

"Okay," Grace scoffs. "Is that gonna be the new apartment joke? It's already tired."

Yuki hides a smile in her pillow. "Perhaps."

237

She looks sleepy and giggly. No longer the lazy dream in Grace's memories, but the real thing.

"Yes," Yuki answers to a question unasked, looking back up at Grace. "You can kiss me, yes."

Maybe Raj was right. Maybe Grace has been selfish. There are decisions to be made. She has a life to live and a home that waits. She cannot spend the rest of her days kissing a girl that tastes like tart red wine. She cannot stay huddled around a radio listening to the origins of misunderstood things. But she wants to. She wants to hold on to this just a little bit longer, before the universe makes her choose.

Soon, she will have to face the rejections in her inbox. She will have to apply for more positions and sit through more interviews. She will have to answer all their questions, and she will not give them the satisfaction of walking out. If there is anything she's learned with Yuki, away from the constant pressures in Portland, it's that it is okay to be the monster. To be the feared creature lurking in the dark with teeth and claws and blood.

She will embrace it. She will stare them down in their fear, and she will demand their time and their consideration and their equal opportunity. She will not let them spin her into a scary story, a thing whispered about and cast aside.

But Grace will also hold on to this good thing,

her good thing, for just a little while longer. She has earned the right for something to be easy. She has earned the right to hold on to this place, this peace, this girl, this red-bricked home.

Just a little longer, she whispers to the universe. *I will cling to it like stardust.*

Fourteen

August comes with humidity and open windows and music speakers blaring from the stoops on the block. It's Grace's birthday month, and the passage of summer weighs heavily on her.

She spends one night of it on Yuki's bed watching *House Party* while Dhorian two-strand twists her hair.

"You need to be committed to the protective style," he says. "Don't let your half-white side break down your edges."

"I'm committed!" she argues. "I don't want my edges broken! I do protective styles! I sleep on silk!"

Yuki gets dressed, hiding halfway behind her closet, ready to make her way to the radio station. She shimmies into some jeans that are more holes than denim. Grace peeks at her, eyes roaming over Yuki's curves and the way her back is shaped like a bow. There's a little bruise on her hip, purpling like wine, and she flushes at remembering how it got there. "You better take care of your edges," Yuki says. "I would hate to be married to a bald-headed bitch."

"Can you go?" Grace whines.

"Please," Dhorian adds. He points at the TV and Grace's hair. "Can't you see we're in

240

the middle of a delicate cultural process right now?"

Yuki holds her hands up in surrender. "I can tell when I'm not wanted." She bends down and pauses, just for a moment, before she kisses Grace on the cheek. There is a lipstick imprint left behind, Grace knows. "Listen to the show tonight?"

"Always," she says, and Yuki gives her a helpless smile. "Text me when you're there."

Yuki rolls her eyes. "Cute how my wife thinks I can't kick anyone's ass if I need to." She blows a kiss at them and the scent of her soap lingers.

In the quiet, with just the TV and the lull of Dhorian's fingers, Grace remembers this is Colonel's favorite movie. She hasn't seen it since she was a teenager and found him watching it in the living room. She was grounded for being in the wrong place at the wrong time with the wrong girl, caught by a cop who knew her father.

She was brought home in the back of a squad car, heart thumping with each mile, eyes trained on the baton and the gun and the cold metal handcuffs. He dragged her by her arm up to their front door, and she listened, standing on the doormat, as Colonel assured him it would never happen again. Not with his daughter.

She was grounded. No phone, no TV, no iPod. Just school and homework and helping Miss Debbie file papers and listening to her endless tirades about how rude and disrespectful and disappointing Grace was to her father. That was the true punishment. So, when she crept down the stairs at the sound of loud music and Colonel—*Colonel*—bellowing with laughter, she didn't expect to see him lounging on the couch, watching a movie about college kids with '90s haircuts and '90s clothes.

She fully expected to be sent back up to her room, but Colonel hadn't minded her joining him. There were two beer bottles in front of him, empty, and he sprawled on the couch, relaxed. "You ever seen this?"

She crept closer, sitting primly on the edge of the cushion. "No. What is it?"

Colonel groaned. He *groaned*. "Damn, Porter. How have I never showed you this? Sit down. I'll start it over."

"You don't have to."

"Got to," he said, rewinding. "This right here is a classic. A staple in the culture."

She sighed, getting comfortable in her own little corner. "If you say so."

"Oh, I say so."

It's a good memory, Grace thinks, brought back to life here.

Dhorian's pager beeps. "Shit," he says. "I'm the on-call resident this week." He completes one of Grace's twists; there are only a few left to do in the back. "You can finish these up, right?"

"Go save Harlem," she says. "You're like Spider-Man."

"Only if it's the Miles Morales version," he says, grabbing his bag and his hoodie from the living room. "Bye, Porter!"

And then Grace is alone. The movie loses some of its appeal in the quiet of the apartment. There's just the hum of the huge fish tank and her circling thoughts. There is Yuki's incense and bottled sea salt and rough-cut crystals. Her mishmash butsudan has small, cutout pictures of her grandmother and dried flower petals and candles and a glass of water she changes out every morning, first thing. It has all become familiar to Grace.

She will miss it, when this champagne-bubble dream pops.

She decides that tonight, in the hours before Yuki's show, she will not brood. She crawls under the covers and pulls out her laptop. The Skype call is dialing before she registers it. It rings and rings, and finally Ximena and Agnes become grainy and visible. There they are, down to the overworked shadows under their eyes and Agnes's lips, peeling and irritated from stress picking.

"Hi," Grace says. She feels herself drawn to them. "Miss you guys."

They are both cuddled on the couch. It has been many years of *will they, won't they, do they, don't they,* and she realizes she has missed that, too: the reliable uncertainty of their relationship status. Ximena holds Agnes around her small waist and buries her face in the shock of blond hair. "Hi, conejito," she murmurs quietly. "We miss you, too. We were just talking about you."

Agnes's eyes flutter open. She looks tired and sharp. "Hi, Porter," she croaks out, and Ximena meets Grace's eyes.

She shakes her head slightly. Grace suddenly feels the entire country between them. She cannot hold Agnes and wait for her sharp edges to dull. She thinks of Raj's words. They all have their hard things. She wants to be there, really *be there,* for this one.

"Hey, Ag," Grace says, because she can, because she must, because she *wants* to support her friends. "Bad day? Bad week? Bad person? Want me to fly back and put them in their place?"

Agnes laughs, and it leaves her like a heavy, burdened weight.

She gives a small smile, and Ximena presses a barely there kiss to her neck. Grace pretends not to see Agnes shudder. "What about if the bad thing is my brain?"

It's always the goddamn brains. "I'll put your brain in its place, if it helps," Grace says, scooting closer to the screen. *I'm here, I'm here, I'm here.* "Me and Ximena have grown rather fond of you over the years. What would we do without our feral white girl?"

"She is feral, right?" Ximena asks. "And that means strong, and powerful and so dangerous that any brain wouldn't *dare* try to fuck with her."

Agnes groans, hiding her face behind a lanky arm. "You guys are the worst," she says.

"Yeah," Grace agrees. "Love you."

"So much it hurts," Ximena adds.

Agnes bites her lip. It'll scab and bleed and heal, like she always does. Like she always has. When Grace looks at Agnes, she does not see a monster. She sees hurt and anger and the scarred remains of fear turned survival.

"I was actually going to call you tonight, start giving you shit about your birthday and becoming old and decrepit this month," Agnes says. "It's not even—"

"Relax," Ximena murmurs, rubbing Agnes's stomach beneath the heavy sweatshirt. "It's a big deal for you, so it's a big deal for us."

A trembling breath. It does not sound like Agnes, who Grace has always known as fierce and utterly composed, even at the height of her shrieking, furious anger. "I got a new diagnosis," she says, looking up into the camera to meet Grace's eyes. "Borderline personality disorder. It's not even that big of a deal, you know?" Grace holds her breath. "It's not like I wasn't already living my life as a major depressive with clinical anxiety with a lovely little sprinkle of self-harm, right? So, what's the big fucking deal?"

There are a lot of words Grace could say. *I'm sorry. I'm glad you told me. It'll get better.*

They all aren't enough.

Instead she says, "You know I love you, right?"

"I'm painfully aware," Agnes replies. She pulls two small pill bottles from her hoodie pocket. "Anyway, I have two new prescriptions to turn me into a semi-functioning person," she says. "They've just been making me sick so far." She smiles, a bitter thing. "Guess you guys are stuck with me. No one else would take in a late-blooming nutjob."

"Hey," Grace says. "As a fellow late-blooming nutjob, I take offense to that." She presses her hand to the screen, like that will help. "Give us a little more credit," she teases softly. "I mean, we liked you well enough when we thought you were just depressed and mean. Especially Ximena, right?"

"Fuck off," they both say.

Agnes sends her an awful glare. "*Anyway.* That's enough emotional vulnerability for a lifetime. I'll deal with it. Whatever."

Grace snorts. "You're already doing better than me," she confesses. "Don't think I've reached the 'deal with it' stage of anything yet."

"That's because you're not as well-adjusted as me," Agnes says. "I'm going to therapy twice a week, but my therapist is driving me crazy. She says she's absolutely positive I'll adapt beautifully to this. Old hag."

Grace laughs. "You can't say that."

Agnes makes a nasty noise. " 'Beautifully,' she said, Porter. Beautifully borderline. Maybe I'll write a book."

Ximena hides a smile behind Agnes's serrated, angular body. "I'd buy it," Grace says. "I'd—" She cannot understand this, what Agnes is going through, but she can understand loneliness so deep you can't reach it, and sadness that consumes everything. She can understand wanting to let your limbs go weak as you sink underwater. "I'd get it," Grace says, and she trusts that Agnes will understand that, too.

Lonely creatures, she has learned, will always find each other.

"Yeah." Agnes sighs. "Your phone is lighting up, by the way. Since when do you have friends we don't know about?"

Ximena lets out a fake cry. "We're being replaced. Maybe Porter was the hip-hop SoulCycle type all along."

Grace ignores their increasing dramatics to grab her phone.

Yuki
11:59 p.m.
are you there?

are you listening?

where are you, grace porter?

"Oh my God," Ximena says, and Grace looks up, feeling caught. "I have never seen you look so lovesick. Is this what married life does to you? You're glowing."

"I'm not lovesick," Grace mutters. "And I'm not glowing. It's just—I'm just—"

"Uh-huh." Ximena hooks her chin over Agnes's shoulder. "Don't get your heart broken, Grace Porter, okay? I'll put you back together, but I won't be nice about it."

Grace doesn't meet her eyes. She fiddles with her phone, navigating to Yuki's webpage.

"I won't. I'll be fine," she says. "Things are good here. Promise."

"Okay," Ximena says. "We'll let you go. Love you."

"So much it hurts," Grace says.

"Gross." Agnes sticks out her tongue and the call disconnects.

She clicks the Listen Live link flashing on her phone and is immediately transported into the world Yuki builds up, each word like a brick in the foundation. She settles in and pretends half her heart hasn't been left in Portland, unable to find its rhythm when the people it's connected to are hurting. She settles in and inhales embers and crushed herbs and wonders if she will remember the smell clearly once she has to leave.

"Tonight, we are talking about the Akashita," Yuki says over the radio. "It's another yokai I'm sharing with you. I think my mom would be livid if she knew this is what I've shared from our culture. But, it's interesting, isn't it?"

Grace listens.

"Every culture has different stories for things that go bump in the night. This one, the Akashita, I couldn't get out of my head for some reason. Maybe it's because there is no way to say if this creature is good or bad. It reminded me of people. We are capable of so much good and so much harm, sometimes in the same breath."

Yuki's voice is melodic and tranquil and quiet.

"The Akashita is a yokai that was first drawn by Toriyama Sekien. It's a hairy beast with claws for hands and a huge, red tongue. You can't see most of its body because it is lost in a black cloud. It is a monster stuck in darkness and it guards, or maybe holds the key to, a floodgate.

"You look up, and there it is. This unknown monster with its unknown motivations. Some say it is a bad omen to see the Akashita. They say that to see it means a terrible drought is coming. Some say it is a protector. It watches to make sure people do not take more than they need, and if they do, they are punished. They are

249

swallowed up whole by this half-hidden thing in the sky.

"Take too much, and you will be eaten. Take what you need, and leave the rest for those that have none. Leave space and room and chance for those that have none.

"I think that's what makes the Akashita so scary," Yuki says. "Not its body or its hunger or the black cloud it lives in. I think what makes it so scary is that you see it, and you don't know whether to feel scared or safe. You don't know what it wants, and if it will shield you or eat you. It is the unknown, the uncertainty, that is terrifying, more than the darkness and the monster that crawls from its clutches.

"I don't know if the Akashita is a lonely creature. I think it could be, with only a black cloud for company. Maybe it is looking for other lonely creatures, thirsty and starving and drought-ridden. Maybe it opens its floodgates like one would hold out a hand. Or maybe it is a lonely creature looking for other, unsuspecting things. Maybe it has embraced its loneliness, and the floodgates wash away all the other fragile, weak things in its way. No one can say, really. No one knows. It's unknowable."

Grace holds her phone with shaking fingers. Yuki's voice is an echo in the background. An echo of all the things Grace feels when she looks up. Uncertain. Unknown. Afraid to be swallowed up and unsure how to ask for help.

Her fingers hover over the keypad. She opens her messages to Agnes first.

Grace
1:03 a.m.
what do you need from me to help?
you don't have to ask
whatevs you need, it's yours

She switches to the long chain of texts with Yuki.

Grace
1:05 a.m.
it was a good show tonight
maybe I am uncertain too

Yuki
1:06 a.m.
i was waiting for you

And then:

Yuki
1:07 a.m.
everyone is uncertain grace porter
sometimes you just have to keep going anyway

Grace takes a breath. It is August. Age twenty-nine is about to begin, and there is still so much she doesn't know. It is the scariest thing in the world.

August 26, 2010

"Hurry up and cut it," Meera says. "It's Mama's butter cake. It's delicious, I swear."

"Give her a minute," Raj mutters. "She only just learned how to make a decent cup of tea. Cake cutting might be a new level."

Baba Vihaan smacks him on the back of the head. They're all huddled around a table at the end of the night. Floors still need to be swept and dishes need to be washed and the till needs to be reconciled but for now, cake.

Grace tucks some flyaway hair behind her ears and bends down. There are three little candles in the center of the cake, burning brightly.

"Mama wanted to come," Meera confesses quietly, fingers picking at the designs on her kurti. "She got tired. She gets tired a lot now."

"Hey," Grace says, reaching for her hand. "It's okay. She needs her rest."

Raj crosses his arms, and Baba Vihaan clears his throat. "She sends her love. Now make a wish. Three wishes."

"Not how it works," Raj says, and he gets another smack on the head. "Just saying."

Grace smiles and stares into the little flames. "What should I wish for?" she whispers, still gripping Meera's fingers. "Any ideas?"

"A car," Meera suggests. "Sharing the Corolla with Raj is getting unbearable. Oh!" she exclaims. "A good semester, obviously."

"Health," Baba Vihaan says. "Prosperity." He rolls his eyes toward Meera. "Maybe a car."

Grace laughs and closes her eyes. "I'll take all of those under consideration."

Her cheeks are still flushed from the mild humiliation of having "Happy Birthday" sung to her. Even stoic Raj joined in, gaining energy from Grace's discomfort. Now she takes a deep breath and blows. She sends a wish out to the universe, and life has taught her she has to mean it, or nobody and nothing will listen.

Good health, she wishes, *for those that need it more than me. A good academic year.*

She hesitates, but the universe does not grant wishes to hesitation. She grips Meera's hand tight and goes to blow out the last candle.

Make my parents proud, she wishes, harder than anything else. Hard enough that she almost sees it take shape. That's what Porters do.

She opens her eyes and begins to cut the cake. She follows the tradition of serving each of them a bite. She serves Baba Vihaan first, then Meera. Raj looks like he won't open his mouth at first, but Grace says please soft enough that the others don't hear. "Please, Raj."

He stares at her for a long moment. He is wary of Grace, wary of the way Meera follows behind her, asking questions about school and life and the universe while they're between customers. But Grace says please, and he opens his mouth for a slice of cake.

"It's good," he mumbles, and she smiles.

"Of course, it is," she says. "Your mama made it."

August 26, 2012

"Hey, Mom," she says. "Just checking in." She stands outside this little Salvadoran restaurant in the city that sells tres leches cake.

"Hey, Porter," Mom says. There is a bunch of noise behind her. She might be in Scotland this month, or maybe it's Madrid. "Happy birthday, baby!"

She smiles in the window reflection. "Thanks. Are you busy?"

She can barely hear Mom when she answers. "We're at a summer festival!" she yells. "It's way too loud, but I'll call you when I get back to the room? We're staying in this quaint little house with—"

The call cuts out.

"Of course," she sighs. She goes inside. The

cake tastes sweet. She eats it alone at a table in the corner.

August 26, 2016

Sharone makes mac and cheese and string beans and fried chicken and a pitcher of margaritas. They sit out on the patio, reclined back and watching the sun go down.

"You're going to do big things," she says. "I hope you believe me when I say I see so much life in you, Porter. You make me wanna go back and do it all again. Your father is so proud of you."

"I was supposed to do medicine," Grace says quietly. "Not this."

"So?" Sharone asks. "You ain't *supposed* to do anything but stay Black and die. Anything you do beyond that is a feat in itself, you hear me?" She lifts up her glass in a toast, and Grace meets it.

"I hear you," she says, clinking their glasses together.

The door opens behind them. Colonel leans against the door, still in his uniform, hat in his hand. "What are we celebrating?" he asks, limping out on the patio to perch on the arm of Sharone's chair.

She gives him a poisoned look. Grace stares down at her lap, into her glass at the little pieces of fruit Sharone squeezed in. She's starting to feel a little tipsy.

"We're celebrating," she hisses, "your daughter's birthday." She turns and plasters a smile on her face. "Baby, get that cake out of the fridge. We'll cut it out here. The bakery messed it up a little, but don't worry, I gave them a piece of my mind."

Grace hurries inside. She hears Colonel's muttered "shit" before the patio doors close behind her. In the fridge, there is a white cake with buttercream frosting. In pink letters on top it says Happy Birthday, Peter.

"Happy birthday, Peter," she says quietly, swiping a finger through the icing.

August 26, 2018

Grace spends the day in the lab. Her neck and shoulders and back hurt from being hunched over one of their older pieces of equipment. She's exhausted, but the distraction is nice.

One of the postdocs that added her on Facebook presents her with a small cupcake and a lone candle.

"I have to watch for these results," Grace tells her. "But thank you."

"You work too hard," she says. "Take a break."

Grace blows out the candle, and some of the icing begins to melt. She doesn't remember what she wished for, or the name of the girl that gave her the cupcake.

August 26, 2019

"Las Vegas?" Grace asks, staring at the tickets in front of her. "You're sending me to Las Vegas as a graduation present?"

Colonel clears his throat. He sits stiff in the chair across from her. "It was Sharone's idea," he says. "She thought you needed to let loose."

"She does," Sharone says. She turns to Grace, grabbing her hands. "You've worked so damn hard, Porter, and in a few months, you'll be done. You deserve to have some fun."

Colonel clears his throat again, and Grace straightens—muscle memory. "Everything is refundable. I advised her it was highly probable you already have things lined up. You're in a competitive field, best to get things moving early."

"I don't," she says, backtracking when his face goes blank. "I mean nothing that won't still be there when we get back." She holds up the three tickets. "Is it for us three?"

"Girl, what?" Sharone asks. "What grown woman wants to go to Las Vegas with their father and stepmom? And who says I want to go to Vegas with y'all?"

Colonel looks upward for strength. "In

other words, no. Take who you want. I assume you'll make sure they're responsible and won't influence you to do anything regrettable."

"Oh my God," Sharone says. "She's never done anything that could even come close to regrettable in her life. Why would she start now?"

They bicker, and Grace goes over the specifics in her head. She can't take Meera, because the trip is set for March, and she'll have class. Grace would love for Raj to come, but she knows how much he loves the tea room. He would never want to leave Baba Vihaan to scramble alone with Meera, even for a few days.

That leaves Ximena and Agnes. She knows Ximena will commiserate while they're forced to Travel While Black, and Agnes won't let her stay in her head the whole time. What happens in Vegas will be experienced fully, and not sidelined by all the stress of completing her doctorate program. She'll set foot in Vegas with her mission completed, her success achieved.

"Thank you," she says, when she finally finds her voice. "I can't wait."

Colonel raises his eyebrows. "Well, you have plenty to keep you busy until then," he says pointedly. "One last semester. Stick to your plan. Don't let the promise of a trip derail you. You have big things to accomplish."

Your plan, he says.

"I know," she tells them. "I'll stick to the plan. I always do."

August 26, 2020

The night before Grace's birthday, she goes with Yuki to the radio station. She sits in the second swivel chair and watches Yuki bring creatures to life with her slow, melodic voice.

Tonight, the show is about selkies. She listens to Yuki talk about seals becoming trapped in human flesh and their skins being hidden from them, leaving them imprisoned with men.

"Sometimes people feel ownership over the things that make us *us,*" Yuki says into the mic. "Sometimes the things that are familiar to us and feel safe to us, remnants of our childhood and old lives, are locked away by someone who wants us to be different and look different and follow their rules. Sometimes lonely creatures are not of their own making."

Grace leaves the room, her nails digging into her palms. Sometimes the stories feel too familiar, too lived. Sometimes Grace does not want to relate to a monster in a story.

She sits in the hallway, earbuds in so she does not hear Yuki wrapping up the show. Grace is engaged in a debilitating round of Candy Crush when a shadow falls over her. She looks up, and

Blue is looking down, big headphones wrapped around her neck.

"You good?" she asks. "Yuki got an idea for another episode, so she might be a few minutes. You know how she gets."

Grace nods. Yuki gets single-minded and quiet and snappish when she has an idea, barely blinking and frustrated with anyone who interrupts her thoughts.

Blue flops down next to Grace, smelling like cigarette smoke and bubblegum and hair grease. "What's up with you?" she asks. "Usually you're in there making googly eyes at your girl."

Grace laughs. The sound echoes in the empty hallway. "I'm not that bad," she says. "I don't know. I've been having this existential crisis about my place in the world and what I'm supposed to be doing with my life and who I even am." She scrunches her nose. "Really inconvenient."

"Oof." Blue bumps Grace's shoulder. "Big mood."

Surprised, Grace turns to look at her. Tonight, she has her braids twisted up into two space buns, and she blinks back at Grace with bright yellow eyeshadow and gold hoops that say *Bitch* across the middle.

"Really, though?" she asks. "Sometimes it feels like I'm too old for this. I'm about to turn twenty-nine. Like, while I was busy getting a

PhD everyone else was figuring all this stuff out. I feel so behind."

"You give other people too much credit, okay?" Blue says. "Everyone's just pretending they have it together, because they don't realize everyone else is pretending to have it together. None of our dumbasses actually have it together." She frowns. "Maybe people with generational wealth and access to resources that allow them to prosper in the middle to upper class? But that's it. Just them."

"Very specific," Grace murmurs.

Blue smiles. "This is late stage capitalism, man. We have debt and will never be able to retire. *Yaaaaay*."

The studio door opens, and Yuki looks down at them. "My 'capitalism is a plague' radar was going off," she says. "Figured I'd come join the fun."

Blue gets up. "Your space girl just needed a pep talk. Be nice to her."

"I'm always nice to her," Yuki complains. "You catching the bus, Blue? We can wait with you."

Blue's already shoving her backpack over her shoulder. "Got a ride," she says. "And when we get back to my place, I got a riiiiide."

Yuki gags. Grace covers her face with her hands. "Get out," Yuki says. "Get out!"

"Don't forget to shut everything down!" Blue yells, cackling as she sprints down the hall.

"Ugh." Yuki gags again.

Grace looks up. "All done?" she asks.

Yuki nods. "It's after midnight. Happy birthday, Honey Girl," she says. She holds her hand out. "Come on. I want to take you home."

At the apartment, she lays Grace out on the bed. She kisses her mouth, and her neck, and her breasts, and the flat expanse of her stomach. She leaves her own matching bruise on Grace's narrow hips and smiles in the dim light at the shuddering noises Grace makes.

"You're so sweet," Yuki croons. "Just like honey."

She threads their fingers together. "Are you sweet everywhere, Grace Porter?"

It is their first time this close, this laid bare. It is the first time Grace sees all of the pink creases and soft skin and gentle curves that make up Yuki Yamamoto. It is the first time Yuki sees Grace golden from head to toe, with gold-dusted goose bumps and sun-colored hair prickling on her thighs.

Grace shakes apart at the feeling of Yuki's tongue on her, *in* her. She arches off the bed, pulled back down to earth by Yuki's fingers. She keeps hold of Grace, so she does not float away.

"Yuki," she whispers, eyes pressed shut. "Yuki, *fuck*."

Yuki looks up. Her eyes are dark, and her lips glisten. She is a monster, a siren, pulling Grace down and down and down. There is salt and burning sea in Grace's lungs. She does not want to come up for air.

Yuki eats her out while Grace comes, shuddering and clenching her thighs around the head of the girl between them. She kisses up Grace's heaving belly, her sweat-slick chest. She kisses Grace's fluttering eyelashes. She pushes back the honey-gold curls so they splay on the sheets like treasure.

"Good?" she asks, mouth swollen.

Grace closes her eyes and nods. Tears streak down the sides of her face as she squirms with oversensitivity as Yuki's fingers keep stroking her.

"Good," she gasps out. "You're so good, Yuki Yamamoto."

It is her birthday, and the summer's end nears. Grace holds on to her good thing with clutched fingers and an aching heart. She holds on for dear life, and she realizes she does not want to let go.

Grace wakes up to a phone full of missed calls and texts. There are voice mails from Sharone and Colonel and Mom. She scrolls through everything sleepily, sending a bleary selfie to the group chat with all her friends back home.

"You should not be allowed to look like that as soon as you wake up," Yuki murmurs, digging her chin into Grace's shoulder. Yuki is bed-mussed and mellow, hair still tussled from the fingers that twisted and pulled at it.

Grace feels heat in her belly at the reminder. She feels heat in her face, and though her brown skin doesn't blush, she still knows it's written all over her.

"Grace Porter," Yuki teases, laughing quietly as Grace hides under a pillow. "Are you *shy?* You didn't seem like it when I had my—"

"Okay," Grace interrupts. "It's my birthday. No jokes. I'm banning jokes."

Yuki grins at her. "Fine." She kisses Grace's neck. There is nothing hesitant, no pause. They have seen the other at their barest, most vulnerable. They have left their soft parts unguarded and raw. "Happy birthday," she says softly. "I think there's probably a surprise waiting for you in the kitchen once you're up."

"A surprise?" Grace smooths out Yuki's hair. She presses gentle fingers to the wine-purpling bruises on her jaw and the tender skin on her neck. Grace really did a number on her. "From your roommates?"

Yuki stretches, and Grace takes it all in. The way Yuki is dimpled and squishy and sharp and thorned all at once. "You've been here all summer," Yuki says, rolling out of bed. Her shirt barely touches her thighs. "They're not just my roommates. They're your *friends*."

"Oh," Grace whispers, though it shouldn't

264

surprise her. She may be lonely, feel lonely, wanting to take the world on by herself, but she has never really been alone. She is still trying to absorb that. "Yeah. My friends."

Yuki holds her hand out. "Come on. I want cake for breakfast."

There is, in fact, cake. Dhorian and Sani present it to her as she sits at the head of their coffee table, and Fletcher sings an off-pitch version of "Happy Birthday." It's not the Stevie Wonder version, and Grace doesn't even call him out on it.

"You guys didn't have to," she says, taking a bite. It's French vanilla with cream cheese frosting, and it tastes so sweet on her tongue. There is a lick of frosting at the corner of Yuki's mouth, and Grace kisses it away. That tastes sweet, too.

Sani frowns. "Of course we did," he says. "It's your *birthday*."

"Your twenty-ninth birthday," Dhorian adds. "It's a milestone. Last year before you're officially old."

Grace stares down at the cake. The blue and purple icing that makes up a night sky. The little astronaut set delicately on top. She is twenty-nine years old today, in a new city with new faces. Later, she will call the old ones, and they will all start to mesh. They will just be her friends, and there will be no distinction.

"A milestone," she repeats, picking up the little plastic astronaut. "I made it, huh?"

"You made it," Yuki confirms. "You can do whatever the fuck you want."

"I want more cake," Grace says decisively.

There is more cake. Fletcher sets up the game system, and then there is an impromptu *Mario Kart* tournament. There is wine, even though it's late morning, and shouting, and even more cake. Grace finds herself sipping a glass, situated on the floor and pressed back against Yuki's legs.

"Why are you so bad at this game?" Grace asks when Dhorian wins again. He's in his scrubs, ready to leave for a shift soon. He's beaten Yuki on this course three times in a row. "Shouldn't you be trying to impress me?"

"I don't have to impress you," Yuki says, clicking Replay. "You already married me."

Grace smiles down at her phone. Everyone has been texting her all day, full of exclamation marks and emojis. Raj and Meera sent a video of Baba Vihaan wishing her a happy birthday, and Ximena and Agnes sent a picture of them in her bed, little party hat stickers edited onto the photo.

Grace checks her email. There is the normal onslaught of brand-sponsored birthday wishes, and she keeps the ones that Yuki can use as retail therapy later. She swipes more of them into the trash, the movement almost therapeutic.

She swipes left and freezes. This one isn't trash. Professor MacMillan.

Dear Dr. Porter,
I hope your summer has been well. I come bearing news regarding our last conversation.

"Shit," Grace mutters. She pushes herself up, phone gripped tightly in her hand as she makes her way down the hall.

"Everything okay?" Yuki asks. Grace hears her familiar footsteps thumping behind her.

"Fine," she murmurs absently, fear and anticipation battling in her. "I just got an email from my advisor."

"And you have to read it right now?"

"Yes," Grace says. "She said it's regarding our last conversation. The one where we talked about jobs. Where we talked about *the* job I was supposed to have when I graduated."

Yuki shuts her bedroom door behind them. "I thought you didn't even want that job. They were total assholes to you. Isn't that why you walked out?"

Grace takes a deep breath. "That's not the point. The point is that I was groomed for it. Professor MacMillan basically said it was guaranteed for me as her mentee. It was the next checkpoint in my plan, and *I didn't get it.* I should have gotten it."

"So, you wanted it even though you didn't actually want it?" Yuki squints at her. "Grace, that doesn't make any sense. Fuck that company."

Grace opens the email. "You don't get it," she says. "It completely derailed everything I'd been working for, and it wasn't fair—"

"You got a *doctorate in astronomy* and it all hinges on one job?"

"You're not listening—"

"I'm just trying to understand—"

"Yuki," Grace says firmly. "Let me read this email."

Yuki walks over to the bed, situating herself hip to shoulder with Grace. "Go ahead and read it. Let's see what she has to say."

As your mentor, it weighed heavily on my mind that the opportunity I facilitated did not have the expected outcome. Like I said in my office, you are a great astronomer, Grace, capable of great things.

You have flourished under my tutelage and harnessed an energy and drive in this field that is unmatched. Such a talented scientist should never be made to feel small. With that said, I have reached out to the company once more and spoken directly with my colleagues there. They have agreed to a second interview, which will serve as a blank slate. I hope you will consider this opportunity to showcase the immeasurable work you have accomplished over eleven years.

In addition, this summer I have had the pleasure of remotely collaborating with Dr. Liz Hawthorne at Ithaca College. She has advised me that they are looking to recruit a junior faculty member and wondered if I had any contacts. They are a small but formidable team in upstate New York, and under Dr. Hawthorne's guidance, I believe you would excel in teaching the same way you excelled in my lab. I forwarded your information, so she should be in touch soon.

As your mentor, I have your best professional interests in mind, Grace. Hopefully these opportunities are a step in the right direction. I would love to hear your thoughts on them.

Regards,
Professor Rebekah MacMillan

"Holy shit," Yuki says. "A department in New York. I mean, Ithaca is far, but it's not as far as *Portland*. Do you think Fletch would let us borrow his dad's car for the drive up?" She flops back on the bed. "And the nerve of that company giving you a blank slate. They are the ones that need a blank slate. They—" She cuts herself off. "Okay, you're not saying anything."

"I wonder what she said to them," Grace says, staring at the screen. "I mean, I was not nice about leaving. Why would they have agreed to meet me again?"

"Does it matter?" Yuki asks warily. "You're not actually going to meet with them again, are you?"

"No." What would be the point? She's not going to give them the chance to make her feel small again. "But, Professor MacMillan went out of her way to set this up for me. It would also be nice to see them admit they were wrong."

Yuki sighs. "Nice, but probably not going to happen. You know that. What about Ithaca? I told you that you'd be good at teaching. Seems like someone else knows it, too."

"It's a bad idea."

"Why? Because it's not some high-tech place with shiny, new equipment?"

Grace turns around, narrowing her eyes. "You heard what she said. They're 'small but formidable.' That means they're understaffed and underequipped and underfunded. How could I thrive there? How could I be the best without the best resources and facilities available to me?"

Yuki raises her eyebrows. "You know all that from an email?"

Grace grits her teeth. "Going there would confirm it. I've worked too hard to just settle. And, like, okay. Maybe I do want to go into teaching. It's a good idea, and it makes sense for me. I want the best university, then."

"What does *best* even mean in your head?" Yuki sits up, fingers twisting in the blankets. "What is best for you, Grace Porter? The best place to prove yourself? The best place to spend the next eleven years running yourself into the ground? Or does *best* mean maybe teaching some snot-nosed freshmen in a place that gives you room to take care of yourself? Where you can learn and grow and even fight for more without completely burning yourself out?"

Grace blinks. "So *best* means Ithaca College? Or just any school as long as it's in New York?"

"You know that is not what I'm saying."

"I don't, actually," Grace says, standing up. She paces the width of the room, fingers digging into her arms. "Tell me what you think *best* means for me after eleven years. It means—settling? Just because it's easier?"

Yuki sits up and meets her eyes. They are both still in their pajamas. Still morning crumpled, but Grace feels like an exposed live wire. She feels it sparking off her fingertips, too hot and too fast. Yuki says, "Since when is easier such a bad thing?"

271

"I don't understand what you're saying," Grace tells her. "What are you saying?"

"I'm saying I want you to *stay*," Yuki argues. "That is what I'm saying, Grace Porter. I want you to stay."

Grace swallows hard. "I do want to stay."

"Then what's so goddamn hard about it?" Yuki stands up, all of her frustration right in front of Grace. "Isn't that what this summer has been about? Getting to know each other? Getting to—" She clenches her jaw. "Getting to love each other?"

Grace angrily wipes her eyes. None of this is fair; it has never been fair. "*Yes*. But that doesn't change anything. The reason I talk about being the best," she says, voice ragged, "is because that is the only way anybody will see me. I have to be the best and do the best. I have to work so hard it kills me, because anything less is just an excuse not to let me in the door. Anything less means I'm not fighting hard enough."

"Why is it all on you?" Yuki asks quietly. "Maybe it means *they're* not fighting hard enough. Maybe it means they aren't the ones that should get your best work."

Grace squeezes her eyes shut. "You don't get it," she says. Her arms sting with red scratches. She feels Yuki trace gently over them.

"You're hurting yourself," she says.

Grace laughs, and there is no joy in it. "I'll

survive." She runs her thumb over an irritated welt. "Porters are tough. I'm supposed to be tough. I'm supposed to be—"

"The best," Yuki finishes. She takes a step back, letting Grace's arm go. She takes another step back. Then another. "Can I ask you something?"

Grace sniffs. She's sure she looks disgusting right now. She feels it. She feels it under the weight of Yuki's disappointment. "Yeah."

"Were you ever going to stay?" Yuki asks. "This summer, were you ever going to make the decision to stay here. With me? Or was I just a stop-gap in the incredible life of Grace Porter? Did you even—do you even—" She blinks up at the ceiling. "Was I ever part of your plan?"

Grace feels something break within her in this moment, the moment where Yuki has moved far enough away that she can't just reach out and touch her. All she can think about is stars, brilliant and glittering and wished upon, and watching them die. A supernova that would echo in her ears if it could. It would reverberate to the core of the earth and shake the foundation.

"I want to stay," Grace tells Yuki. This has been her mantra of the summer. All of the moments of holding on tight to this good thing—Yuki—and not letting go leading up to this, right here. "I want to figure out how to keep all of it, my career and my dreams and you." When she takes a breath, it hurts. "I don't know how."

"And will you even try?"

Grace looks away. "I want to," she says again. "But if staying here means I have to settle for something *less,* how can I? I had a plan, Yuki, and it was perfect. Being an astronomer that never accomplishes anything great because I settle for easy, just because it means staying here, with you, was not in it."

Yuki nods, mouth trembling. "I think maybe your definition of *best* doesn't fit anymore," she says. "I think that's because the parameters of your grand plan have changed. It's okay to admit that. It's okay to admit that something can be *best* just because it makes you happy, and not because you had to tear yourself apart to get there. And I'm—I'm sorry that's not me. I'm not what's best for you, am I, Grace Porter?" She runs fingers through her hair and turns toward the door, her back to Grace.

"Where are you going?"

"I don't know," Yuki says. "I just don't think I can be here right now." She holds herself like a fragile thing guarding her soft guts from the claws of the lonely creature in front of her. "Happy birthday, Honey Girl." And with that, she walks out of her bedroom. The front door shuts not soon after, and there is silence from the living room. Even the video games have gone quiet.

Maybe this is the universe's answer to her

wishes. No, she cannot have all of it. No, she cannot have easy.

Grace feels sadness and frustration and hurt. She feels shame and anger, and she doesn't know where to direct it all. Her ears are echoing with the distant roar of a silent supernova.

She decides she does not want to be here when Yuki gets back. Colonel said it, months ago, that she was so much like her mother. That she ran when things got hard. Well, this moment, this collapsing star moment, is hard. She does not want to know the aftereffects of an eradicated star. She does not want to see it reflected on Yuki's face.

There are many things in space Grace Porter wants to explore. Galaxies and voids and formations and births.

This is not one of them. A supernova is a silent and resounding and terrible thing. She does not feel brave enough, strong enough, Porter enough, to linger in its wake.

Fifteen

Florida feels unfamiliar and alien after a summer in New York.

She stumbles outside Miami International Airport, about an hour from Southbury, and crouches down to watch the cars and taxis. She doesn't know what kind of car Mom drives now. It used to be a hand-me-down pickup truck. Grace hopes she upgraded to something more comfortable.

The conversation in the hours leading up to her flight were quick and messy. It was held in whispers, Yuki's door locked to keep her roommates out even as they knocked persistently and tried to coax Grace out. *We're your friends, too, Porter,* they said. *Are you seriously going to leave? Wait for Yuki to come back. Just stay. Just talk to us, Space Girl.* It was Grace, struggling to speak as she packed up her bags, throat tight as she told her mom she was coming down.

Please, Grace said. *Please, Mom, I just need to get out of here. No, not Portland. Can I just tell you when I'm there?*

Eventually, it is a pickup that comes to idle in front of her. It's not the old rusty thing that Grace remembers, but a newer, gunmetal-gray truck. A young white guy gets out, hair pulled into a bun and torn jeans and a flannel shirt. With his sleeves rolled back, she can see he has tattoos all the way up his arms and creeping up his neck.

Grace is leaning against the wall by Arrivals, shoulders hunched and eyes down. His eyes find her anyway, and he takes a few steps closer. "Hey," he says, a Southern accent drawing the word out. "What are you doing?"

"Waiting," she says shortly. She is used to the aggressively liberal white people of Portland. In Yuki's small corner of Harlem, no one talked like this. No one looked her up and down, as if they were trying to figure out where she belonged. "I'd like to get back to it, if you don't mind."

She knows her eyes are red and swollen and puffy. Her hair, only half contained under Yuki's cap, has frizzed up under the humidity. She doesn't want to have to remember all of Colonel's lessons. Stand up straight. Meet their eyes. Talk clearly. Don't back down, but don't be too aggressive.

Grace is tired. She doesn't want to fight. She wants to be left alone.

"You don't recognize me, huh?" he asks, coming closer. She leans back. "I'm Kelly. I guess people really do look different over a video."

She eyes him warily. "Mom sent you?"

He smiles, putting his hands in his pockets.

"She did. You know, video didn't really do your hair justice, either. Gold as anything."

"Yeah," Grace says. "Okay."

In the car, Grace damn near breaks her neck keeping her eyes trained out the window. Kelly fiddles with the radio, going from country to pop to some old-school jazz. She can feel his eyes on her.

"Mel talks about you all the time," he tries eventually. "She spends more time taking pictures to send to you when we're traveling than she does looking at things herself."

"Cool."

He clears his throat. "You know how long you're staying?"

"Nope." The scenery passes by in a blur. Trees and earth and blue skies. "Sorry."

He makes a surprised noise. "Don't apologize. It's your home." He looks a little older up close. Not by much, but there are laugh lines by his eyes and mouth and little wrinkles in his forehead. She noticed gray around his temples when he leaned down to get her bag. "Mel and I are glad to have you here."

Grace closes her eyes and doesn't answer.

They don't talk the rest of the ride.

She doesn't open her eyes again until the truck comes to a stop. Kelly turns the engine off, and she peers out the window. Somehow, she expected the house to change just because she

278

has. But it looks the same, nestled behind big green trees.

The orange grove trees line up in neat rows. They spring white flowers and orange starbursts that will soon be ripe enough to pick. It's almost harvest season, and Mom and all the seasonal workers will be out in the sun for hours. Grace is too old now to watch from the tops of the branches. She is too old to hide between the leaves and brambles.

The front door to the house swings open, and Mom comes running down the steps. "Grace Porter, you had me worried sick!"

Grace is enveloped in strong, tanned arms. Mom smells like citrus and weed, and Grace relaxes in the hold. She leans into it, inhaling deep, and she doesn't want to let go.

God, it shouldn't feel this good just to get a hug.

"Kelly, take my kid's stuff up to her room," she murmurs, still not letting go. "Don't just stand there." She huffs when he disappears into the house. "He better not touch anything on that stove while he's in there."

Grace laughs softly into her mom's bright blond hair. It feels like coming home. It feels like all the memories have sprung to life. It feels like she is skidding to a stop, and she can take that breath.

Mom rubs her back, and Grace squeezes her

eyes shut. "You haven't turned my room into an office or something?" she asks, her voice soft. "I don't visit enough to keep it."

Mom finally pulls back. Her eyes are a little red, too. "What do you take me for? It's always your room, whether you're here or not." She pulls her toward the house. "Come in," she says. "Enough standing around out in this heat. Come in here, my beautiful Sunshine Girl."

In the house, Grace sits while Mom works at the stove. She peers at the oven. "What did you make?"

"Started getting it together when you called," she says. "That's why I sent Kelly to the airport. Easier to let him do that then mess with my recipe." She pulls out a pan. "Made some good ole-fashioned lasagna. Used to be your favorite thing to eat when you were feeling down." She looks over, hesitant. "It still is, right?"

Maw Maw, Colonel's mom, taught Mom how to cook. *You can't give my grandbaby that bland-ass food.* Mom got really good at lasagna. She made it when Grace brought home grades that were less than stellar. She ate it the night she broke her arm falling out of a grove tree, and the night she whispered, voice trembling, *There was a girl at school, Mom. She's really nice, and she has pretty clothes, and we held hands at recess.* Mom cooked lasagna that night, while Grace hiccupped over her plate, and even Colonel had some.

She remembers Mom making lasagna the last time she was here. Grace was working on a project; she doesn't remember which one. She kept her head buried in her textbooks the entire time. Mom made lasagna for her the last night, and it was the first meal they shared the whole visit.

In the time between, whenever she had a bad day, she had other things. She curled up at one of the tables in the tea room and split gulab jamun with Meera until they had to get back to work.

She had wine, and movie nights, and tearful confessions on their little rusting balcony. She had a voice on the radio telling her stories of scary things. But no lasagna. None of Maw Maw's cooking passed down.

"Yeah," she says, voice strained. "It's still my favorite."

Mom sits across the table as Grace tucks in. It tastes good. It tastes like warm nights and full bellies and comfort.

You're going to ruin that girl, Colonel used to say. *She'll be soft, and then what? She's got to face the world one day, Mel.*

Those were whispered arguments in the living room. They were unaware that Grace lurked in the doorway, fingers clenched around the frame.

Mom had asked, *What's so bad about being soft?*

Grace waited, but she never heard Colonel's answer.

Now there's just Mom, blond-haired and brown-eyed and tanned from being outside. There is just Grace, swollen-eyed and summer-freckled. There is a ball cap that does not belong to her, but she can't take it off, not yet.

She opens her phone and scrolls past all the messages until she gets to just one.

Yuki
1:34 a.m.
i didn't know when you said
you didn't believe in monsters
you meant you didn't believe in me too

Grace bites her tongue. It could be easy, Yuki said. As if Grace hasn't worked over a decade to get here. It *could* have been easy, if Grace's perfect plan had worked the way it should. But it didn't, and it wasn't.

Yuki knows that things are not easy, not for either of them. Not for girls like them. All things cannot be as easy as their summer was, hidden from reality. Grace believes in them, believes in Yuki, but she does not know how to believe in the world around them.

"You wanna talk about it?" Mom asks.

Grace looks up. She's being looked at with patience and kindness she doesn't feel she deserves. "Not really," she mumbles, shoving food in her mouth.

Mom sighs. "Wanna tell me why Sharone and Colonel had no idea you were flying down here until I called them?"

She swallows. "Not really. Not yet." Grace has been ignoring those calls.

"Shit, kid. You're really gunning for me to win Parent of the Year, huh?"

She shrugs. Mom could send her home. *Home,* back to drizzling Portland. Grace isn't really in a position to argue.

"So," Mom says. "You don't wanna talk about it, and your father doesn't know anything." She stares at Grace, looks at her long and hard. "How about we really lean into this, then?"

Grace looks up. "What do you mean?"

"It was your birthday yesterday." She smiles at Grace's shocked look. "I've never forgotten your birthday, even if I'm in a different country for it."

"Okay," Grace says quietly. *Okay, sometimes I thought you did. Okay, I did not think my birthday was as interesting to you as Prague and Auckland and Madrid.* "So, what?"

Mom exhales heavily. "You might as well take advantage of me being the cool, laid-back parent," she says. Grace follows her toward the cellar stairs. "Wanna split a bottle of wine and forget all our problems for a little bit?"

"Yes," Grace says, shoulders loosening. "I really want to do that."

"Tomorrow," Mom says, pointing a finger at her, "you fess up. Today, we drink. Fair?"

The freedom is a welcome reprieve. "Fair," she says.

None of it is fair, not for her or the girl she left behind, but Grace picks out a bottle of red and pops the cork. Everything else can wait for now.

Mom wakes Grace up just before dawn hits. She was dozing lightly anyway. There are no glow-in-the-dark stars for her to count, and she has grown used to the constant, rhythmic sounds of New York City. Here in the groves, there is no city noise. There is just a bit of a breeze through the windows if you're lucky, and the bugs chirping all night.

"You getting up?" Mom asks. "It would be mighty nice to go for a walk with my daughter and catch the sunrise."

She rolls over, blinking in the early light. "Do I have to?" she asks, even as she gets up. "I would rather stay in here and feel bad about myself, honestly."

Mom sits on the edge of the bed as Grace stumbles around the room, looking for something to put on over her flimsy sleep top. "That's not very good for you," she says. "You wanna hear a little story?"

Her first thought is no. She's done with stories. She's done with stories that say she is made up of the same stuff as the cosmos. She's done with stories that say she is a lonely creature looking for more.

But Mom used to sit in that same spot and tell Grace stories to get her to sleep. She used to tell Grace stories about the roots of trees, and how they found friends beneath the soil and dirt and earth. How they held hands and became strong, strong enough to grow like lightning out of the ground and reach to the top of the clouds.

Grace does not want to hear any more stories, but she sighs and says, "Yeah, sure," as she pulls a T-shirt on.

"My therapist gave me the idea, actually," Mom says, and she winks. "What? Kelly got me into it. Drinking away my problems only works sometimes, Porter. It's just not sustainable. Anyway, this was, I don't know, maybe a year, year and a half ago. I was thinking of selling this place."

"You never told me that," Grace says, sitting down hard on the bed. "You never said anything."

"What would you have done?" Mom asks her. "That steel-backed Porter will is good for a lot of things, but it wouldn't have changed my mind. Not much could." She leans back, eyes distant, like the memory is drifting right in front of her.

"What did?" Grace asks quietly. She always

thought Mom had just as much a connection here as Grace did. Even while she tried to find herself in spiritual healing and wellness retreats around the world, Grace never thought she would want to leave this place behind for good. "What made you change your mind?"

"It was so funny," Mom says. "My therapist said, 'If you go, what will happen to all the oranges?' And I said, 'Lady, I don't care, honestly.' I just wanted to get away, I think. I've never been like your father in that way. Too much rigidity and planning and rules make me run for the hills. Make me feel crazy, you know that."

Grace snorts, pulling her knees up to her chest. "Yeah," she says. "I know."

Mom looks at her. "But it got me thinking. What would happen to the oranges? Whoever I sold this place to, they'd still sell to the grocers, I'm sure, right? But would they still go to the fresh market in town? Would they haggle with Mrs. Pinkerton, or Tracy, who's got those three little boys all by herself? Would they peel a few of 'em and let the kids get juice all over the stand? Would they help their parents get some fruit and vegetables that won't leave them broke until the next paycheck?"

She shakes her head. "It got me so fired up. I thought, there's no way some rich businessman is gonna partner with the local fruit box company and send all the bruised and too-small oranges out at a discount. He would just let those oranges sit and rot and spoil the earth, wouldn't he? And I couldn't let that happen. I couldn't stay in bed and feel bad for myself. I had an orange grove to run."

She bumps Grace's shoulder. "Sometimes your mom can be very dramatic, you know? But, I'm still here, so I guess all the drama worked out. And I know exactly what kinda homes these oranges are going to. Sometimes you just need to know that what you're doing makes a difference, at least for some people. Now c'mon. C'mon."

Grace follows her outside, but her thoughts are on stray oranges. Her thoughts are on bruised things being left to rot, unless there is someone to pick them up and give them somewhere to go. Her thoughts are on taking care of people who take care of you, and not leaving, because who will take care of them if you go?

The night dissipates, and everything is glowing and orange: the sky, the trees and the sun creeping past branches that look like they go on forever. Mom keeps humming a little tune that Grace picks up, both of them like two chittering birds in the early light.

She checks her phone. There are messages from Yuki's roommates—Grace's *friends*—she can't bring herself to read. Ximena, Agnes, Raj and Meera spammed the group chat overnight. Grace grits her teeth at the wave of guilt that rips through her. They have their own lives, their own problems, but here she is wishing they could solve hers, too. To hold her hand and stroke her hair and say they'll fix everything.

Agnes
3:01 a.m.
what have you done now, dumbass

Raj
3:15 a.m.
i should have brought you back with me

Ximena
3:18 a.m.
call me now!!

Grace isn't calling her. There's nothing for her to say. *I am too scared to come home. I am not as strong as you thought I was.*

I am running. I am running. I am running.

"Think you're ready to talk about it?" Mom asks.

"I just—" She waves her phone. "I'm letting so many people down." She clenches her jaw tight enough that it hurts. "I worked so hard and so many people believed in me. I'm letting everybody down." She curls in on herself, gasping through the words.

"Hey," Mom says quietly. She brings Grace

in close. "Let's go sit, huh? That'll be good. That'll be good, Gracie." Gracie, like she's a kid again.

They end up under a grove tree, one that's been nearly cleared of all the fallen fruit beneath it. Mom leans back against the trunk, and Grace falls into her lap.

She is like a child all over again.

"Shhh," Mom says, running gentle fingers over her back. "You'll get yourself all worked up. Just calm down."

"I messed it all up," Grace cries. "I don't know what I'm doing, Jesus." She wipes her nose, feels the burning and stinging of it. "I'm—I'm—"

"What?" Mom asks quietly. "Tell me. Go on."

"I'm *lost*," she sobs. "I don't know what I'm doing, and I hate it." It comes up like black sludge, like tar. It's been buried, and it comes up now. "I hate not having things figured out." She shivers, even in the warm morning. "I should be trying harder. I hate that even now I just want things to be perfect. I hate myself for thinking they need to be that way."

"Oh, honey," Mom says. She leans down and kisses Grace's head, her wet face. "Have you been bottling this up all summer?"

Grace can't help the terrible, monstrous laugh that erupts from her. "I think I've been bottling this up for a lot longer than a summer."

"Why didn't you say anything?"

"I don't know," Grace finds herself snapping. "Maybe because you're always searching the world for *peace and clarity,* and I didn't want to get in the way of that."

"Okay," Mom says. She tenses slightly. "Maybe I deserve that, and I'm sorry, Porter. I haven't always been around like I should have been, but I'm here now. Let me help."

Grace sniffs.

"Let me help," she whispers fiercely. "Let me try. Tell me how it's gotten this bad."

A million years ago, Yuki told Grace she needed to get her head out of the clouds. To look down, and see all the people down here, wanting to be with her. Grace looks, and Mom is waiting. She wasn't always, but she is right now, and Grace decides in this moment, that is good enough.

"I got married," she breathes out. "I got so drunk in Las Vegas, I met a girl, and she made me laugh, and we kissed and danced. Then I married her."

"Jesus—"

"That's the good part," she says. "It was stupid and reckless, but it's not the bad. It was never the bad."

"What is, then?" Mom asks. Her voice strains with caution. "If it's not the—the drunk marriage in Vegas, and Jesus Christ, Porter, I don't know how it's not—what is?"

What is?

290

• • •

Here is the thing about the tar, the sludge, the inky black poison. Once it starts its ascent out of your body, there is nothing you can do to stop it. It tastes like volcano ash and fire, and you must taste it, and gag on it, and ultimately, you must spit it out. There comes a time when you cannot swallow it down any longer.

Everything that is buried will be unburied. Everything that is pushed down will find its way out. It is the way of the universe.

Here is an origin story that Grace tries to forget: she was not always dedicated to being the perfect daughter. After her parents' divorce, she was angry and spiteful and full of teenage rebellion. She did not want to be like Colonel, inflexible and regimented and reserved. She did not want to be like Mom, absent as she backpacked through country valleys searching for serenity and balance and her *free spirit*.

So, she acted out at school. She messed around with the wrong girls. She skipped class. She found herself at parties where the cops showed up, even though she *knew* how it could go. But Colonel and Mom would hate it, just like Grace hated being uprooted from Southbury and transplanted to the other side of the country.

It didn't last long.

"Colonel was so mad," Grace tells Mom. "I know you both talked about it, but he was so mad. So—*disappointed*." Colonel sat her down at their dining room table. He was going through another round of physical therapy back then, and the last thing he needed was Grace's insurrection.

Through pain and gritted teeth, he laid down copies of her transcripts. He laid down a copy of a police report that said Grace was disorderly and trespassing. He laid down college admissions packets and a bulleted list.

This is your plan, he said, *which you will stick to, and I mean every goddamn letter of it, Porter. I've worked too hard to watch you throw away your future. Do you understand?*

Yes, sir, she said, and that had been the birthplace, the true beginning, of Grace Porter's Grand Plan. Everything else fell to the wayside. She would be the Porter her father expected. She would be the Porter that did not burden her mother's newfound tranquility quest.

"So you felt obligation and guilt," Mom says. "God, Porter, I thought you just *loved* astronomy, that's why you became so single-minded about it."

Grace closes her eyes and remembers. It wasn't until that first astronomy course that she thought, *The universe has everything mapped out for me. I cannot go wrong, because I am it, and it is me. It is a plan, but not Colonel's,* she thought. *This is a plan I can do myself. I can prove to him that I can do it myself.*

She talks about seeing face after face that was not like hers in the department, and once, a lab manager asking if she was lost, because this was for astronomy students, and liberal arts was on the other side of campus.

"I had to work so hard," Grace says. "I couldn't mess up, because *they* weren't messing up. They didn't think I was supposed to be there in the first place." They said as much, and she knows it is twisted privilege that her lighter brown skin kept them reserved to sly remarks only.

"Even when you came back here, you were always working," Mom says. "Every summer and break you came back. I left you alone because I didn't want to break your stride. I didn't want to interfere."

"I wish you had," Grace says. "I should have told Colonel, because he's dealt with it in his own way, but I wanted to handle it myself."

She remembers presenting research in her master's program. She never told anyone, not a single soul, about how they ripped her apart. About how multiple academics complained to the board and said there was no way the work was her own. About how the conference kindly and quietly and firmly asked her to leave a day early. She would be refunded for the remainder of her trip to avoid further confrontation. Ximena and Agnes asked why she was back early, and Grace locked herself in her room for two days.

It was worse, Grace remembers, in the doctorate program. It was worse, because Grace remembers all the academic recruiters' events. She watched as white people in ironed suits and pencil skirts glanced over her résumé, her list of achievements. Queer and Black and under the tutelage of their favored professor at the university. Professor MacMillan said, *This is my shining star, Grace Porter,* and she watched as their lips folded and their smiles turned brittle.

I think they liked you, Professor MacMillan told her. *Kid, you're going to have your pick of any institution in the country when you're done here.*

That hasn't been true. Grace knew it wouldn't be true, even though she wanted it to be *so badly*. She wasn't what the recruiters had in mind. She was not the future of the sciences they wanted.

Mom rubs her back, the motion soothing and calm. "I wish I could fix it, Porter. I wish you didn't have to feel like you can't make mistakes. I wish people weren't so caught up in maintaining their status quo that they don't see how things could be so much better. How you could be so much better than anything they've ever seen."

"I have to be perfect," Grace says. "I have to be *excellent*. I have to be the best. I can't be anything else. It makes me feel sick that I'm not. It makes me feel worthless."

"None of that," Mom says. "No more of that talk, okay? I listened—I listened to you tear yourself down, Grace Porter, and now you're going to listen to me. You can do whatever the hell you put your mind to, just by being you. Fuck anyone that disagrees. You are not worthless."

Grace takes a deep breath, burrowing her face in her mother's shirt. She feels helpless and tired and aching. "I don't know how to stop feeling like this." She's twenty-nine now, and she's spent so long this way.

"Can I ask you something?"

Grace nods.

"Have you ever talked to anyone about how you feel?" she asks. "Not your friends. I mean a professional. Have you talked to anyone like that?"

Grace thinks, *Wouldn't you know if I had?* That is the inky poison and sludge talking.

"No," she says instead. "I was too—" *Scared. Terrified I'd find out I'm stuck like this.* "Busy. I thought there was something wrong with me, because nobody else seemed as hell-bent on succeeding as me. Nobody else seemed like they couldn't handle the pressure. It's just me, there's just something wrong with *me*." She wraps her arms around her torso, feels her nails dig into skin, and she presses hard. Grounds herself.

"Okay," Mom says. "Can you just hear me out for a second?"

"A second," Grace tells her.

Mom smiles, and they both pretend it doesn't

waver. "You know Kelly used to be a crisis counselor. He knows a lot of people that could help. It might be hard, but maybe we could look for somebody. Maybe you'd prefer a Black therapist. Someone that understands what I can't."

Grace blinks. She's too old for this. Too old to be held. Too old for this crisis of self, but it persists nonetheless. "You think I should talk to someone?"

"Maybe give it a chance." Mom tilts Grace's head back so she can meet her eyes. "It's not exactly the same, but I was like you for a long time." She smiles at Grace's suspicious look. "I know, I know. But when you were younger, I thought plans and lists and perfect organization would give me control. It didn't, though. It just made me worry more."

Grace nods. "If I control everything, it can't go wrong. At least that's how it feels."

"I know," Mom says. "So what do you say? Will you let go of that control for a little bit, and talk to someone about it? Even if it's just to make your poor mom feel better?"

"Yeah. Yeah, okay. It can't make anything worse."

"Okay, then," Mom says decisively. "We'll talk to Kelly. He doesn't need to know the details, but he'll help you find somebody good, I promise. Now," she announces, groaning as she reaches up to stretch. "These old bones are hurting from being on the ground for so long. How about you and me head in and whip up some breakfast. French toast?"

In the kitchen, Kelly is already up. He's got the radio on the local pop station and the griddle going on the stove. "Howdy, ladies," he says, giving a little salute. If he notices their red, puffy eyes or the way Mom holds tight to Grace's hand, he doesn't say a word. "I got French toast coming up if anybody wants."

Mom smiles. "You sit down, Porter. You want orange juice? Or mimosas?" She shakes her head. "Okay, that was a terrible suggestion. We're having orange juice."

Grace smiles, a small little thing. "Okay. Orange juice it is."

Kelly sings along to the radio.

"And tada!" he yells, waving the spatula. "How many do you want, Porter?"

"Two, please."

He slides two on her plate along with a bottle of syrup. He slides two more onto Mom's plate and pecks her on the lips. Out of the corner of her eye, Grace watches him wipe her eyes and fix her hair.

"Everybody good?" he asks, silverware hovering over his plate.

Mom nods, and Grace hesitates. *Let go of that control for a little bit,* Mom said.

Let go, Grace Porter, she thinks. *You can't control everything. You've seen that.*

"Kelly," she says. "Mom said—she said you knew some people."

He tilts his head. "Sure. I know a lot of people. Can you narrow it down?"

Grace peeks at Mom, who stuffs French toast in her mouth. "I'm eating," she says unhelpfully.

Grace sighs. Meera once said the Grace Porter she knew wasn't a coward. Well, Grace has been having a hard time remembering that version of herself.

Let go.

"Therapists," she says bluntly. "If you know anybody that I might be able to talk to—I would, like, appreciate it. It would be cool to find a Black woman, but if you can't—" She shrugs. "As long as they're good. Please."

Mom's hand finds hers under the table and squeezes.

"Yeah," Kelly says, regaining his composure. "Yeah. Let me make a few calls, okay? Absolutely."

"Cool," she says.

Back upstairs in her room, she sends out a mass text in the group chat.

Grace
7:32 a.m.
life update: in florida with my mom.

maybe gonna have my eat, pray,
love moment???
will report back soon.

She opens up the chat with just Ximena and
Agnes.

Grace
7:35 a.m.
i'm the shittiest person alive but
idk how long i'll be gone
colonel def won't keep helping
with rent
i might have an idea

She pauses. She opens the group chat again.

Grace
7:38 a.m.
meera if you want my room
it's yours i know you've been
dying to move away from home
just ask ximena and agnes
about it, okay

She sighs, fingers trembling as she holds back
from spilling it all in the text box. She wants to.
She misses the comfort of her friends. She misses
how that felt easy, too.

Grace
7:40 a.m.
i'm gonna figure my shit out hopefully
love you guys so much it hurts

She turns her phone off. She has so much work
to do.

Sixteen

Time passes strangely when you don't have a routine or a grand plan.

Grace spends her mornings in the groves. Sometimes it's her and Mom. She talks about the things Grace did not notice during her sporadic visits in the years before. The changes to the fresh market, the weird yuppies that have moved to downtown Southbury, Mom volunteering at the yearly circus that's put on by the fire station.

"What do you do?" she asks, peeling a small, bruised orange she's saved from the ground. "Walk the tightrope?"

"Look," Mom says. She puts down her basket and picks up three, four, then five oranges. "I was the opening act." She laughs and starts to juggle.

Sometimes it's just her and Kelly. They don't talk much. Thankfully, he knows not to ask about school or jobs or her summer in New York.

Sometimes he asks about her favorite planet (Venus) or if she's ever seen Halley's Comet.

"That only comes every seventy-five years," she says quietly. "The last time was 1986."

"Oh shit," he says. "I could have seen that."

"Probably. What were you doing in 1986?"

He gives her a mysterious smile. "That's a long story, Grace Porter. You up for another lap around the groves?"

She finds herself spending chunks of time in therapists' offices. The first one is an older white woman named Barbara-Jean Marie, who wears a long denim skirt and Skechers and baubles for earrings.

"So, tell me a little about yourself, Grace," she says, hands tucked under her legs. Her gold-rimmed glasses make her eyes look huge.

Grace fiddles with the frays in her jeans. Her foot taps an anxious rhythm. "You can call me Porter if you want," she mumbles.

"Porter?" Barbara-Jean Marie crosses her legs. "That's your last name, isn't it?"

She shrugs. "Colonel—my dad—he's military. Guess it just kinda stuck."

"Ah," Barbara-Jean Marie says. She writes something in her notebook. "So, from a young age you were exposed to the imperialistic ideals of the American military regime. Talk to me about that."

The fifty-five minutes drag in silence. Barbara-Jean Marie's pen hovers, and Grace stares resolutely at the clock.

The second therapist is a Black man named Davis Redman. He has flower-adorned crosses on his walls, and gospel music plays softly in the background. He hums along with it, reaching out for Grace's hands. She lets him, only because she is not sure what else she is supposed to do.

"You feel that?" Davis asks. "That's God right there, Miss Porter. You hear that? That's God."

"Okay," she says.

He releases her hands. He's wearing an Easter-blue suit and white shoes. "Have you ever been to church before? Real church, the kind that has us sisters and brothers speaking in tongues, stomping our feet, singing in His name?"

The last time Grace went to church, it was an Easter Sunday, perfect for Davis Redman's suit. Maw Maw shoved her into a scratchy lace dress from JCPenney with a little shawl over top. Grace kicked the pew the whole service, while the pastor hollered and yelled and sang along with the aunties in the choir. She didn't understand half of it, but she understood the eye Maw Maw gave her if she kept kicking that damn pew. She understood the stale strawberry candies were to keep her quiet and still.

"Not in a long time," she decides to say.

Davis Redman shakes his head. "That's where a lot of the youth have gone astray. I believe with the power of talk and prayer, you can heal."

Grace scrunches her nose. She hasn't prayed in even longer. "I don't think that's what—"

"God!" Davis Redman shouts, and Grace jumps. "God can fix all, if you let him. Can I get an amen, hallelujah?"

Grace leaves. She sits on the curb and waits for Mom to pick her up. She's late, of course, but Grace lets the apologies wash over her. She spends the rest of the day in her room, pretending to be asleep.

The third therapist is a Black woman named Heather Huntley. Her office is homey: a desk, two lounge chairs, potted plants along the wall, a yellow-orange lamp. She has some photos on the bookshelves of her and a huge, hulking dog. Her dark skin gleams under the light, and when she shakes Grace's hand, she smells like cocoa butter. Her black box braids hang over one shoulder and are adorned with little plastic jewels.

"Nice to meet you, Grace," she says, and Grace figures being called by her given name isn't actually a sign she should walk out and forget the whole thing. "How are you doing today?"

She sprawls across the chair. "I'm okay. Can I just get some things out of the way first, though? I'm a lesbian," she says, holding Heather Huntley's eyes the way Colonel taught her to. "I'm not religious, so I don't think praying it away will work. I call my father Colonel because he was in the military, and it's probably a little fucked-up, but it's stuck now. While we're on the subject, I don't want to talk about the inherent imperialism in America's military-industrial complex." She pauses. "At least not here. I could probably talk about it somewhere else. I don't want you to think I don't find the discussion important."

Heather raises her immaculately arched eyebrows. She makes Grace feel grungy and unkempt in her oversize T-shirt and ripped denim overalls and backward BARNARD cap.

"Noted," she says, sitting back in her chair. "Anything else you want to get off your chest?"

Grace mirrors Heather's position in her chair. "I have a doctorate in astronomy that I'm trying to figure out what to do with," she says. "The thought of spending the rest of my career doing research with a bunch of privileged people who don't understand me and days filled with racial microaggressions makes me want to scream. I want—I don't know exactly what I want." She huffs and crosses her arms. "Oh yeah, my mom said to mention that feeling out of control in situations makes me feel extremely anxious." She thinks about the anxiety that makes her scratch at her skin, makes her want to bury it deep in her marrow where it can't get to her anymore. "I also probably have a perfectionism problem?"

"Well, I'm glad you mentioned it," Heather says. "That's probably important for me to know."

Grace shrugs.

Heather stares at her. Grace glances at the clock. It ticks down.

"You seem pretty straightforward, Grace," she

says eventually. "So, I'm going to be straight-forward with you, too. Sound good?"

Grace narrows her eyes. "Depends," she says carefully. "What are you going to be straightforward about?"

"You," Heather says. "I want you to tell me why you're here. Then we can decide, together, if this will work."

Grace clenches her jaw. The words force themselves from between her teeth. "I'm here because I want to get better," she says. "I don't want to feel worthless just because I'm not working myself too hard."

Heather tilts her head. "Can you tell me a little about what you mean by getting better? Do you think you're sick?"

Grace is quiet. Years ago, when Agnes was still a biting, bloody, angry thing, the hospital called her sick. That's what they told Ximena when she was assigned as her companion. *She's sick,* the nurse said. *Not just under the bandages, but in the places you can't see.*

Agnes was sick in the places no one could see. No one can see the heaviness that's settled into Grace's ribs, either. No one can see the poison and sludge building up in her chest.

She doesn't know what happens if she lets someone see it all.

"Grace?" Heather asks quietly. "Can I ask what's going on inside your head right now?"

"I was just thinking," Grace says, and is surprised to find her voice is hoarse. "I let people tell me what I was feeling for a long time, and I avoided understanding it for myself. I didn't want to know. I just wanted it to go away." She stares at her knees. "How do I do that?"

"I don't know if it ever goes away," Heather says. "But it can get better. It gets better when you confront it, and hold it up to the light, and start the process of breaking it down."

Grace looks up. "You know in space, things don't break down like that."

"No?"

She shakes her head. "There's no air to facilitate weathering and disintegration." She clears her throat. "Maybe that's—maybe that's why I was so drawn to it, the universe, all of it. Nothing breaks down. But here, everything does. People do."

"Is that what happened to you?" Heather asks quietly. "You broke down?"

Grace shrugs. "I think it was hardwired into me."

"I don't know about that," Heather replies. "But maybe that's something we can work through together."

Grace sniffs, folding into herself. She is exposed, but she does not run. "You read my intake questionnaire?" she asks. "What do you think?"

"Well, I—"

"Please," she says. If she is going to do this, she is going to pull out the ugliest things. She is going to hold them up to the brightest light. She is going to take the biggest hammer and break all the shit down. "It'll help if I just—"

"If you hear what I think?" Heather finishes, and Grace nods. "Okay," she says. She clears her throat and shifts through the pages in her lap. "Well, first, your relationship with your parents seems complicated in very different ways."

"Yeah," she says. "That sounds about right."

"Well, that's something we can talk about," Heather says. "If you want."

Grace nods, eyes on the papers in Heather's hands. "Are you going to diagnose me or something?"

"I don't want to rush anything. There's plenty of time for us to determine what's going on."

Grace presses her face into her knees. It's not quite her blanket world, but it's close. "You know how sometimes you just need someone else to rip the bandage off, and then you can do the rest?"

Heather sighs. "This is just our intake session," she says, "but I think *you* think you're sick. I think you're sad and anxious, and you don't want to feel like that anymore. I think, for all intents and purposes, you want to get better. But I don't know what *better* means for you. Maybe it's medication. Maybe it's talking to me. It's definitely work. It will be hard, daily work."

There is silence in the office. The clock ticks. *Tick. Tick. Tick.*

Grace remembers Colonel's face when she told him something felt wrong. "I don't feel right," she said. "It feels like I'm suffocating. I don't know if I can—"

"You can," Colonel said, face hard. He stared her straight in the eyes. "You will."

"But—"

"Porter," he said. "They recruit you out of high school for a war you got no business fighting in, and they tell you to come home and celebrate. They tell you congratulations and welcome back, and they give you nothing. They tell you to keep a smile on your face, so you do. You hear me? That's how you survive. That's how you make something of yourself. That's how you stick to the plan." He pushed back from the table, groaning as his leg started to give out. "Congratulations," he says. "You're making it through some tough shit. Now you smile. You never let them catch you otherwise. You understand me?"

She understood.

"Yes, Colonel," she said, and she was left sitting in their kitchen alone. "I understand," she whispered to a silent room.

In a different room now, she sits in that same silence. Heather waits, carefully putting her papers to the side. Maybe a minute passes. Maybe more.

"Are you okay?"

She unfolds herself and peeks up at Heather. "I don't want to feel like the world will end if I take a breath. I don't want to feel *guilty* anymore for taking care of myself. I don't want to stay in bed and stare at the wall and blame myself because I didn't execute some perfectly ordered plan. I want to try to get better."

"Okay, Grace," Heather says. "We can work on it. All that anxiety, all that sadness, all that guilt." She sets her pen down. "You know, it makes sense you've been feeling this way. As Black women, we're conditioned to work twice as hard just to end up in the same place. We're called strong and fearless. We're never really allowed to be vulnerable, are we? So, that's what we'll work on. We'll work on being vulnerable and kind to yourself, and that voice that tells you it's wrong? That you have to keep going past your breaking point? We'll break it down."

Things don't break apart in space.

This is not space.

When she gets in the car, Mom asks, "So how did it go?"

Grace squeezes her eyes shut and cries. She cries at digging her hands in some of that sludge and getting permission to let it go. Clear it out. Break it down.

"Shhh," Mom says, rubbing her back. "It's gonna be okay, kid."

Grace, with everything she's got in her, wants to believe that's true.

Seventeen

It's early October and the start of the harvest season. Grace sees Heather once a week. She has a psychiatrist and a prescription for two small pills she takes every day.

She doesn't know if they're working yet, but she takes them each morning dutifully. She wonders if this is how Agnes felt, with Grace and Ximena watching over her like it was part of their morning routine, wondering if these little pills would help untangle the wires in her brain.

So, Grace takes her pills. Heather suggests a hobby. "School locked you into a routine for a long time," she says in one of their sessions. She's wearing a pink suit that looks like a sunset. It's hard for Grace to feel mad at her, and sometimes she *does* feel mad, when Heather looks like a sunset. "Maybe getting that routine back will help orient you a little."

"What should I do? I don't have any hobbies."

Heather smiles. "I can't give you all the answers. I can only give you the resources and help you navigate through the journey of finding them on your own."

So, Grace works at the fresh market four mornings a week. It's good work. The heavy lifting and haggling of prices distract her. She and the other vendors hide under their booths and eat fruit when it gets too hot. It's good.

She comes home stained with orange juice and a little money in her pocket—half she gives to Mom and Kelly, and her share split with one of the grove workers, Yosvani, since he helps her lug the crates she brings to the market. She collapses on her bed even though she needs a shower because she smells like citrus and the cucumbers from the next stand over.

Mom knocks on the door and tosses her phone on the bed. "Somebody's been asking about you," she says, sipping at what looks like a margarita.

It's only noon, but honestly all Grace can think is *mood*.

"Who?" she asks. She turned her own phone off after that ridiculous group text over a month ago. She knows she will have hell to pay when she finally enters the real world again, but it feels—not necessarily good—but right, sorting out the mess in her head without worrying that she will look weak in front of anyone else besides Heather.

Soon, she thinks. But not yet.

Mom plays with her straw. "Colonel James Porter," she says brightly. "Or, Sharone, but you know. He's been wanting to talk to you."

Grace shoves her face in her pillows. If she suffocates, it would solve a lot of her problems. Heather would probably say that's unproductive.

313

Heather also made her talk about the expectations she always felt—*learned*—she had as a Porter, and so talking to Colonel feels like pressing on an open wound.

"What if I just didn't call him back?" she asks. "He would let that slide, right? He would totally let that happen, right?"

Mom slurps her drink. "Sure," she says. "I'll let you believe that if you really want to."

Grace lets out a long sigh. "I don't want him to be disappointed in me. I'm not—I'm not doing anything we agreed on. I ripped the plan to complete shreds." She looks up at Mom. "He'll never forgive me for that."

"There's nothing to forgive," she says. She perches on the edge of the bed. "Listen, I know you've always been eager to meet his expectations. But, Porter, they're *his* expectations. You just have to be his kid. Our kid. You're not perfect, and God knows you never could be, with parents like us." She leans over and kisses Grace's hair. "I think you're doing pretty good, though."

Grace groans. "Can't I just have a minute?"

"Sure," Mom says again, standing up. The liquid in her glass never wavers. "You have one minute, then you should probably make that call. I believe in you, Grace Porter," she says over her shoulder.

Grace stares at the ceiling. Last week Kelly

put up some plastic stars for her. They're not the familiar ones from her room in Portland. These are Florida plastic stars that glow blue instead of green. These are still Grace's stars, in Grace's room.

She picks up the phone and dials.

"Hey, Mel," Sharone answers. "I didn't think I'd hear back from you so soon."

Grace swallows. "Yeah, me, either," she says. "Hi, Sharone."

She hears a door shutting before Sharone whispers into the phone. "Porter, is that you?"

She clenches her hands in the bedsheets. "It's me. I'm here."

"And thank Black Jesus for that," Sharone says. "You really had Mel calling to give us updates on you? At your big age? Since when do you up and go silent on us? You owe us a little more respect than that."

Grace nods before she realizes she can't be seen. "I hear you. I won't do it again, I promise."

"I know you won't," Sharone says, "because I would be on you like white on rice, little girl."

Grace huffs. "I won't," she repeats. "I swear. Can you be nice to me now?"

"Can't hear you," she says. "Colonel's asking for the phone. Bye, Porter!"

Grace's stomach flips. She hears the soft murmur of Sharone's voice and the low timbre of Colonel's. In her mind, she comes up with a

315

dozen different excuses that aren't the truth, but she knows she has not spent the last few weeks wading through insecurities and doubts, little by little, just to tell a lie.

A throat clears, and she straightens against her will. "Porter," Colonel says. "How nice of you to call. It's been a while."

Grace winces. "Hi," she says. "I'm sorry it took me so long."

"Are you?" he asks. "The last time I spoke to you, you gave no indication that you were planning to disappear to Southbury after your research ended. I'm assuming that means they didn't offer you a more permanent position."

Fuck. "So, you should probably sit down," she says carefully. "There's something I need to tell you."

"And sitting down would make it more palatable?"

She lets out a silent, drawn-out scream. "Probably," she ends up saying. "I didn't—there was no summer research project in New York," she confesses.

Colonel is quiet. Grace knows his processing face, the way he looks like a robot rebooting. "You quit the project?" he asks.

"There was no project," she blurts out, frustrated. "There was never any project in New York." She goes for it. "I lied. I was in New York all summer, but not for that."

316

The call ends. Grace blinks at the screen. Not even a whole thirty seconds later, it rings again. *Colonel.*

"Explain yourself," he says immediately.

Grace sits up in the bed. "You didn't listen to me," she stresses. "I told you I needed to *stop* for a second, and you just wanted me to keep going!"

"That's what parents do, Porter," he says calmly, evenly, but she can hear the thunder in his voice. "We don't tell our kids to stop. To give up. To quit. Mine didn't teach that to me, and I certainly wasn't going to pass it down to you."

She feels frustration burst in her. "I didn't give up. I went to college. I went to grad school. I got my fucking doctorate—"

"You will watch your lang—"

"I didn't quit," she snaps. "You don't get to say I quit, because I didn't, because I wanted to make you proud, and you still aren't. That's the only thing I need to give up on."

She's breathing hard, the words ripped from the disturbed earth within her. It's slow-going, hammering away at all the things that have been buried deep. But those words split through and feel like a relief.

Now neither of them says anything. She checks to see if he hung up again. No, he's still there.

"Do you think that's what this is about?" he asks finally. Grace can't place his tone. It's unfamiliar. "Do you think I'm not proud of you?"

She shrugs, unsure. She angrily wipes her eyes, frustrated they're betraying her.

"Grace?" he calls, and she inhales sharply, because he hasn't called her that in years. She was still a kid, *a little kid,* the last time Colonel called her by her given name.

"I'm here," she croaks. "What else am I supposed to think? You walked out of my graduation." She sniffs. She hates this. She's used to having that good old-fashioned Porter control, but now that she's started exploring her feelings instead of shoving them down, it's like they have a mind of their own. "Everyone knew you were there for me, and then you weren't. You just left."

She wants to say *You left me,* but that isn't true. By the time Sharone and Grace emerged from the small auditorium, Colonel was sitting right out front on the steps.

He makes a small, aborted noise. "I didn't leave," he says, like he's picking the thoughts right from her brain. "I was right outside. I could still hear them calling your name, and the way the kids in your program clapped for you. God knows, I could hear Sharone's loud ass," he says. He pauses, and Grace's fingers clench around the phone. When he speaks again, his voice is rough and almost angry. "I have never left you. Not once. Not once since the war messed up my leg, and I was sent home. Not once, Porter."

She goes to argue, but stops short. Once Colonel was home, *really* home, he took her everywhere with him. To the base, out in the groves to help him work until his leg couldn't take any more pain, and he refused her help as he limped back to the house. He took her to physical therapy, where Grace watched him push himself almost to the brink of tears, but he never stopped. He left the groves and life here, and he took Grace with him, kicking and screaming as they flew away from the only home she ever knew.

Colonel never left Grace.

"You want to know what I saw that day?" he asks. "At your graduation?"

"Yes, sir," she says. She wants to know what he thought of *her* that day.

He takes a deep breath. "You were the only Black girl in that doctorate program," he says. "You were the only Black person in that room besides me and Sharone. I saw those kids, and I saw their parents. While you were backstage preparing, I saw those parents talking to the faculty like they had known each other for years. I knew in my gut, Porter, those parents would do anything for their kids. Not—" He stutters. He never stutters. "Not just that. They *could* do anything. There was no resource or connection they couldn't use to make sure their kids made it. And I couldn't blame them, because I would do the same. That made me angry. It made me so angry, I walked out of the auditorium."

"What are you saying?"

"I had connections, *good* connections, in the medical school," he says. "I sat in that auditorium, and I saw those parents shaking hands and schmoozing, and I knew how hard it was going to be for you. I already knew, but that cemented it for me. And I knew I couldn't help you there."

Grace feels anger whip through her. "You never said. You made me think it was me. You made me think you were disappointed in *me*."

"I've been telling you for years," Colonel counters. "You just weren't listening."

"I can't," she decides suddenly. It's too much at once, the way Colonel's words and behaviors start to click into place. He never *said*.

"I can't do this right now. I know you've been calling, but I can't—I can't have this conversation right now. I should, but it's too much right now, and I don't care what Heather has to say about that." Immediately, she bites her tongue hard. She let down her guard, and she said too much.

Colonel latches onto it immediately. "Who is Heather?" he asks, instead of an explanation. Instead of putting into words why he left Grace to decode his fears about her future and think they were directed at *her* instead of her field.

She collapses back on the bed. She stares up at

her Florida-blue stars. They tell her to be brave, so she is. "Heather is my therapist," she lets out, bracing for impact. "I got diagnosed with major depressive disorder and anxiety," she says clinically. "I see her once a week. It's been great, actually, so."

"Why do you sound like you're waiting for me to argue with you about it?"

"Because I tried to tell you something was wrong," Grace says. "You told me to grit my teeth and smile through it, and I know what you meant. I still do. But now I'm sleeping in my childhood bedroom, and I see a therapist once a week, and I have to take these two little pills every day, and I wish I hadn't pushed myself so hard."

Colonel is quiet, so quiet. She doesn't know if that's better.

"You had a plan," he says finally, sounding tired and human. "I wanted you to finish it. I wanted you to go further than anyone ever expected you to. That's all I ever wanted for you, Porter. I wanted you to follow your plan, because you worked so hard for it. I can't feel bad about that."

Grace inhales a shaky breath. It feels like someone has laid a stone on her chest. "I wish you did," she confesses quietly. "I wish you felt bad, and I wish I didn't understand why you don't."

She hears noise downstairs. She hears Kelly's and Mom's voices.

"I have to go," she says. "I have to go now, okay?"

"Porter," he says suddenly, sounding rushed. She waits. "Call soon. I know Sharone would love to hear how you're doing down there."

Grace is tired. Running away from the weight of her problems was tiring, but standing still with two feet planted firmly on the ground takes all her energy. "What about you?" she asks, feeling a surge of bravery. "Is this your way of cutting me off from the Porter name?"

"You're always a Porter," he says firmly, brooking no arguments. "Porters, we—"

"No offense," she says, closing her eyes, "but I need a break from what Porters do. I want to figure out what *I'm* going to do."

"Okay," he says, backing down for what could possibly be the first time ever. "I'll save it for another time."

"So, you want me to call you again?" she asks.

Colonel clears his throat. "Call soon, Grace," he says.

The call ends.

She keeps the phone pressed to her ear long after the screen goes dark. *Call soon, Grace.*

Hope mingles with frustration. But Colonel has never left her, not once. She holds on to that.

"It's so hard to let go of wanting to please him," Grace says, lying sideways in a chair across from Heather. "Being angry at his unattainable expectations is so much easier than accepting that the only ones I have to meet are my own. And I *am* angry, you know? But *then,* it feels unfair to hold on so tight to my anger toward him, when I set it aside for Mom in case she decides to up and leave again."

Heather hums, tapping her pen against her notebook. "I'm just theorizing here," she starts, "but it sounds like maybe it's time to think about what you want, as Grace Porter, outside of your parents' expectations and feelings and desires. Outside of what they want for you or themselves."

"I don't even know where to start," Grace says, voice cracking in the middle.

"You don't?" Heather asks. She gestures between them. "Then what do you call this, what we're doing right now?"

Grace closes her eyes. In her lap, she rips a piece of notebook paper into small, careful pieces. They're still trying out alternatives for the moments she wants to pull and pinch at her skin. It's like she can hear Heather in the back of her head like a self-help version of healthier coping mechanisms. "Holding it up to the light," Grace recites. "Breaking it down. Making something new out of it, right? Something that's just me."

She hears a satisfied noise. "You're getting it

now," Heather says. "Soon, I'll be the one on the couch."

"And I'll be the one with the trendy suits and the immaculate braids?" She plays with her Bantu knots. It's one of the easiest styles for this humidity.

Heather laughs. "I know a lot of girls like the twist-outs and wash-and-gos, but I don't have time," she says. She fishes a card out of her bag and hands it over. "That's the African braid shop I go to. Give them my name, and they probably won't overcharge you. Protective styles save my life."

Grace remembers the feel of Dhorian's gentle hands twisting her hair. "Yeah," she agrees. "We're in agreement there."

Kelly picks her up today. Mom gave her a key so she can drive herself around, but Grace doesn't trust herself not to take the car and never come back. She's okay letting them pick her up. It's another routine. It's something she can't run from.

"Hey, Porter," he says. He's got some Norah Jones playing today, just loud enough that Grace can guess he was singing along before she got in. Kelly's a weird guy, but he's got a good heart. "Doing okay?"

She shrugs. "Been worse," she decides, and he fist-bumps her.

"So, listen," he says, once they're idling in

324

the driveway and drinking milkshakes from McDonald's. "I got something to ask you."

She narrows her eyes, trying to think of what he's going to say before he says it.

"Your mama makes that same face," he tells her. "That 'how can I outsmart you right now?' face. Y'all look like you're planning three ways to manipulate a conversation."

"Military tactic," Grace says, slurping through her straw. "I have four, currently. Colonel says you should always have five, so give me a minute."

Kelly laughs. "Well, this ain't no coup, Grace Porter. I just wanna ask you something."

She studies him for a moment. Crow's feet at his eyes, his brown-and-gray hair tucked up into a little bun. Another plaid shirt rolled up to the elbows and a Dolly Parton T-shirt underneath.

She inclines her head.

He takes a deep breath, fingers tapping against the steering wheel. "I know you and Mel are still working out your issues, and that ain't none of my business. But you know we're planning on getting married here on the grove soon. And I know it would mean a lot to her if you officiated the wedding." He gives Grace a quick look. "Only if you're comfortable. I won't breathe a word of it to her if you say no."

Grace's eyes go big as her head. "You want me to do what?"

"You can do it all online," he says. "I'll pay for it. I already googled everything. You just have to, you know, get ordained. And then the county clerk's office will ask for some stuff, but it's just paperwork." He turns in his seat and stares at Grace curiously. There's a huge rip in the knee of his jeans. She focuses on that. "What do you think?"

"You want me to do it?" she asks. Her head is spinning. Heather would tell her to calm down, to focus, to breathe. She would tell Grace to find the source of her anxiety, like a peach pit in the middle of her stomach, and grab it tight. So, Grace grabs it tight. Her hands tremble around it. "*Mom* would want me to do it?"

Kelly shakes his head. "It's not really about me, but yeah," he says. "And, of course, Mel would want you to do it. Do you know how much she talks about you? How proud she is?"

Grace blinks fast and turns her head away. *No, I don't know,* she wants to say. She swallows because she does not want to be overcome by the salt and the sea today. She can't talk, because it is there in her throat: the ocean coming to claim her.

"Would you want to?" he asks gently. "You can say no, I swear."

She clasps her fingers tight in her lap so they don't shake. The last wedding she remembers is her own. The stumbling steps up to a church. A priest, dressed as bright as the overhead lights as they recited some vodka-sodden vows. A hand in hers. *I do. I do.* A kiss to seal the ceremony. Desert flowers. A fence. A lock.

A beautiful girl she misses desperately.

She reaches around her neck for the chain and key. On her ring finger, a small gold band she refuses to take off.

Kelly is asking her to be a part of their love story. Grace was in her own love story once. She couldn't find a way to make the love story fit in her plan. She couldn't find a way to make Yuki fit. And now she is being asked to bear witness, to officiate, Mom's wedding.

She is glad, really, that Mom has found something easy with Kelly. Something that does not require a sacrifice or breaking your own heart. She wants to be a part of something good like that. It would not feel like being left behind by Mom, if she were a part of the something good and easy.

Grace turns to Kelly and nods.

"You'll do it?" he asks, mouth twitching into a smile.

"Yeah," she whispers. "Yes. Of course, I'll do it."

In the house, Mom cries when they tell her. She hugs Grace so tight it hurts. She smells like oranges and smoke. She says, "Thank you so much, Porter. I know I haven't been around like I should. I might not even deserve it, but it means so much that you said *yes*. I'm so happy to share this with you."

Grace presses her face into her mother's hair. It is the same way she used to press close when she was a child and hiding from monsters.

"You're here right now," she murmurs softly. "We're both here, together, right now."

"We are," Mom whispers fiercely. She holds Grace as she shivers. "I am so goddamn proud of you, and I hope you believe that."

Grace squeezes her eyes shut. "Can you say it again?"

Mom laughs quietly. "I'll say it till I'm blue in the face. I'm so proud of you. You're doing so good."

After, Grace finds herself sitting on the edge of her bed with her phone in hand. It's been turned off since August, gathering dust in her drawer. There's a voice in her head that says she isn't ready, that she has more work to do. But Grace will always have work to do. This—being kind to herself, not trying to be perfect, not hurting herself in her quest to find the best and be the best—will always be work. It will take all that's within her to learn that she does not have to grind her bones to dust, that needing to stop, needing to breathe, needing other people, is not weak.

She is full to bursting with wanting to talk to her friends. Wanting to show them all what she has accomplished here, but even more, wanting to hear about them. Saying, *I am getting stronger, strong enough that you can lean on me, too.*

Plus, there's no way she can officiate a wedding without having at least one of her friends in the crowd.

She turns on her phone. She ignores all the notifications that immediately come through, swiping away before she can read them. She opens a chat, the group chat with all her friends in Portland that have become family.

Grace
4:45 p.m.
i'm here now
are you there?

Her phone buzzes with incoming texts. None of them call, which is a relief. She needs a little more time before she can speak any words out loud. She needs time to hold them up to the light, and make sure these, at least, do not break down.

The messages come through, filled with comfort and outrage and love. Grace presses her phone to her chest and laughs.

Eighteen

She cries the first time she sees Ximena and Agnes on-screen after what feels like months and months and months.

She rushes home from the fresh market, catching the attention of Saffiya, who runs the vegetable stand on the alternating days with her father.

"Where are you going in such a hurry?" she asks, eyes sly under her floral hijab. "You usually stick around and try to get free food."

Grace frowns. "You're exposing me so loud right now," she says, and Saffiya laughs. "I just have an appointment, I guess? Let's go with that."

Raised eyebrows greet her. "A girl?"

"Yes, but not like that," she says, and ignores the ache. "Some friends from back home."

Saffiya waves her hand. "Far be it from me to keep you, Grace Porter," she says. "But you know Old Maria likes you best. She always gives you the best papayas."

"Maybe because I don't call her Old Maria," Grace points out, shoving her backpack on. "Try calling her by her name and see what happens!" she calls, racing for her bike.

"No fun!" Saffiya yells back, as Grace disappears into the autumn sun.

So, she cries when she gets home and boots up her laptop and sees Ximena and Agnes. She doesn't just cry; she sobs, rib-cracking things that she tries to hide behind her hands.

"Porter," Ximena says, a laugh in her voice. "Are you that happy to see us? It hasn't been that long, has it?"

Grace nods, because it has been that long. It's been that long since she's had Ximena's uva de playa jelly or laid in her lap or shared her bed, the two of them whispering under the sheets like girls at a sleepover. It's been that long since she's smelled her ridiculously expensive coconut oil and the little bit of calendula oil behind her ear. Grace nods, because it has been that long, and she cries enough to fill all the days that have passed.

Agnes leans in. Grace sees the dark circles under her eyes, the way she peers at Grace warily, like she isn't sure what to expect.

"You think she's a ghost?" Ximena asks her incredulously. "Why are you looking at her like that?"

Agnes blinks, aware that she's been caught out. "I'm not looking at her like anything," she says. She crosses her arms. "Hi, stranger." And Grace hides a smile in the folds of her mouth.

She knew if any of them would be angry with her, it would be Agnes. She wishes she was there with them. Agnes could lash out and scratch and bite, and she could feel that Grace was real in a way that's difficult through a computer screen.

"Hi," she murmurs. "Missed you. You've been doing okay?"

Agnes scoffs, and Grace waits. Ximena sits quiet between them. She doesn't get it, the way Grace and Agnes work. She doesn't try to get in the way of it, either. *"Aggie,"* Grace says. "I'm sorry, I swear. I was just—I needed some time."

"Don't start crying about it again," Agnes tells her. "I can only take so much."

"Agnes," Ximena hisses.

Grace sniffs dramatically. "No more crying," she says. "It was gross anyway."

Agnes *humph*s and slouches on the couch. Her near-white blond hair is hidden under a navy blue NASA beanie that Grace recognizes as her own. "Fine," she says eventually. "I won't hunt you down and gut you. But this is the last time you disappear off the face of the earth. Next time you take us with you." She stares her right in the eyes. "Promise?"

Grace and Ximena both valiantly pretend they don't hear her voice tremble.

"I promise," Grace swears. "Southbury's boring without you guys anyway. Nothing happens here except orange picking and, like, gossiping with my therapist."

Agnes raises an eyebrow. "You got a therapist?" She looks impressed. "Tell us everything."

Grace shrugs, but she can't help the smile that pulls across her face. "Yeah. Her name's Heather," she says. "She's, like, disgustingly beautiful and competent and more put together than I will ever be. It's annoying."

"I bet," Ximena says dryly. "I mean you only have a dumbass PhD. Loser."

"Don't be mean to me." She pouts. "And don't think I didn't notice neither of you guys said you missed me back. That doesn't hurt or anything."

"I missed you," Ximena says primly. She nudges Agnes. "This one shares the bed with Meera sometimes because she says it just *feels like you* in there. I don't know how, considering Colonel had a lot of your stuff moved back to his house. I think Agnes might miss you more than anyone." She widens her eyes in fake disbelief when Agnes groans next to her. "Oh shit, was that supposed to be a secret, cariña?"

"Fuck you," Agnes mumbles, and slumps down so far she disappears from the screen. Ximena leans down and kisses her head obnoxiously. "And fuck you, Porter, for having Meera sublet."

"You guys love Meera."

"We do," Ximena agrees. "She's giving our poor little demon here a complex. Can't imagine why." She rolls her eyes.

Agnes reappears, glaring. "She's so—" She stutters, and her hands flail. Grace tries so, so hard not to laugh. "Cute," Agnes finishes angrily. "She makes me this amazing tea and rasam rice since I'm trying a new set of meds and they make me feel like shit. Plus, she sings in the shower. She *sings* in the shower."

"This is bad?"

"She has a wonderful singing voice," Ximena explains.

"It's beautiful," Agnes spits out. "And have you ever talked psych with her? God, her mind is just—"

"Ah," Grace says, suddenly understanding. "I get it. You have a crush on her."

Ximena bursts out laughing, nearly folding in half. "*Such* a crush," she emphasizes. "I didn't even know Agnes could *give* heart-eyes like that to someone."

Agnes makes a face. "I can think of someone else I give them to," she snipes, just to see Ximena get flustered. "Anyway, yes. I have a crush. It's terrible. Let's move on." She tilts her head at Grace. "What about you, Vegas Girl? Is the wife picking wheat and barley with you on your Florida farm?"

"Okay," Grace starts, mostly to give herself some time to gather her thoughts. She knew they'd ask about Yuki, of course they would. That doesn't mean she knows what to say. That doesn't mean she wants to say anything. She hasn't even talked to Heather about all the details of Yuki Yamamoto. "First of all, it's an orange grove? We pick oranges."

Agnes narrows her eyes and leans in. "Not what I asked," she says. Ximena leans in, too, both their faces too close to the screen. "Spill it."

Grace tries to smile. The thing that comes out is shaky and painful. "Not much to spill," she says, refusing to look at either of them. She looks at her blue stars instead. It's strange how much comfort they give her. "I thought I—" She shakes her head. "It doesn't matter what I thought. I had the chance to start trying to incorporate *her* into my grand life plan, and I didn't want to give an inch. It felt like giving in, giving up. I always wanted, needed, to be the best, and she asked me what the best meant for me." Grace grits her teeth. "I thought my best couldn't possibly include her, because that would mean settling. I—" She shrugs. "I haven't talked to her since my birthday. I left New York that night."

"Oh, Porter," Ximena sighs. "Why do you never think you deserve anything good without having to kill yourself for it?"

Despite her best efforts, Grace has to blink away some more stupid tears. She hates unburying all these feelings. She hates having to open up. She wants to fall back on her old Porter attitude because it kept her guarded and safe.

She doesn't feel safe, having her soft underbelly exposed like this. Heather would say it's progress, but Grace is allowed to hate it. She has to be allowed to hate it.

"I'm working on it," she says. "My idea of best was—is still—so skewed. How could it mean a beautiful girl that—that I started to *love,* and who started to love me, too?"

"Love?" Ximena repeats quietly.

"I should have told her," Grace says. "I should have told her what was happening in my head instead of getting so defensive. But I didn't want her to know, really know, how screwed up I was. How terrified I was of doing it wrong. I wanted Yuki to think I was strong and fearless and unintimidated. I didn't want her to see me as weak."

"You know being vulnerable and honest is not weak," Agnes says. It was one of the first things she learned in group therapy after she was discharged, and she held Grace and Ximena to it, too. "It takes so much courage to be open with people and to let them help when you need it. It takes strength to tell someone you're scared, you're terrified. That you're *not* perfect."

"Yeah, I know." Grace wipes her eyes. She went to New York City in the first place because she felt deep in her bones that Yuki saw her. Saw the Grace Porter that was not perfect. The Grace Porter that was lonely and scared. "I let all my fear control me. I wasn't honest, and I left."

"You left her behind," Agnes says.

Grace swallows hard. "Yeah," she says. "I did. I thought it was the right thing because she didn't *get* it, you know? But now, I just want to apologize. I just want to listen. I want to be honest with her about everything."

"Jesus." Ximena looks at her with such tender sympathy. "None of that makes you a bad person. You know that, right?"

Grace rolls her eyes. "I'm learning that." She lets out a long, heaving breath. "Can we not talk about this right now? I don't want this to be all about me. I'm working on being a better friend."

"You were already a good friend," Ximena says softly. "But, fine. Let's talk about something else."

Grace lets their voices wash over her. She listens to Agnes complain about Meera some more, how she's perfect and beautiful and kind and whip smart. Ximena complains about Raj being tight-lipped about the Boston deal.

"He says he'll only tell us the news once he talks to you first," she scoffs. "Like, of course Meera knows, but she's not budging, either. You guys are like a cult."

Grace smiles, burying herself in her bed. "We're just close," she says. She wonders, though, what the news is. She wonders, thinking of a drunk, angry, defeated Raj slumped over a table in Harlem, if any news would be good news. "Meera has been blowing my phone up. I'll have to chat with them soon. It's just—"

"A lot?" Ximena guesses.

"Yeah," she breathes out. "It's hard. This living in the real-world thing? Facing my problems head-on? A hundred percent don't recommend."

Agnes leans over and starts flickering the side table lamp on and off. "Welcome to hell," she intones somberly.

"Oh, hey," Grace says, sitting up. "I do have other news. I'm going to officiate Mom's wedding."

"No way," they both say. "We want details," Ximena says.

Grace loses herself in their rapid-pace conversation. It feels good to connect with them again, to hear their voices, to see their faces. They are just the first in the long line of people Grace has to reconnect with, and the first is always the hardest.

She won't let the fear and doubt keep her from moving forward.

It only takes her another day or two to call Raj.

"I'm sorry to be calling now," she says when she hears his sleepy and confused voice. It's 5 a.m. in Southbury, 2 a.m. in Portland, and she's given up on sleep. "And I'm sorry that the first time I'm calling you after weeks of silence is because I need advice. You can be angry and yell at me later, but right now—" Grace gathers her nerve "—I just need my big brother for a minute."

She waits, hating herself for a long moment.

"Okay," Raj says finally. "Yeah, I'm here. What's going on?"

She collapses on the front porch steps. "Remember when we were in New York?" she asks. "And you said you were envious of me because I got to choose my dream job, and I was being selfish for leaving just because it got hard?"

"Oh my God," he says. "I was mad drunk when I said that. I already apologized, and Meera laid into me about it. She even threatened to tell Baba, okay? I didn't mean it."

Grace clears her throat. "You had a point," she says. "I knew the field was going to be difficult to navigate, but I thought if I pushed long enough and hard enough, it would just bend to my will."

She closes her eyes. "But what if I was right to step away? What if I make my own career, instead of going after the most prestigious job? What if the best job is one that makes me happy and satisfied? Does that make me selfish?"

Raj sighs. "You've never been selfish. Stop saying that."

"I've been selfish in more ways than I'm comfortable with," she presses. "I don't need you to protect my feelings. I just need you to be straight with me. Would you think less of me?"

She can picture his face. The tightly pressed lips, the annoyed look in his eyes. The way he runs his hands through his hair in frustration until the curls turn into a mess.

"I think," he says, sounding tired, "since it's you, and you're my fucking *sister,* I want you to do what's gonna make you feel good. So, what do you think that is, if not going after the most exclusive jobs in academia?"

She feels her shoulders drop in relief. She trusts Raj, she believes Raj, and sometimes she needs his opinion. "I never said I want to leave academia altogether," she says. "I've been told I'd be a good teacher, and I've been thinking about it. It would be nice to inspire some students the way I was. I don't know. They could see me and know that there is room for all of us in astronomy and the stars and galaxies."

"Then that's what you'll do. I think that sounds like a brilliant idea," he says simply. "Okay?"

"Okay." The line is quiet for a long minute. She leans against the railing and presses the phone closer to her ear. "Is this the worst time ever to ask about the Boston deal?"

He groans, and Grace smiles at its familiar sound. "Go ahead and twist the knife," he says. His voice sobers and quiets, like he's trying to make sure no one hears. "It went through. The White Pearl Tea Room, coming to an east coast near you." His voice, even at a near whisper, is dry.

"And how do we feel about that?" she asks. "Raj, I'm—"

"If you say you're sorry one more time, I might actually scream," he interrupts. "It is what it is, and besides, it'll be cheaper to come visit you this way. I'll be way closer."

"You know you don't have to feel okay about this," she tells him, and Heather's voice echoes in her head. "Your feelings are valid, however mean or resentful you think they are."

"What's this?" He laughs. "Did you go to Florida and gain some wisdom?"

"Something like that. Mostly someone gets paid to be wise for me."

"Good," he says. "One of us needs to be wise. I mean, it's been me for *so* long—"

"Shut up."

He falls quiet. "I've been trying not to think about it," he admits. "If I think about it, I'll get angry. If I get angry—"

"Yeah," she says. "Yeah, I get it. But you don't have to hide it from me, okay? I know why you're hiding it from Baba Vihaan and even Meera, but not from me. I wasn't there for you like I should have been, but I'm here now. I swear I am."

"I believe you," he says. "Dibs on the next late-night breakdown, then."

"Deal," she says.

• • •

Only Kelly is in the house when Grace treks in. "Mel's getting an early start in the groves," he calls lazily, squinting at his laptop. "I'm ordering your wedding officiant materials now, by the way," he adds, catching her eye before she disappears upstairs. "Last chance to run away screaming."

"Been there, done that," she says. She leans against the doorway to the kitchen. "It still feels a little weird," she admits. "Me and Mom still have so much to work out, you know? I still have so much to work out. It's a process. But I still want to do this."

"Positive?" he asks.

"Order it," she says immediately. "I said I wanted to, and I do. Really."

"Sounds good, kid," he says. "Go on and git now." Grace takes another step up before he calls again. "And, Porter?"

"Yeah?"

"It'll be good to talk it all out with her. It never feels right to let things fester, that's what I've learned. Shoving things down just breeds resentment."

"I hear you. Thanks, Kelly." Grace shuts and locks her door when she finally makes it upstairs. She has to force herself not to just fall into bed.

There is something she wants to do. She wants to use the eleven years she spent working and researching and sacrificing and finally decide

342

where that will lead her. She can forge her own path. It does not have to be tumultuous and difficult. It just needs to be chosen by her.

Dear Professor MacMillan,

I hope you have been well. I apologize for the delay in my response. I did in fact receive your last email with the opportunity to interview again with Kunakin, Incorporated.

I am sure the offer has since expired, but I want to let you know I would not have accepted. They were not accommodating, welcoming or respectful of my value as a person or an astronomer. As someone that appreciates your knowledge in the field and the people within it, I would not recommend Kunakin to my fellow peers. I hope that doesn't come across as ungrateful. It would have been a mistake for me to begin my career with them.

I have been thinking a lot about my next steps. In your email, you also mentioned a junior faculty position at Ithaca College. While I am unsure of feeling challenged in that kind of small environment, teaching has sparked a strong interest within me.

The reason I am an astronomer now

is because of my first class of Intro to Astronomy with you. I felt a part of something bigger, more complex and more formidable. It was there that I learned the vast universe has room for not just those who value science and logic, but those who are drawn to the romance and mystery and poetic storytelling it compels within us.

If I can be of service to a student by introducing them to a field in need of more diverse and unique stars within its system, than I will have done my duty to all that it has given me.

Are you able to set up a time to discuss this with me? I am currently in Florida, but in the next few months, I believe I will be in a better place to explore faculty positions. I'll mention now that I have a preference for academic institutions in the surrounding New York area.

I look forward to speaking with you. I am not just grateful for your tutelage, but honored to be held in your esteem. You propelled me toward the cosmos, and I will do my best to move others forward and farther into the unknown.

Warm regards always,
Dr. Grace Porter

Nineteen

"You busy?" Grace asks.

It's the middle of the night, and there's a storm raging outside. Grace follows the familiar path of the house in the dark and finds Mom in the living room surrounded by scribbled-on paper.

Mom looks up, hair clipped back and round, multicolored glasses perched on her nose. There's a bottle of wine on the coffee table and an empty glass. "Last-minute changes to the seating chart," she says, gathering the mess up. "You'd think getting married would be easier the second time around. What's up?"

Grace steps in hesitantly. "Do you have a second to talk?" she asks. It is not just insomnia that keeps her up, but the thought of business unfinished. Of reconnecting with the people important to her, except there is still a girl left. A girl that hunts monsters and blooms roses.

Mom moves her papers aside so Grace has room to sit. "More than a second, kid."

Grace sits. She plays with her nails, bites her thumb. Tries not to pull at her skin. She left the slime Heather suggested upstairs and wishes she had it. It reminds Grace of quiet mornings in a car with Sani. "I reached out to Professor MacMillan," she says, "about jobs. About

345

looking into some teaching opportunities." She takes a deep breath. This is her choice that she made. "I told her I wanted to look in the New York area."

"Ah." Mom leans back, surveying Grace. "With your wife, the elusive Yuki."

Grace plays with some of the tendrils that have come out of her pineapple bun. "I have to—" She shakes her head. "I want to make things right with her. I just *left* because I was scared. I left her behind." She looks at her mom. "It feels terrible to be left behind because someone has their own issues to work on."

Mom swallows hard, pulling her legs up and mimicking Grace's posture. "A feeling you're familiar with, huh?"

Grace shrugs. "I just never understood it," she says. "It felt like you were always on an airplane, off to another place to find yourself. I never understood why you had to go away. Why finding *you* had to be so far away from *me*. Why—" It's hard being this honest. It's hard opening up your wounds to prying eyes. "Why couldn't it include me, you know?"

Mom lets out a long exhale and fixes her gaze out of one of the big bay windows. The rain outside swells into a Florida storm where the wind beats against the screen door and the trees look like they might shake apart.

"There's a lot I could say," Mom says. "There

are a lot of things I've said to my therapist that have been long overdue for you to hear. But I don't want to make any excuses to my kid." She meets Grace's eyes. "It was never about you, but you're right. You should have been a part of it. I was so focused, for a long time, Porter, on being my greatest self, that I didn't even realize I wasn't being my whole self. And my whole self includes an amazing daughter that needed to know both her parents were supporting her, and were proud of her, and loved her. That she was not second. You have never been second for me, and I should have done so much more to show you that."

"Yeah," Grace says, voice warbling. "Yeah. I needed to hear that, I think."

"It was a long time coming." Mom reaches out for her. "You were in good hands, you know, all the times I've been away traveling the world. Colonel did a damn good job with you. From the moment you came screaming into this world, he said he'd move mountains to make things easier for you, things I couldn't always understand. He'd burn down the world for you."

It's Grace's turn to avert her eyes. The rain comes down in a thick, humid curtain. The wedding is soon, and she makes an idle wish that the stormy weather lets up for it.

"I know," she says softly, squinting through the window. "I do know that." She is trying to know that and understand it. It does not mean that either of her parents are perfect or that she will always agree with them. It means that all three are on their own journeys, and sometimes the paths will intersect, and sometimes, they will not. "Thanks for saying it."

"Sometimes we have to say things we should have said a long time ago," Mom tells her. "We want to make excuses or rationalize or say we had good intentions." She raises her eyebrows. "What would you say to Yuki if she asked you why you left her behind?"

And isn't that the big question? Grace is making plans to move back to New York in the next few months. She wants to get to a place where being vulnerable and honest and scared doesn't feel like she's at her worst. They are just things that make her up, like the stardust and ashes of the universe. "I think I have to figure that out," she says. "I wanted to find my way and be better, and I cut her out. She was—she *is*—a part of it."

"Well, Grace Porter," Mom says, "maybe that's something she needs to hear from you."

The words stay with Grace. She finds herself curled up on the small nook in front of her bedroom window as night drags on. There will be no sleeping here, not when she feels this buzzing need under her skin. She pinches and pulls at her homemade slime, trying to distract herself from her anxiety, and feels fireflies beneath her skin.

This is a habit she is still working to break, like all the other terrible habits she is trying to break.

What would you say to Yuki?

She presses the record button on her phone. Suddenly, Grace finds herself desperate to create that same intimacy she felt the first time she heard Yuki on the radio. Like someone was seeing her, the deep-down, wretched part of her. The part that was monstrous and lonely and pushed aside.

"If I could say anything to you," Grace starts, "I would say that this is scary. Talking to someone you can't see and hoping they are there, hoping they are listening. That's terrifying. I don't know how you do it." Would Yuki even listen to this? Would she see Grace's name and swipe this recording right into the trash?

"I'm afraid of a lot of things. I'm afraid of failing. The thought of it makes me feel sick. I'm afraid of not being perfect, which my therapist would say is ridiculous. Nobody is perfect. Not me or you or my parents or our friends. Not the people that rejected me, and not the people that will see that I have claimed the stars as mine. The first class I ever took, I knew astronomy was mine. The same way I saw you that night in Vegas in that overpriced, overcrowded bar and claimed you as mine. My wife, my siren, my lonely, monstrous creature."

She hopes Yuki will listen.

"I talked to my advisor. I told her I wanted to

look at some faculty positions, some teaching opportunities, in New York. Maybe it's presumptuous of me. You might not even want to see me again, but I—" Her nails dig into her palms. "I've spent a long time trying to be the best. The best daughter, the best protégé, the best astronomer. Anything less meant I was doing something wrong. Any deviation from my perfectly crafted plan was wrong, and *fuck,* how I almost stuck that landing. But then I stormed out of the interview for the job I was groomed to get. For a job I was never going to *actually* get. And then I *married you.* How could the great Grace Porter recover from that?

"I've had a lot of time to think about what I wanted to say to you. I don't want to give you excuses or rationalizations or good intentions." Mom's words echo in her head. "I was terrified. I was scared. I wanted to be the best, even if it meant working myself into the ground. Even if it meant breaking my back to prove I deserved a seat at a table I had no desire to sit at. Even if it meant leaving you behind. If I could say anything, it would be that I'm sorry. You asked me before I left what *best* meant for me, and I'm still learning what that looks like. But I know it means I take care of myself. It means I'm kind to myself. It means I support my friends and my family, and I don't let the guilt take over when they support me back."

Please be listening, she thinks. "I know it includes your midnight radio show and all the lonely creatures and monsters and stories that come with it. It includes your weird-ass roommates, our friends. It includes *you,* Yuki Yamamoto, because *best* for me means being happy and—*God*—being in love with you."

Grace feels out of breath by the time her mind catches up with her tongue. She feels like she has run an entire marathon, and the finish line is right there, if only she can keep going for a little bit longer. "Are you there, Yuki? Are you listening? Because there is so much I want to say to you, and I made a promise in a chapel in the desert that I don't plan on breaking. Till death do us part, we said. That bejeweled priest asked if I, Grace Porter, took you, Yuki Yamamoto, to be my lawfully wedded wife, and by every power I have within me, by the endless and thunderous universe, I do, okay? *I do.*"

Grace ends the recording and sends it before she can doubt herself. Like how people send their wishes up to the moon and wait for an answer, Grace sends hers to join them. *Please be listening,* she thinks. *I am here. I am here. I am here.*

Twenty

The day of the wedding finally comes.

Grace's arms and legs are sore from helping set up the outdoor wedding tent and wobbling on ladders to string up extravagant fabrics and lights and little flowers.

She's in her room making sure her suit is immaculate. It's a deep purple, the color of nightfall. She went to the African braiding shop like Heather suggested, and they put her hair in thick, jumbo box braids. The woman put purple and silver threads in them that twinkle and glimmer when they catch the sun. The braids hang down Grace's back, and she glows when she looks in the mirror.

Thankful for a mild temperature day, the suit makes her feel put together and settled. "What do you think?" she asks.

Meera leans in, her face too close to the screen. "Come closer to the phone, and do a turn," she commands. "Move back a little. It's tailored so well."

Grace sighs. "My father is military. You think I'm not a stickler about my suits?"

Meera rolls her eyes, smiling quickly when she realizes Grace can see her. "You'll look so good when you're dancing at the reception," she says dreamily. "Some beautiful woman will twirl you, and your suit jacket will flare so perfectly."

Grace frowns. "Where did this beautiful woman come from?" She straightens her bejeweled choker in the mirror. "There is no beautiful woman dancing with me. Just Kelly, and like, Mr. Cooley, who doesn't know how to keep his hands to himself."

"Did you tell him you're a lesbian?"

"I told everyone I'm a lesbian," she says. "Maybe he thinks it's a phase."

"Well, tell them to back off," Meera says loyally. "You look amazing, by the way."

Grace smiles. She sits at the vanity, so she can actually talk to Meera for a second instead of yelling at her from across the room. "Thank you," she says. "You know I wish you were here, right?" Ximena and Agnes arrived yesterday afternoon. They're only staying for the weekend, and Grace wishes they could stay longer, or that she was going back with them to Portland.

Meera shrugs, ducking her head. She's taken over Baba Vihaan's office to talk to Grace, and she looks unbearably small in the middle of all his things.

"Meera," she says, her voice gentle. "You know that, right?"

Meera nods quickly, and when she looks up, her face is contorted into something that

353

is supposed to be a smile. "I know," she says, mouth trembling. "It's just—ugh. Yeah, I know."

"Tell me," Grace says quietly. She is trying; she is trying so hard to be here and present. She is trying to be the best friend she can be. "You can tell me."

She's not expecting it when Meera starts to cry.

"Hey," she breathes out, reaching for the phone like she can touch her. "Do you need Raj? What's wrong?"

Meera hiccups, carefully wiping her eyes. "He's not here," she gets out. "He's at another meeting for the new tea room, and soon he'll be living in Boston. He'll be in Boston, and soon enough you'll be in New York for good, and it'll just be me here."

"That's not true," Grace says carefully, though her chest feels tight. "Baba Vihaan is there. All your cool, young and hip college friends are there." She pauses, mouth twisting playfully. "Agnes and Ximena are there," she teases, "and I know they *loooove* being around you." Meera covers her face with her hands, embarrassed.

"Shut up," she mumbles. "God, you're as bad as Raj."

"Older sibling privileges," Grace says. "It's our job. You know what else is?"

Meera sighs, fiddling with her hair. "What?"

"Not leaving you." The sincerity of the words comes from somewhere deep inside her. "Even if we're not there, we haven't forgotten about you. You don't just stop being our little sister."

"I know," Meera says, sounding stronger than she did a few minutes ago. She meets Grace's eyes and nods. "I know. Now go away. I'm going to call Agnes and Ximena so they can show me the wedding decorations."

"You could have just asked *me* to show you," Grace complains. "You guys are going to be so gross and cute, aren't you?"

"Shut up," Meera says. "As if you don't know Ximena is, like, ridiculously beautiful inside and out, and Agnes is the coolest, kindest person ever. I'm hanging up now. Bye!" The call disconnects.

Grace laughs and slips her phone into her pocket. She decides to take a short walk around the groves, on the side hidden away from the guests. She will breathe in the smell of citrus and earth, and she will breathe out all her anxiety and swirling thoughts.

But by the time the guests start arriving and people begin looking for her, all Grace has done is work herself up into an anxiety spiral about officiating. And, her shoes are dirty.

"Them things look a mess," Saffiya says, when Grace greets her at the front of the tent. "Go inside and clean yourself up, Grace Porter."

"I have to—" she starts, but Saffiya snatches the wedding programs out of her hand. "Fine, I'm going. Thank you."

She cleans herself up. She knocks the dirt off her heels, dabs sweat off her forehead and tries to remember her speech.

Somehow, she makes it back outside in one piece. She feels stuck in her head, and it's hard to breathe. It feels like she's inside a washing machine, spinning around so fast that everything on the other side of the glass blurs.

Heather says to focus on one thing when she gets like this. *Focus on one thing, Grace, and hold on to just that.* Only, there is not just one thing to worry about now. Grace is officiating a wedding. Guests begin to sit, watching her for direction. Mom and Kelly are depending on her to do this perfectly. She is trying so hard and—

"Hey," someone whispers, grabbing her arm.

Immediately, Grace relaxes. She knows that voice. She knows that shampoo and that lotion and that presence next to her. "Ximena," she says. "Fuck, I'm—"

"Freaking out," Ximena finishes. "Yeah, I could tell. But Kelly is on his way down, and the music will start soon, so you need to get it together."

Grace blanks out. "I can't," she says, shaking her head frantically. "Oh my God, I can't do this." She grabs Ximena's hand tightly. "Why did they ask me to do this? I don't—I'm not—"

"You can," Ximena says firmly. "You are." She's in a bright pink dress that pops against her brown skin. Her thick, curly hair is pushed into a high puff. "What did Heather tell you?"

"Focus on one thing," Grace parrots obediently, feeling dizzy. "There's too many things. What am I supposed to—"

"Focus on me," Ximena says. She points to a row near the front where Agnes slouches down and gives them a lazy wave. "That's where we'll be. Focus on me and Agnes, okay?"

She gives Grace a push, so hard that Grace stumbles to the front of the tent just as Miss Darla starts to play the opening notes on the piano. Grace looks back at Ximena, wide-eyed.

"Go," she whispers loudly, so Grace goes.

She takes her carefully typed-up paper out of her breast pocket. It has been opened, folded and opened again. It opens for the last time just as Kelly appears at the end of the aisle and walks up.

She takes a deep breath.

She tries to smile as he makes it up to the front next to her. "You look wonderful," he says, leaning in carefully. "Do you need me to hold your hand?"

Grace glances at him, just as the curtains pull back and reveal Mom, ready to make her walk down the aisle. "Why would I need you to hold my hand?"

He looks down. "So that only one of them is shaking," he says blandly, and Grace grips one hand around her wrist in response. "Suit yourself." He adjusts the cuffs on his neat, pressed suit and tucks some gray-brown hair behind his ears. "Mine are shaking, too, just so you know."

"Thanks anyway," she murmurs, and she refuses to look at him when he laughs, quiet and low.

Mom walks down the aisle as Miss Darla plays the wedding march. She doesn't falter, doesn't stumble as she walks toward them. Grace wonders if she was this sure walking down the aisle toward Colonel. If her eyes were this wide. If her cheeks were flushed with heat and happiness just like this.

Grace commits it all to memory.

Mom reaches them as the music ends. She has makeup on, enough that her eyes sparkle and her mouth is a pretty apple red. She smiles at Grace first, then Kelly, and Grace thinks, *I am a part of this. I am a part of this moment and this happiness. I am not left behind, but in the thick of it.*

"We are gathered here today," she says, in the hush of the crowd, "to wed two people that have found love."

Her hands shake. She meets Ximena's eyes and watches her whisper, "I love you so much it hurts." She finds Agnes, who has sunglasses on but is smiling wide, despite how much she is trying to project a devil-may-care attitude.

"There are a lot of things I don't know about my mom," she says, glancing down at her paper and deciding to go off script. "There are so many things I don't know and so many things I am discovering by being here. I am learning that she works hard in the groves, never asking anything of anyone that she wouldn't do herself. I am learning that she drinks one, sometimes two, glasses of red wine every night, and she prefers company while she does it."

The crowd laughs, and Mom reaches out to grab her hand. Grace blinks and squeezes back.

"I have learned that she is capable of many mistakes and is not without flaws. My mother is not perfect," she says, voice trembling. "But she is also capable of great love and understanding."

Grace glances over to Ximena and Agnes, her anchors. Focus on one thing, and she focuses on a piece of her family, her chosen family, that settles her and makes the spinning stop.

"I have learned that she is a part of a wonderful community. It is full of people who want to help, and do good, and feed others, as is their path in life. They grow so they can feed. They wake up at sunrise, so they can pick the fruits of their labor, and deliver them with gentle hands to those who need it most."

Mom ducks her head, and Kelly gives Grace another smile. She thought she would have regrets, standing up here, but she feels hopeful. For love, for their future.

She looks out at the crowd again. There are familiar faces everywhere. Grace squints into the sun, toward the back of the tent, and her breath catches at the person looking back at her. She would recognize that uniform anywhere. Colonel raises his eyebrows and tilts his head. *Well,* he seems to say. *Are you going to let this trip you up?*

It won't. She is a Porter, and she said she would officiate this wedding. She said she would marry Mom and Kelly, so she will.

"We are gathered here today," she says, voice loud and clear, "to unite two people who have found love in our strange, chaotic world. Kelly," she says, turning toward the man who will soon officially be her stepdad, "you are kind and patient and wise. Most importantly, you always cook so much food, and it's *seasoned*. Incredible."

There is warm laughter, and he looks pleased. Grace sobers and grips her paper tightly, even though she has given up on reading from it. "Thank you for taking care of Mom," she says softly. "If I have to respect and live with a white man, I couldn't imagine a better one than you."

He does laugh then, loud and long. He pulls Grace into a tight hug. She doesn't feel uncomfortable like she did the first time she saw him, approaching her at the airport. She feels familiarity and comfort—he's someone who will look out for her. He lets go, and she has to wipe her eyes quickly before she continues.

"Mom," she says. Mom grips her hand so tight it hurts. Grace doesn't let go. "You are trying, and I am trying. I am so grateful to share this day with you, and I am so glad you found someone to make you happy."

Mom pulls Grace in, too. It's a different hug than the one shared with Kelly. This hug says, *I'm sorry.* This hug says, *I am here.* This hug says, *I am trying and you are trying.* This hug says, *Nobody will be left behind.*

"No one makes me as happy as you, kid," she whispers fiercely. "No one could ever compare to you." Grace closes her eyes, and for a moment focuses on this one thing: the smell of Mom's perfume and her trembling arms and the way she holds on like a promise. *I will not let go again.* Grace focuses on that one thing, and her brain is quiet. Mom and Kelly share vows that are sincere and genuine and intimate, and her brain is quiet.

She clears her throat when it is her turn to make this official. "Let's get you married." She raises her voice. "Mom," she says. "Do you take this man to be your husband?"

Mom turns to face Kelly, glowing like the sun. "I do."

"And, Kelly?" she asks. "Do you take this woman to be your wife?"

His eyes are only for Mom. For him, it is just the two of them. "I do," he says, sure as anything.

The *I do*s echo like a memory, a memory of the same words uttered in a church in the desert. She doesn't try to push it away. She just lets it be.

"Melodie Martin," she says. "Kelly Nichols. I now pronounce you husband and wife." She lets out a relieved exhale. "You may kiss the bride."

The crowd stands and applauds as Mom and Kelly kiss. She looks out, and Ximena meets her eyes. "I love you," Grace whispers, "so much it hurts." She feels good seeing all the people from their community brought together for this day. She looks toward the back, and there is Colonel. He catches her eyes. Grace stares back, and she smiles. He doesn't return it, but his parade rest relaxes just a little bit.

She'll take it.

Miss Darla starts the piano again, and Grace takes in the music. She takes in the happiness. She takes in the fact that she is here with most of her family. She is here, and not lost, spinning between stars and galaxies. Mom and Kelly start to walk down the aisle, and Mom looks back to make sure Grace is following.

"I'm here," she says quietly.

The piano plays the start of another song. It's about new beginnings. It is honest, and it is love, and it is real. She commits it to memory.

Grace feels like herself again at the reception.

It's in a different tent. The ceiling of this one is entwined with gold lights that illuminate the oncoming night. She walks through to see all the people engulfed in gold, to see Mom and Kelly engulfed in gold, and she relaxes. It's over. She did it.

She collapses in relief next to Ximena and Agnes seated at a table by the back. Agnes leans on Ximena's shoulders as she downs a glass of champagne. They sway a little to the music.

"Hey," she says. "Hi, I'm so happy to see you."

"Hey, hi," Agnes says. "I'm getting drunk." Next to her, Ximena nurses what is probably ice water. "Tell her to get drunk with me."

"She won't," Grace says at the same time Ximena says, "I won't."

They catch eyes, and Ximena glares. Grace grins. "She likes taking care of you too much, Agnes," she says brightly. "Weird kink, but whatever." She ducks from the shoe that tries to swat her. "Not la chancleta!"

"Don't get comfortable," Ximena snipes when Grace sits down. "Someone is looking for you." She gestures toward the other side of the tent, and Grace's stomach flips before she turns around.

Colonel, standing stiffly and proudly, watches her.

"Shit," she mumbles. "Did you know he was coming?"

"Yeah," Ximena says. "He texted me all his flight details, and we even shared a drink at the airport bar. No, of course I didn't know he was coming."

"Maybe he didn't see me." Grace stays stock-still. "Is he still looking?"

"Yep," Agnes says, starting on Ximena's glass of champagne. "It's almost like he recognizes his own daughter. Strange."

"Okay." Grace glowers at the two of them. "I'm going to go talk to Colonel because that is actually better than sitting here being mocked. How do you feel about that?"

"He's still looking," Ximena says. She inspects one of her painted, jeweled nails. Grace stomps off.

The walk from their corner to where Colonel has planted himself feels like miles. There are a million questions swarming through her head. Mom never mentioned inviting him. Colonel never mentioned coming. Granted, Grace only answers about half his calls, but it's the principle of the thing. She tries to get ahead and figure out his angle, but he has always been unreadable and two steps ahead.

She comes to a stop a few steps in front of him and resigns herself to the fact that he has the upper hand.

"Colonel," she says, straightening. She meets his eyes, chin tilted up. "I didn't know you would be here."

"Yes," he says evenly. "I asked your mother to keep it a surprise."

"Why?" Grace blurts out, frustrated. "Did you want to trip me up? Were you trying to disarm me or something? I'm not coming back to Portland, not yet," she says, surprised by her own decisiveness.

She has seen Colonel in many moods. She has seen him angry and disappointed. She has seen him in pain, near out of his mind lying in a hospital bed. She has seen him scared, convinced the ghosts of his past would burst through his own front door in the middle of the night.

She has never seen him surprised. The expression is unfamiliar on his face.

"Porter," he says, eyebrows furrowed. "Is it really that far-fetched that I just wanted to see my own daughter and maybe wish an old—" His lips twist, unsure. "Maybe just wish your mother the best?"

"Maybe," Grace responds, but she knows, deep in the pit of her belly, it's unfair. Some days, her brain reshapes Colonel into a villain of her past. Sometimes, it's easy to believe. It is much harder to believe the person she looked up to as God for so many years is just a man. He is just her father.

"I didn't mean that," she says. "I'm just a little taken aback."

He holds his hand out. She eyes it warily. She cannot think one move ahead, let alone two. She takes it, out of options, and is amazed to be led onto the dance floor.

"We're dancing?" she asks, as he positions her arms around his tall, broad shoulders. His arms rest on the side of her waist. It is the closest thing to a hug Grace can remember ever getting from him. "Okay, we're dancing."

"An astute observation," he murmurs, taking the lead. "Glad to see all your education has paid off."

She tenses. She hasn't told him about her plans for her career, and she certainly won't do it while he's looking at her. When she broaches the subject, she would rather not have to see the reaction on his face.

"Relax," he says, voice almost, *almost* apologetic. "I'm not going to ask you about it. Tonight is a night for celebration. It's a wedding."

Her shoulders relax minutely. "But tomorrow is fair game?" she guesses, and one of his eyebrows flicks in answer. "Where are you staying?"

"Your mother offered me a room in the main house, since they'll be away on their honeymoon, but I—" He glances at Grace, and for a moment, just a blink, he looks like the man who needed so desperately to leave this place. "I declined," he finishes, composed once more. They make another turn to the beat, and his voice is low when he says, "Some memories don't need to be revisited."

Grace has been trying on some bravery lately. "My therapist would probably disagree with you," she uses it to say.

Colonel shrugs. "Well, it's a good thing she's not mine," and she is struck speechless.

The song starts to wind down, and she and Colonel slow their dancing. As the next song starts, something faster and upbeat, she pulls away and wraps her arms around herself. "Well."

"Let's have lunch tomorrow," he says abruptly. "There's an acceptable place near my hotel. I'll text you the address. I suspect there are some things you and I should discuss."

She swallows hard. "Yes, sir," she murmurs, staring at the spot over his shoulder so she won't have to meet his eyes. "I'll be there."

He nods at her, as if unsure how to make his leave. She will make it easy for him.

"I'll just—"

"Grace—"

She freezes. She holds her breath and watches her father struggle to find words. He always has words, whether they are short and succinct or weighted and heavy. Now, though, he flounders. Grace watches, entranced.

"You did well today," he says finally. He's

never been prone to fidgeting, not like Grace, but he rolls his shoulders and clears his throat. "I watched you stand in front of all those people, and in front of your family, and you were every inch the Porter I always knew you were. I was—proud."

She lets out a stumbling, disbelieving laugh. "Thank you," she manages. "I—"

"Yes," he says quickly, cutting her off. He clears his throat again and takes a step back. "I'll greet the newlyweds and then take my leave. Give my regards to Ximena and Agnes, yes? I'll see you for lunch tomorrow. Be on time."

"Yes, sir," she says, arms clenched around her waist like she's trying to hold everything in. "I'll be there."

He inclines his head, and then he is gone.

Grace doesn't remember the walk back to the table. Ximena and Agnes move so she can take the space between them. They flank her on both sides.

"That bad?" Ximena murmurs. She holds up a glass of champagne and a small water bottle. "How are we feeling?"

"Water, please," Grace says. "It wasn't that bad, actually. Maybe that wasn't Colonel at all. It was probably a clone." She closes her eyes. "Well, mystery solved."

Agnes snorts and leans on her. "Great job, Nancy Drew," she says.

"I'm Bess," Ximena says immediately. "You're George."

Agnes shrugs. The champagne has made her languid and agreeable. "I always knew George was gay. The many Carolyn Keenes can't fool me. And don't get me started on The Baby-Sitters Club."

"Don't get started on The Baby-Sitters Club," Grace and Ximena both plead. Agnes sticks her tongue out and slouches back down. Grace takes her hand in consolation, and it's a testament to how peaceful Agnes is feeling that she doesn't pull away.

Grace lets the world spin around her. She can see Mom and Kelly holding court at the elaborate sweetheart table set up for them. Mom is smiling and glowing, bright and gleaming. Kelly watches like the sun rises and sets on her command.

The buffet smells like Caribbean food. Old Maria and her sister cooked for almost a week leading up to this. Grace's stomach grumbles at the smell of curry and brown stew and the buttery scent of roti.

People are dancing and laughing and the room fills with love. There is so much love spilling out from this tent. Grace feels it on both sides of her, between her two closest friends, who press close and do not let her go. There is a small, hollow ache, somewhere deep inside her, but she is learning that she is made up of many small, hollow aches. She will continue the process of exploring them, one by one.

Ximena's phone lights up and she makes a choked, surprised noise. "Shit," she says. "I forgot your mom asked me to bring in the other case of champagne ten minutes ago."

Grace tilts her head. "Did you set an alarm for it?" she asks, leaning over her shoulder. "You're turning into me."

"I like to be prepared," Ximena says primly, getting up. "I'll be right back."

Grace shakes her head. "No, I'll get it," she says quietly. "I could use some air anyway. All this carefree happiness is more than I can bear. Where is it?"

Ximena glances at her phone. "On the front deck. Tucked in the corner closest to that cherry blossom tree."

Grace nods and starts to untangle herself. "Got it, boss. I'll be right back."

"I can go," Agnes says. She fluffs up her hair under her pink beret. "It'll give me a chance to show off my outfit."

Ximena stares at her. "*Porter* is going," she says carefully.

Agnes crosses her arms and tilts her head like a challenge. "*Porter* had a long day," she says. "I think she should stay here."

"Believe me," Ximena mutters fiercely, "you've made it quite clear what you think."

370

"Then maybe you should—"

"Okay," Grace cuts in. "I'm going to go get the champagne, so you two can have this—is this a lovers' spat? Is this foreplay? I'm flattered that you would involve me, but—" she leans down to kiss Agnes's cheek, then Ximena's "—maybe another night. Be right back."

She feels their eyes on her as she disappears into the crowd.

Outside the tent, the world becomes quieter. She shivers as a night breeze rolls in and blows through the grove trees. *Hello again, Grace Porter,* the crinkle of the leaves says.

"Hello," she whispers back.

She makes her way through the dimly lit path toward the main house. The porch lights are on, and the same gold string lights from the tents are twined down the railings. She stops to admire them. Everything looks gold kissed. If there is any truth to the story of the sun favoring her at birth, tonight she could believe it.

On the porch, there's the box of champagne, already loaded on a cart ready to be wheeled out. She grunts with the weight and starts the annoying job of getting it down the steps.

She turns around, trying to decipher the probability of dropping the whole thing, when she realizes there is a light coming from the groves. A flashlight or something. There is someone out there.

"Shit," she says. She sighs and stares up at the sky. "I am way too Black for this."

She waits and watches, but the light does not dim. "Okay," she says. She opens the case of champagne and pulls out a bottle. "We're going to 'white girl in a horror movie' this shit." She carries the bottle out like a baseball bat for protection.

With the bottle in hand, she moves quietly through the trees. These paths are familiar to her. Whoever is out there does not know these groves like she does. Grace gets close to the mysterious light and holds her bottle out. Whoever this is doesn't stand a chance.

"Who the hell—" She stops, the bottle coming just shy of the person in front of her. "Yuki?"

Yuki turns around. Her black hair gleams in the light. Her half-moon silver piercings glint. Flowers bloom, her very own cherry blossoms, from the exposed parts of her skin. "Are you going to kill me with that, or can we open it?" she asks.

Grace tries to recover from her shaking adrenaline. "What are you doing here?"

Yuki shrugs. She looks very small out here. "I don't know," she admits. "I heard there was a lonely creature lurking in these orange groves. I wanted to see for myself." She looks intently at Grace. "And I heard from some friends of yours that there was a wedding."

"And which one did you come for?" Grace leans against an orange tree. If another breeze comes through, it might just take her with it.

Yuki sighs. "I thought about going to the wedding," she says. "But I couldn't. It made me think about . . ."

"Us," Grace breathes out, and Yuki nods in agreement. "I thought about you the whole time. I *missed* you, like my body knew if I was standing at a wedding altar, you were supposed to be there with me."

Grace takes in the girl in front of her. She's wearing a high-waisted leather skirt with a striped button-up tucked in. Her face is done up with shimmering, dramatic makeup. There are metallic barrettes holding her bangs back. She's barefoot, and her feet are speckled with earth and soil. She is beautiful, and Grace aches for her.

"Were you really out here walking?" Grace asks. "Were you out here the whole time?"

Yuki shrugs again. She doesn't meet Grace's eyes, not yet. "I can see the appeal, I guess," she says. "Almost got myself lost walking in these groves, trying to figure out if I wanted to talk to you. I was so angry. I am *still* so angry. But I'm here, and I hate to waste a trip."

Grace swallows. It hurts. It all hurts. "Well, I'm glad you came," she says. "I should have asked you myself, but I don't know if I could have handled it if you said no."

Yuki meets her eyes finally. "Don't you know, Honey Girl?" She plays with her collar. It's pressed neat, like she wanted to make an impression. "I said *yes* to you once, and I haven't learned how to say anything else, since."

Grace steps forward. "I'm guessing you got my recording. I was—I don't know how you do it," she confesses. Yuki stares at her, illuminated by moonlight. "It was scary. It was terrifying. I don't know how it doesn't terrify you to get on your show and—"

"Talk about monsters?"

"Be honest," she says, and Yuki's teeth clack together. "How you can be vulnerable to so many people. I'm not quite used to it yet."

Yuki mirrors Grace and takes a step forward, too. She waves her phone. "Is that what this was? You being honest and vulnerable? You said a lot of things."

Grace nods. She bites her tongue hard, but not enough to bleed.

"Was it true?" Yuki presses. "That you're sorry for leaving me? That you're looking for teaching jobs in New York?" She crosses her arms, glaring. "That you—" Her voice gets stuck.

Honesty, Grace thinks, is jumping into the blue-green sea. It is letting the salt burn your lungs. It is about reaching out at the bottom of the sea and saying, *I heard you singing. I heard the song you sang for me. Stay, please, with me.*

"That I love you?" she finishes. "It was all true. I was scared and angry and trying so hard to be the perfect everything. I'm learning to deal with all of that, but yes, I love you. That's not something I have to work through."

Yuki lets out a slow, trembling breath. "I didn't understand exactly what you were going through. I didn't understand that it would make you *leave,*" she says. "I just wanted you to be with me. I wanted you to see that maybe I could be part of your perfect plan. I would have tried to live up to the great Grace Porter for the rest of my fucking life. Because," she says softly, "that's what you do when you're upside down in love with someone."

Grace laughs. One of the hollow, aching spaces inside her starts to fill. She shoves her hands in her suit pockets. "And what about now?" she asks. "Are you still upside down in love with the great Grace Porter?"

"Our friends coordinated this whole scheme of getting me down here," Yuki says. "You think I'd let them do all that for a girl I don't love?" She ducks her head and wipes her eyes. "Grace Porter," she murmurs, "why did you leave me behind?"

Grace looks at the girl in front of her. "Remember how you asked me what *best* really meant to me? What does *best* mean anyway, if I'm not happy? What is best if the people I care about come second? I realized my idea of best left no space for anything that didn't tear me apart in the process. It barely left space for *me*. I didn't know how to deal with that, how to reckon with that truth, that revelation, so I left. I left you behind, and I'm—fuck, Yuki. I'm *so sorry*."

"I'm sorry, too," Yuki says, looking shaken by Grace's openness. "I never meant to put more pressure on you. I shouldn't have expected you to have all the answers, you know? God, nobody does. I certainly don't. I just wanted to be one of your answers. One of the things you would fight for, too."

She stares Grace down, her voice going fierce. "I'm still so angry with you, but if we do this, if we keep doing this, you don't get to disappear on me again. We talk and we fight and we *stay*. We said in good times and bad, and I don't know about you, but I have been having a bad time these last few months. Would not recommend."

Grace lets out a real laugh now. Her vision is blurred. "Would not recommend," she agrees. "Good times and bad," she repeats, "I'll be here. You asked me, you asked all your listeners, and I'm a few months late, but I'm here. I'm listening. Lonely creature to lonely creature. Now, I'm asking you," Grace says. It hurts. She keeps going. "I'm asking you."

Yuki nods. She looks past Grace at the big tent

376

filled with carefree people and sun-gold lights. They reflect in her eyes.

"Okay," Yuki says. "Ask me." It sounds like an echo.

There is a siren singing Grace a song. It must have looked into the very core of her to know which song to sing. It is a sad song, because sometimes the world is sad. It is a hopeful song, because sometimes the world is hopeful.

"Ask me."

Grace asks.

Yuki catches the words in her mouth, and she tastes citrus-sweet. Yuki kisses her, and Grace is lit up from the inside, like the sun has been buried within her all along. She is favored, or maybe the gold lights from the wedding tent illuminate what she's been searching for.

Grace asks. She does not hesitate. The universe waits for her; the girl in front of her waits for her.

"Grace Porter," Yuki says, when all the guests have gone, and the house is quiet with just the few people staying. Sunrise approaches in the distance, and the yellow and gold and honey rays reach out toward them. "Did I ever tell you why I was in Las Vegas?"

Grace looks at her. Yuki lies in her lap, mouth kiss-swollen, fingers curled around the bottle of champagne. "No," she says quietly. "You never told me."

Yuki smiles. "Monster hunting," she says. "We crowdfunded to get that trip paid for, and I didn't find a thing." She glances up. "I was so frustrated about going back home with nothing. I went out on my last night to at least have some fun. And then I found you."

"And then you found me."

Yuki shivers when Grace runs fingers through her hair, careful of the barrettes. "Maybe you heard me," Yuki says, "that night in the desert. Maybe you heard me singing you a song even back then." She holds her pinky out. "Finders keepers. No take-backs. Promise me."

Grace curls their pinkies together. "Promise," she says. "No take-backs. You're stuck with me now."

Yuki shrugs. "That's okay. Heard there was a monster lurking down in these groves anyway." She closes her eyes, like she trusts Grace will watch for the scary things in the lingering shadows. "Heard it was favored by the sun, even."

"Sounds like bullshit to me," Grace tells her. "But I believe you," she says. "Maybe I believe in your monster, too."

Acknowledgments

Honey Girl is a labor of love and community.

First and foremost, it would not exist without the writers who did sessions with me every single day, all of us working so diligently and also complaining about how difficult it was to meet our word goals. This book would not exist without Natasha, who read every single chapter as it was written. For my very first audience of one, you mean the entire world. After it was written, Brie, you read the entire first draft. You gave me notes on what worked and what didn't. You told me the notes that soared and the ones that fell flat. My work has always thrived under the weight of your proverbial red pen, and this is no exception. Ellen and Shooky, I still remember everything you said about that first draft. Thank you not just for your time, but for your kindness and attention and unwavering enthusiasm. The *Honey Girl* that exists today would not exist if I did not have y'all pushing me to new and extraordinary heights. You believed in this story before I even knew what it was.

To my self-proclaimed mentors C+L, I learn something new from you every single day. Y'all are humble and welcoming and wise beyond measure. I hope I can pay it forward like you have done and continue to do. I hope I can pass along another author's book one day and open the first of many doors so someone can perhaps take a chance on them, too. Y'all are the blueprint, and your work is more than just the books you write. It is the hands you extend to lift people like me up. I hope I can be as cool as you when I grow up.

To the incredible team at Root Literary, spearheaded by the most badass agent in the biz, Holly Root, there are no words. Holly, you once told me my writing voice was like a vibrant blue house. There would be people who thought it was too much, not for them, not their cup of tea. And that was fine. You told me there would be people who loved that blue house. Thank you for loving the blue house. Thank you for fighting so fiercely for me. Any author who has you in their corner is on the winning team. I am so, so happy to work with you, and this is just the first blue house of many. We are going to paint this whole town.

To the people bringing this book to life: Park Row Books, there is not a thank-you big enough. Roxanne, Lia, Lindsey, Linette and everyone involved with the Park Row/Harlequin/HarperCollins team. I am so happy you all connected with my book and worked so hard to get it into the hands of many, many readers. It means everything. Laura Brown, you are an incredible editor, an incredible professional and an incredible ally to have to give this book a chance in the market. From our very first phone conversation, I knew you understood *Honey Girl* and what I wanted to say. You dug into the muck and the weeds and you helped me pull up the roots so the real story could be planted. Your ideas helped create a revision that sprouted from the ground something strong and distinct and spectacular. I consider *Honey Girl* a triumph, and that would not be without your expertise.

The words inside are not just the heart of this book. Its essence has also been captured on the cover. This book would not be this book without Gigi Lau and Poppy Magda's incredible vision. This book cover is one for the ages. In my opinion, it is one of the greatest I have ever seen. The talent and artistry and vision you both executed to give us this stunning portrait of Grace Porter is a remarkable feat.

Thank you, Maureen and Dana. You were the first industry professionals I ever talked to about *Honey Girl*. You are bright and kind and passionate. Any book that you work on is a book that is good and valuable and needed. This world and this industry can be very difficult to navigate, but I know that the reins you hold are in good hands.

I would not have reached this point at all without the support of my family. Mummy, thanks for always being on the other end of the phone. Thank you for helping me get to where I wanted to be my whole life. Thanks for teaching me that it is okay to fight for what I am owed. Thank you for always having an answer, whether I listen to it or not. Muffy, thank you for always listening. Your words of encouragement mean more than you know. Missy, you are the best sister anyone could ever ask for. I have loved you from the moment Muffa brought you home. You are my best friend, and everything I do is so you can be proud of me.

To the amazing writing community that I now find myself a part of: y'all are magnificent. You all have phenomenal stories to tell. I am thankful for the words you write and the support you give. I am so proud to call you peers. I am so honored to own your work and to look forward to everything of yours in the future.

Thank you to NAO, whose *Saturn* album became the soundtrack for each writing session. Thank you to KNJ, who told me to keep going. Who told me it was worth it if it relieves a pain from one hundred to ninety-nine or ninety-eight or ninety-seven. Thank you to my brain for its weird obsession with space and the ocean and the natural world. There is so very much of it to explore. Shout-out to fan fiction and fandom and tropes. You merely adopted AO3. I was born into LJ and FFN, molded by it.

Thank you to Black girls. You are the inspiration, the culture, the center of it all.

And finally, thank you to those who came before.

This is only the beginning. Nice to meet you.

Center Point Large Print
600 Brooks Road / PO Box 1
Thorndike, ME 04986-0001 USA

(207) 568-3717

US & Canada:
1 800 929-9108
www.centerpointlargeprint.com